> My dear Ann,
>
> How wonderful ... ... you. Here is your copy as promised.
>
> By the way I have hidden the secret of life in the early chapters. Find the "key" if you dare.
>
> David.

© 2011 David J. Shibli
The Cayman Conspiracy

No part of this document may be reproduced or transmitted in any form, by any means (electronic, photocopying, recording or otherwise) without the prior written permission of the author.
david@shibli.ky

This book is a work of fiction and any resemblance to persons living or dead is entirely coincidental.

Preface iv

Acknowledgements v

About the Book vii

Chapter One 1

Chapter Two 15

Chapter Three 25

Chapter Four 33

Chapter Five 41

Chapter Six 50

Chapter Seven 64

Chapter Eight 71

Chapter Nine 82

Chapter Ten 90

Chapter Eleven 100

Chapter Twelve 113

Chapter Thirteen 134

Chapter Fourteen 155

Chapter Fifteen 168

Chapter Sixteen 191

Chapter Seventeen 203

Chapter Eighteen 215

Chapter Nineteen 230

Chapter Twenty 234

Chapter Twenty One 247

Chapter Twenty Two 257
Chapter Twenty Three 261
Epilogue 281
Dedication 284

Preface

The Cayman Conspiracy was written in the late 1980s during a time of intense, personal struggle in the author's life. The original cassette tapes that contained the manuscript had long since been lost and only two physical copies remained. One was with the author and the other was sent to a publisher in London. In 1990, the author was living as a homeless person on the streets of Manhattan where he would push hotdog carts to survive and it was during this time that he made a private decision not to publish.

During a brief personal ceremony in a homeless shelter in New York in 1991, he quietly slid his copy into a trash can and it was forgotten about....or was it?

Incredibly, 20 years later, the winds of providence unearthed the last surviving copy of the manuscript that had found its way back to an old family friend's house. During a recent trip to the U.K. in May 2011, the author was reunited with his original work and read it again.

Deeply moved by the intensity of the characters birthed by his young imagination and astonished by the prophetic nature of his story, he concluded that the manuscript had remained hidden for such a time as this.

You are invited on a thrilling adventure that links the high stakes world of casino gambling with the sleepy Cayman Islands of the 1980s, a place where gambling has always been and still is illegal.

Acknowledgements

The Cayman Conspiracy would never have existed if it were not for the influence of various people in my life and although it is impossible to name everyone; this is my best effort.

First and foremost, I would like to give the greatest thanks to my mother and father for loving me and giving me such a privileged start in life enabling me to draw upon the gift of a great education in all the challenges that I have faced to date.

I would like to thank Sr. Mary Philomena, my cherished headmistress for her continued support over the years.

My brothers, Simon, Jeremy and Dominic and their wives, Tracey, Nikki and Funda deserve mention for treating their *broken* brother with great respect.

I want to thank Dave Pike and his family who were responsible for protecting the last surviving copy of the manuscript for twenty years as it laid safely in their house while the years passed by.

I'm grateful to all my friends from St. John's, Ratcliffe and Cotton College with whom I have accumulated many treasured memories.

A special mention is due to Simon Boardman, Gary Bates, Paul Gibbons and Andy Gabriel without whom I would never have made it through university.

I will also give praise to my talented children, Josephine, David, Christina and Daniela and their moms, Kayla and Osiris.

For services rendered and professional encouragement, I would like to thank Julie Arnall and Stuart Diamond.

I would like to give a special mention to Mary Ethna Williams whose inspiration at the rebirth of this project was so influential.

Finally, I reserve sincere and personal thanks to you, the reader, as you join me on this journey that is The Cayman Conspiracy.

About the Book

Set in the Cayman Islands of the late 1980s this book introduces the complex, yet flawed character that is Joe LeRice, an expat Englishman living in the Cayman Islands by virtue of his father's work. As a child, Joe falls in love with the islands, its people and with one girl in particular. He vows to return and after struggling through university, he does so and marries his childhood sweetheart, Rachael Downing, whose father has since become a prominent politician.

Rachael's father, Arthur, has been tasked with evaluating a proposal from a gaming consortium based in Las Vegas, requesting exclusive gaming rights to the Cayman Islands and the permission to build a fabulous beachfront casino. This promises to inject millions into empty government coffers, solving many fiscal problems that currently prevent them from improving the national infrastructure.

Arthur is torn over this issue which comes to a head during a visit to the islands by the principals of *Eastern Promise Gaming Inc.* including the seductive siren, Kate Clementier. Finally, the issue comes before the Cayman Islands Government's Legislative Assembly for a vote.

Accidentally, Joe comes across a letter to Arthur from a Brogan Higgins in Vegas warning him not to trust *Eastern Promise Gaming Inc.* believing the organization to be responsible for the gambling problems of his brother and his subsequent death.

With very little evidence, Joe decides to trust his gut and embarks on a mission to go to Vegas to try and find out if *Eastern Promise Gaming Inc.* has been implicated in any criminal activity that would consequently negate their application for a business license in the Cayman Islands.

On the way to see Brogan Higgins in Vegas, Joe meets young Bobby, a tough, streetwise hooker. Strangely they bond, Joe being struck by her refreshing honesty as much as she is by his naive vulnerability.

Unable to find any evidence that would legally prevent *Eastern Promise* from operating in the Cayman Islands, Joe and Brogan aided by Bobby formulate a daring plan that takes on the gambling consortium at its own game.

During the execution of this plan, Joe comes face to face with his painful past and must overcome personal demons that have almost destroyed him as a young man.

Chapter One

As if dragged down invisibly by the thousands of dollars wagered on it, the busy roulette ball fell from its faltering orbit towards the swirl of numbers below. After a couple of speedy ricochets, it picked its spot.

"Sixteen. Red," announced the croupier matter-of-factly, as though she had already known. She placed a column-shaped object on the sparsely populated number, reminding her who to pay.

Groaning gamblers watched as their losing bets were swiftly scraped off the green, baize table and dumped into the greedy receptacle at the side of the wheel.

The few winners, suddenly more adept at mental arithmetic, quickly calculated their returns, if they hadn't done so already. The experienced croupier, displaying tactile perfection, didn't even need to look at the chips as she counted them. This display of dexterity was marveled at by the new players and taken for granted by the old hands.

One of the old hands, Higgins, bit hard into his lower lip suppressing the profanity that would have followed the 'F' that had just formed on his mouth. He had lost again. Dregs of table etiquette tightened his bite.

He tore his concentration from the feverish betting frenzy and sat up in his chair. He looked at his watch, if only through pure habit. There was nowhere he had to be, no wife at home, no supper on the table and no kids to play with. He had forfeited all that two years ago. So the fact that it was eight p.m. was irrelevant.

Shaky hands sent up spirals of cigarette smoke that wafted

across his face, urging him to join in. Before obliging, he paused to run his nicotine-stained fingers through his head of grey-flecked, black hair. His once-handsome face was now haggard with neglect and blotched with alcoholic overindulgence, removing any possibility of arguing the downside of his forty years.

He could not remember if his gambling had led him to drinking or if his drinking had led him to gambling. That was all a long time ago. The two seemed to go hand in hand these days; chips in one and a cognac in the other. His third hand was an ashtray that usually held a filterless cigarette, whose raking flavor completed his ritual of self flagellation.

He felt as though he was drowning, choking on self-hate. How had he gotten himself into such a dire strait? He waded back through the hazy avenues of his memory. Wandering back a few years to his favorite bar, he had been enjoying an after-work drink with some of his colleagues and, feeling a little high, he had decided to take a taxi home.

He found himself talking about casinos with the enthusiastic driver. At this point, he had been living in Vegas for three years and had always avoided the bright lights that he felt were for the tourists, besides which, his demanding job selling mining equipment in this state of Nevada had kept him well away. If that wasn't enough, his wife and two young children would sap any surplus energy that he was fortunate enough to come home with.

However, every so often, he and some of his colleagues would spend an evening together as they had done that night. Higgins had found himself believing the driver's story that a little gambling could supplement an ailing income. Coincidentally, recent months had been fairly lean for Higgins' sales figures and with a few drinks under his belt, he had found himself agreeing to a little detour to the *Eastern Promise Hotel & Casino*. Such was his rapport with the driver, they even went in together.

His first impression was one of unbridled opulence. It was incredible; this place wove the fabulous wealth and deep mystique of the Orient into the perfect spell. The faithfully-reproduced architecture had to have been whisked here on a magic carpet directly from the pages of *One Thousand and One Nights*, he had mused.

When he had turned to share his wonder with his new friend, Higgins had suddenly found himself alone, the moist ten-dollar note for his fare still clenched in his hand. In futility, he had looked around for the driver, until the welcome offer of a complimentary drink dissolved any prevailing concern. Well, now that he was here, he might as well see what all the fuss was about, he thought.

At a glance, everybody had seemed too preoccupied with the many ongoing attractions to notice a new face and that suited Higgins as he observed the various games. Surprised at their simplicity, it wasn't long before he had taken the plunge and joined in, getting used to the feel of the toy currency that enabled him to play these fun games. He remembered sitting at the roulette table for the first time. Every spin, he would rub his imaginary magic lamp with hope and more often than not, the genie had obliged. Such excitement, followed by the cashing in of his pile of play-money for the real thing was the icing on this sweet cake.

It was through pure luck rather than good judgment that he had won at first. Penny, his wife, was treated to a rash of useless gifts that she would have happily exchanged for his company. Over the following months they had grown apart, Higgins unable to wrench himself away from his new home and Penny feeling helpless. He persisted even when his beginner's luck had long since run out. Soon he had begun to lose; heavily.

Higgins knew that he had given his cherished Penny no choice but to leave, and although he had seemed incapable of preventing it, he could not understand it. He didn't want it, but he couldn't stop it. All of his efforts were thwarted by the inexplicable rush that he would feel just thinking about the spin of the wheel. He knew the only way out of this whirlpool was down, how much further, he had no idea, but he sensed that he would soon find out.

Warnings from his wealthy brother, Brogan, who had lived in Vegas more than twenty years, reverberated in his ears: "You haven't got a hope in hell. Can't you see that? What the fuck do you think these places are, benevolent societies?"

"I can win next time. I'm overdue for a change of luck. I know it"

"You poor, stupid bastard. You just don't see it, do you? What is it with you, drugs, or what? No sane man would pull your kind of shit. You've thrown away Penny, your friends and your money; you ain't got a scrap of self respect left in you."

"Ok, Big Brother, I hear you, loud and clear. I'll quit soon, I promise. Listen, I've had a few unexpected expenses recently and I was wondering if you could perhaps...?"

"No fucking way!" Brogan had slammed the door of their relationship, anticipating yet another cash request. Brogan had given up and angrily pushed past the empty shell that had once been his beloved brother. Tightly wrapped in his selfish cocoon, Higgins had never even seen the tears in Brogan's eyes.

With his mental soliloquy now ended with the usual self-justification, the craving for another cigarette abruptly tossed Higgins back into the present, his dire situation almost perfectly described by the paltry few gaming chips that were clutched in his sweaty left hand.

He would have to make his move soon. He couldn't sit there all night staring into space, could he? Perhaps a few more minutes, he compromised. For the first time throughout this ordeal he plucked up enough courage to admit that he was afraid. Who wouldn't be in these circumstances? Only yesterday, his car had been repossessed by the dealer; his sales job was on the line and he was four months behind on his mortgage repayments. His only asset was his wife's refusal to demand alimony against the vehement insistence of her unsympathetic lawyer.

Penny had pleaded with her husband and tried to introduce him to professional help but he had always scorned her efforts with an effluent of denial, refusing to accept that his recreation was not normal. Her worst moment had been when her drunk, angry husband had come home after another losing spree in that damned casino when he had actually raised his hand to her, and beaten her, leaping over that invisible threshold of marital trust.

She had confronted him about the missing money that she had been saving up for their eldest child's seventh birthday party. Scavenging around, Higgins had found it in a biscuit tin in one of the kitchen cupboards. He promised himself that he would pay it back. The tin, like the promise had remained empty.

Even the tears that Penny had shed after lighting the single birthday-cake candle for the seventh time had failed to dampen his burning need to bet. Before this incident, Higgins was one of those men who despised aggressive men. He was the kind of man who would butt into an argument to defend the honor of a woman whom he didn't even know. Now he had tasted the bitter pill of scorn that he had once prescribed. He was one of them. A wife-beater!

This shocking about-turn had twisted his values into worthless words, only to be spouted in barroom dialogues with anybody unfortunate enough to have struck up a conversation with him.

It was usually at this point that the desire for the anesthesia of his favorite cognac would rescue him from further anguish. He looked around for the cocktail waitress hoping that the agony in his heart was not evident on his face.

Kerry's eyes met Higgins' and she strutted over, determined not to look foolish in the skimpy outfit that came with the job. She felt a certain pity for some of these hopeless fools, but it was soon forgotten when their leering attitudes insulted her dignity. Higgins was scum. He hadn't always been; but she had seen many a man change like this over the years. Anyway he tipped well and she had mouths to feed. She smiled, "The usual, sir?"

"You got it," drawled Higgins and with a display of male inadequacy, he ogled her from behind as she went about his request, conning himself that she enjoyed serving him.

She knew he was staring and she wore his glare like a millstone of resentment as she poured out the cognac, putting in an extra shot to keep him at bay a little longer. The drink was free, but the service was an intangible extra. Higgins acknowledged this with the usual tip that he could ill-afford, but like all good gamblers, he was a seasoned liar and a master of paranoia.

He searched for any hint of a come-on in Kerry's uninterested face. Once again, they drew opposing conclusions.

It was now time to talk business. Higgins knew that he would have to ask for a line of credit to support this evening's gambling. He accepted this as a last resort, because of what had happened the last time he took credit. After getting a line of credit, then losing and hurrying out, he bumped into what appeared be a friendly fellow-gambler. The new friend had seemed to read his thoughts and over a parting cognac, referred him to a loan-shark. He had quickly realized that these people were deadly serious about getting paid back. Now he was broke again and the sharks would be circling; he would have to win some of his money back. This was ridiculous, he thought, but since he had run out of scapegoats, punishing himself would do no good. He decided to press on. Sheepishly, he made eye contact with Charlie, the pit manager.

Immediately, Charlie seized the upper hand and strode over to the hapless Higgins. Charlie lent a sympathetic ear to the request for credit before picking up the nearest house telephone. He dialed a single digit and stared into one of the many security cameras as though he were talking directly to someone. He was.

"Yes, Charlie. What is it?" asked Luca Telesino, the general manager, giving Charlie the chance to put into words what he had spent the last hour watching on one of his screens.

"Mr. Higgins needs a marker, sir," confirmed Charlie.

"So I've noticed, Charlie. What are you waiting for?"

"How much?"

"Two grand. No more. No less. If he loses...No, when he loses, send him up to my office."

"Will do, sir," said Charlie, relishing this extra responsibility that he was called upon to execute every so often after another sucker had got in way over their head.

"Will two thousand be enough?" asked Charlie turning to Higgins. He was already filling out the credit voucher in anticipation of the standard response. Higgins agreed with the speed of a scalded cat, afraid that they might change their mind.

The whole sum was converted directly into chips in accordance with house rules but it was not until he could actually feel them in his unsteady hands that Higgins felt the waves of relaxation flow over him.

At last, he was safe. Now he could win his money back and some dignity to boot. Now holding the edge, this stack of borrowed chips would buy his ticket from this hell; only time would tell if it would be a return ticket.

That old winning feeling was coming back to him. Very shortly, Lady Luck would be sitting beside him and it would be time to play. An arrogant smirk held his next cigarette which he lit with his gold-plated, Dunhill lighter, remembering to avoid the flame that always seemed to jump higher in this charged place. He had bought it after one of his early lucky spells. If he had taken the time to look back over his fortune since owning it, he would have dropped it like a red-hot coal, but he exercised his right to be superstitious when it suited him.

He sipped some more of his cognac and sensed Lady Luck sidle up to him with promises that warmed his heart. The bitch sang like a Siren and Higgins was set on joining Ulysses as the only other survivor of the forbidden melody. Unfortunately for Higgins, he had no friends left to secure him to the mast of sanity and sure enough, his sinking ship was quickly dashed against the rocks.

Fickle Lady Luck had only needed an hour to lose all of Higgins' money. Charlie scoffed through the episode, actually enjoying the pathetic entertainment that Higgins was providing. Like the hard-core gambler that he was, Higgins played it to the bitter end, geeing himself up with fist clenches, clichés and ludicrously comparing himself to a Spartan warrior facing unfair odds. He even changed his emergency five-dollar note into a single chip and placed it on thirteen. The number stayed true. It was over.

A burly security guard invaded Higgins' wreckage. "Excuse me, sir. The general manager would like to see you in his office. I've been instructed to accompany you."

Like a zombie, Higgins stood up, unable to attain his full five feet ten. He slipped his lucky lighter into a pocket of his tatty, checkered jacket and followed until they reached the private staff elevator.

The guard used his control key and launched them to Telesino's nerve centre on the thirty-fifth floor. Higgins restrained the urge to make light talk as his chaperone stared at the door throughout, anxious to complete his task and not incur the infamous wrath of Luca Telesino. They duly arrived and a faceless heavy held open the door to his boss's office.

Like an errant schoolboy summoned before the headmaster, Higgins shuffled in and behind a huge wooden desk he could make out a patch of black, thinning hair that peeped over the rear of a large, leather swivel-chair. Sensing the arrival of an expected guest, the chair spun around to reveal Luca Telesino wearing a black tuxedo and a yellow smile. He rose, confidently filling out his stout six feet.

"Ah, Mr. Higgins, come in. I've been expecting you," Telesino started in a paternal tone. "Sit down. Please."

Higgins obliged.

"Correct me if I am wrong, Mr. Higgins, but I am led to believe that you are experiencing severe financial difficulties at the moment?"

He paused to await a reaction. None came; he drew the appropriate conclusion and continued, "I would like to give you the chance to redeem yourself." He paused to let his words sink in. "If you perform satisfactorily, we may be able to forget the two thousand dollars."

Higgins wondered what the catch would be.

The erudite Telesino went on, "In addition, I am sure that my cousin would also be willing to waive the ten thousand that you owe one of his loan agents."

Shit! Higgins thought. *The loan shark was tied up with this man's cousin!*

"Hey, wait a minute!" Higgins blurted out. "That was five grand, not ten!"

"If you are that unfamiliar with the terms of your agreement, Mr. Higgins, I suggest that you read the fine print again. Interest usually accrues on such transactions and yours is no exception."

Telesino's voice took on a sharper edge. The ominous warnings sliced through Higgins' resistance. He was prepared to listen to any alternative. It didn't even have to be reasonable.

"What do I have to do?" surrendered Higgins.

"Follow me, please," commanded Telesino, waddling over to a digital pad on the wall. Rapidly, he punched a few numbers in and the wall appeared to vanish, revealing what seemed to be a control room. Paid eyes were scanning the plethora of television screens and ignored the newcomer.

"This is power, Mr. Higgins, absolute power. All legal, I might add. Once our customers come through the doors, we know every move that they make. How much money they spend, what they drink, the brand of cigarettes they smoke, if they need a loan, you name it."

"Where do I come in?" appealed Higgins, acutely aware of his sudden nakedness.

"We would like to have the pleasure of entertaining some of your friends," explained Telesino.

"Like free advertising, you mean?" said the hopeful Higgins.

"Something like that," replied Telesino with a frown that insinuated it was not that simple.

This business was beginning to sound sinister to Higgins. He weighed up his options and gave up almost immediately.

Telesino continued, "All you have to do is convince some of your friends that they should spend an evening playing our tables. One new person each week will be sufficient. I will be watching for you."

"Is that all?" asked Higgins, almost relieved. His sales experience would come in handy for this strange task, he thought. It was simple enough. He didn't even have to bring his victims back again, did he?

"What if they don't come back?" he asked.

Telesino looked at him, grinning. "You did."

Past memories smashed to the forefront of Higgins' brain. What had brought *him* back? Free choice, surely? What about that taxi-driver? And what about his incessant craving to come always to *The Eastern Promise* and nowhere else? There had to be some devious way of making people come back? Or was it just a basic human weakness that they preyed on? Whatever it was, it had destroyed him. He recalled the levels of depravity that he had sunk to, and finally, he had found his last scapegoat.

Higgins suppressed the rising urge to throw up. His thoughts flashed back to Brogan's warning. It was too late now and he accepted it. Higgins found himself nodding vacantly, ignoring the veiled threats of violence that were now spewing from the mouth of

Telesino.

After a slippery handshake that blended Higgins' sweat and Telesino's nature, Higgins was shown the door. Telesino returned to his observation room and patted a machine as though thanking it for a job well done. A magnetic tape in the device played continuously, singing its silent song that accompanied the easy-listening music in the gaming-room. It didn't work on everybody, but it appeared to have an excellent success rate on drinkers and other fools seeking meaning to their lives. Once the victims kept coming back, the slightly unfair mathematical odds of the games would do the rest.

The security guard had waited to escort Higgins back into the public domain. During the descent of the elevator, Higgins wondered if he really had the courage to inflict a similar fate on other fools such as himself. He doubted his resolve. A few fragments of humanity were still nestled in his fragile code of existence.

The claustrophobia of the lift was gratefully diluted with the metallic swish of the doors that announced their arrival on the ground floor. Higgins now sensed the poisonous aura with belated disgust. He glared at the cameras before sneering at Charlie, who was busily assisting in the recruitment of the next slave. Higgins quickly made his exit into the warm Vegas evening strangely relieved that his downfall had been aided.

He found a payphone and dialed Brogan's number. After three rings, Higgins heard the familiar hissing sound that was the beginning of the recorded message. He decided that this may be for the better considering his unswayable plan of action. "...and if you leave your name and number after the tone, I will return your call as soon as possible. Thank you."

Higgins pressed the receiver to his ear enduring the piercing, electronic beep. His grip tightened and he was shaking with a hybrid feeling of fear and anger tempered with love. He paused, desperately reaching for words to convey the spectrum of his emotions.

"Brogan. The bastards got me," he quivered. "It was a set up; some kind of thought control. I never had a chance. I love you. Tell Penny..."

Click. His time was up. With no more change in his pocket, he'd have to leave it at that. Brogan would be able to handle Penny, he thought as he turned to go back to *The Eastern Promise*. Mentally, he kissed his children goodbye as he looked up to the thirty fifth floor and beyond.

Higgins marched back inside the tall building and rode the public elevator as far as it would take him which was two floors below Telesino's lair. The thirty-third floor appeared deserted and he made his way to the emergency staircase. The fire escape key was hanging in a glass case on the wall. Higgins smashed it with his hand ignoring any pain and unsightly blood. He winced with pain as he twisted the key in the lock, struggling to overcome its history of inactivity. It gave way and he pulled the key back out, in the hope that it could help him two floors up. He was right, but there was a welcoming committee and Higgins' gashed hand turned the carpet red.

Two oxen-like men grabbed him by the wrists, and forced his hands behind his back before they frog-marched him back into Telesino's office.

"Mr. Higgins. I am most disappointed with your obvious violent intent. I may not give you another chance."

"Spare me the bullshit." Higgins was pleased with his new found valor. "You should be put away, you evil bastard."

"I take it that you don't wish to make amends for your outstanding obligations," Telesino concluded, still maintaining his grasp of a bank manager's vocabulary.

"I'll see you in hell, mister!" Higgins shouted, struggling in vain.

"I don't doubt that Mr. Higgins. But by the time I arrive you should be settled in," smirked Telesino. He turned to his henchmen coldly and snarled, "Get rid of this piece of shit."

The blood from Higgins' cut hand had compromised the grip of one of his captors. He sensed this and swiftly twisted the hand free from the surprised goon. This motion swiveled him to face the second man whom he surprised with an accurate punch to the jaw. The recoil bought Higgins a few vital seconds and now free, he steadied himself on the heavy wooden desk before launching himself towards Telesino with the desperation of a wounded animal. As his hands vainly sought to induce a fatal stranglehold, Higgins heard a sickly crack that was his last memory.

Chapter Two

Joe LeRice soaked up the last rays of the Caribbean sun. His recliner had long since ceased to be at the best tanning angle, but that didn't matter. There would be many more days like this, he thought as he felt the cool caress of the south-easterly that rustled the coconut-laden palm trees. He sat up and gazed into the crystal sea watching it stroke the sandy beach like a doting mother brushing her daughter's golden hair.

The beautiful Cayman Islands, once remembered as *The Land That Time Forgot*. Joe smiled as the country's motto seemed to form in his mind, *"He hath founded it upon the seas."*

Joe knew who the *He* referred to. It was not Christopher Columbus who was attributed with the discovery of these islands in 1503, but rather the Divine Artist who had created this masterpiece. Columbus had obviously not been ashore because if he had, he would never have chosen to return to the shackles of civilization.

At first the three islands were referred to as *Las Tortugas* on account of the copious green turtles that once adorned the virginal beaches. During their egg-laying season, these turtles would come ashore to bury their clutches as they had been doing for thousands of years. That was before advanced European sailors had discovered the delights of turtle meat. Their population swiftly dwindled and, ashamed yet unshakeable, man was forced to choose a more suitable name for these islands having nullified the original one.

Las Caymanas was the next choice, taken from the Spanish word for alligator. In fact, the alligators referred to were probably huge iguanas that are now extinct in this particular environ and rather than sentence some other innocent species to a similar fate the name stuck.

Over history's ensuing course, the islands became a genetic melting-pot simmering with an unusual recipe of genuine settlers, pirates, freed Negro slaves and indigenous Caribbean Indians. The most enduring ingredient proved to be the British seasoning which even today, gives these islands a distinctly colonial flavor and an English mother tongue.

Folklore has it that the now international tax-haven reputation of the Cayman Islands was a direct result of gratitude shown by King George III who is said to have removed all forms of taxation from the islanders following their heroic deeds during the *Wreck of the Ten Sails.*

Toward the end of the eighteenth century, a convoy of ten British merchant ships was sailing past the eastern end of Grand Cayman and during the stormy night, the leading ship ran onto a reef several hundred yards from the shore. In an attempt to warn the others, it flashed a signal which was mistaken for a benign command to follow. The splintering of the timber and the shouts of the ill-fated mariners alerted the sleeping islanders who quickly mobilized a small flotilla of whatever was remotely seaworthy.

The rescue attempt was a brave success and it is reported that not a single life was lost in the course of that momentous night.

Over the following years the islands remained relatively obscure, although the men forged themselves a reputation as master seamen. A Caymanian sailor was always, and still is, a respected member of any ship's crew due to his almost boundless knowledge of his mother, the Sea, who had protected and nurtured him from birth, sharing her deep mysteries with him.

With the arrival of the first seaplane in 1953 piloted by Owen Roberts, and the subsequent construction of the airport that still bears his name, the Cayman Islands were primed for a mighty explosion of growth that would shatter any effort to retain the status quo.

The Caymans were established as an alternative vacation destination during the 'sixties, its virgin reefs desired by insatiable scuba divers, anxious to follow in the fabled footsteps of the master, Jacques Cousteau.

The more astute business people set about creating homes for the wealthy visitors and banks for their money, away from the prying eyes of the taxation beast that ravaged their assets back home.

The 'seventies saw an unparalleled, condominium construction boom on Grand Cayman that threatened to turn the glorious *Seven Mile Beach* into a writhing concrete snake.

Every major financial institution had watched these developments with keen eyes and after they had dipped their toes into the inviting waters, they decided to dive headlong into the establishment of the western hemisphere's most sophisticated and secretive financial market.

Not surprisingly, undesirables soon took advantage of the confidentiality of the private banking system, flying in on their personal jets to deposit vast sums of cash in their secret accounts. This gave an effective way of laundering their ill-gotten gains with the added advantage of avoiding tax. The Caymanian government became wise to these tricks and passed a series of laws that required depositors to prove the validity of their cash. In drug-related investigations it then became possible to enforce the divulgence of the suspected baron's account details.

Although not openly discussed, it has become extremely fashionable for the more privileged members of our society to have private accounts at one of the five hundred or so banks registered in Georgetown, the capital, which does not even cover a square mile. Foreign-owned, private shell companies soon outnumbered the population, which at last count in 1989 stood at 25,000, only 1500 of whom do not live on Grand Cayman, mainly in favor of Cayman Brac. A mere handful occupy the sleepy Little Cayman.

With the advent of the telex machine, the Cayman Islands boasted more machines per capita than any other country in the world.

Bewildered by this sudden and relentless development of their once peaceful land, many Caymanians still view most foreigners with a justifiable caution.

One foreigner who had almost forged total acceptance was the late Sir Richard LeRice, Joe's father. In the late 'sixties, Richard LeRice, a civil engineer, had been one of several professionals dispatched to the Caymans by the Foreign Office in answer to a plea for assistance from the islands' government. They desperately needed help from the motherland in establishing an efficient bureaucracy to leash the impending expansion. Richard LeRice became so dedicated to the people with whom he had worked alongside, that he was invited to stay on as a consultant to the government even after his Foreign Office contract had expired.

After a knighthood in 1975, Sir Richard was killed in a tragic plane crash two years later when engine failure forced his Cessna into the sea during a routine six mile 'hop' between the two smaller islands, Cayman Brac and Little Cayman. Floating debris yielded a wallet containing a few sodden banknotes and a photograph of his wife and son. On the back a fading inspiration could just be made out.

"Richard, to yourself be true."

No body was found and it was probably fitting that a man so vibrant in life should not have been seen in death; reduced to a flaccid corpse, planted into a hole in the ground and watered by a river of diplomatic tears. A memorial was erected to him on Cayman Brac.

After the accident, a fifteen year old Joe and his mother returned to England permanently. Joe's young life had been spent commuting between public school and his father's job, but he clung quietly to the memories that he had collected in the Cayman Islands and he promised himself that one day, he would return.

In 1980, the year in which his mother died from cancer, and not helped by a broken heart, Joe had almost dropped out of university and decided to spend some time in the islands, amongst the memories of his youth.

Still reclining, he recalled that visit which was to shape the course of his life and bring him back forever to this *Land That Time Forgot*.

The seeds for his return had been planted in his adolescence. During that time of his life, Joe had found someone whom he enjoyed being with; she was a pretty, Caymanian girl, whose different culture had given her a set of homely values that were in refreshing contrast to manufactured, teenaged Britain.

Joe was determined not to be one of the millions who carried fond recollections of their childhood sweethearts through their compromised lives. Having tried as hard as he could, he could not forget that honey-brown girl whose face was firmly imprinted on his soul.

On returning to Cayman Brac, Joe had been pleasantly surprised to find out that Rachael Downing had not married, as so many young island girls seemed to do. Instead, she had embarked upon several correspondence courses in a bid to further her career with local government. Impressed, yet guilty for harboring his own plans to drop out of university, Joe had decided to struggle through the final year of his studies before returning. Many nights of passionate love beneath the bright, Caribbean moon ensured that they would both have something to look forward to.

If his future was to contain Rachael, then it would have to be in the Cayman Islands and Joe knew that he had to find a career to preserve those conditions. He did. After a small wedding, he had used the last of his inheritance money and bought a plot of land on Grand Cayman. With Rachael's help he had secured a loan to build a house on it. He had worked on the site every day spending hours helping, even after the workmen had long since gone home. He had sold the property for a healthy profit and over the next five years, he had built up one of the most successful property development companies in the Cayman Islands. In fact, this evening was one of their first in the brand-new house that Joe had built for his wife.

Joe turned his admiring gaze towards Rachael as she lay just a few yards away. As she slept, her hair cradled her face in a pillow of auburn, and Joe spent a few minutes appreciating the part that she played in his happiness. She and Joe were so different that their relationship served to strengthen the theory that opposites attract.

Rachael had achieved a respectable position with the legal department of government and could easily have followed her father into politics, but there were more important things on her mind. Rachael's greatest desire now was to hear the patter of tiny feet, perhaps a couple of pairs.

Joe found these thoughts stimulating and with a naughty grin he concluded that if Rachael had not yet conceived, it was not for lack of trying. Just imagining making love to his wife, Joe became aroused and played out the scene in his mind.

The sun was slowly sinking below the waves and like a drowning artist, it painted its last skyscape. In a breathtaking spectrum of colors that ranged from a rich yellow to a deep blood-red, skillfully blended on Nature's blue canvas, it submerged in a fleeting flash of green and was gone.

This seemed to be the signal for hungry mosquitoes to emerge from their inactivity and search for their precious food, blood; preferably human. With the high-pitched whining of the first unwelcome insect in his ear, Joe decided to rescue his wife from the impending raid. Moving his six-foot frame quickly, he scooped his wife's warm body into his wiry arms and smiled reassuringly at her as she awoke, pleasantly surprised at reality commencing where her dream had just left off.

"Mmm. Kidnapped by a horny pirate," she teased, "Don't tell my husband."

"I promise," whispered Joe. Rachael winked at him, drawing a smile from her captor. As well as being the gateway to her sensuality, her eyes were unique to look at. Their shape was slightly oriental, a legacy from a Chinese great-grandmother and the pupils were lost in an animated sea of green whose waters it would take a lifetime to chart.

Joe maneuvered himself and his prize between their two recliners and strode past the kidney-shaped pool to the patio door. Enjoying his firm grip, Rachael slid the door open from her vantage point so that Joe would not have to put her down. A cool wave flowed over them. The central air-conditioning had performed perfectly and the formation of goose pimples on Joe's tense arms sped him to the bedroom.

Joe set Rachael down gently on their bed, her arms still wrapped around his neck. She did not want to let go and Joe came forward to kiss her in appreciation of this. They slid under the solitary top sheet and turned to face each other.

They came closer together, probing each other's warmth, searching for opportunities to please one another. They both knew when the time had come, and when it did, they merged slowly and deliberately, savoring the moment. Rachael's hands ran down Joe's sides. Her touch was electric. Her legs began to quiver and she gripped him tightly with them. He sensed her urgency, moving faster and faster spurred on by her pleading, breathless voice. He felt profound waves swelling from deep within and he could not stop. She did not want him to, and they exploded into mutual climax, dissolving in pure emotion. Satisfied, they lay together, Joe's head resting on his wife's pert breasts.

About a half hour later, Joe gingerly eased himself away from Rachael's lingering embrace and succeeded in leaving her asleep so that she could finish the dream that had left her face so serene. He padded out of their bedroom and treated himself to a shower in the guest bathroom. The strong jet of water massaged his entirety and he opened his mouth to savor the cool flow. He would have stayed longer but his awareness for water preservation in this hot climate got the better of him. He pushed in the shower dial, instantly stopping the flow. The sudden silence was broken by the ringing of the telephone.

"Shit!" Joe chimed in. He padded out over the white tiled floor leaving glistening pools of water behind with each footstep. He managed to intercept the call, his calm voice concealing any inconvenience.

"Joe LeRice."

"Hello, Joe," said a voice that Joe recognized immediately as belonging to his father-in-law, Arthur Downing.

"What are you and Rachael doing this evening?" he enquired.

"We hadn't really thought about it. If there's nothing exciting going on, we may go to *Benjamin's Roof* for dinner." replied Joe.

"Well, if you haven't made concrete plans, perhaps you'd like to be my guests at a dinner function tonight?"

"Where?" asked Joe.

"At the *Hyatt Regency.*"

"Why? What's happening?" asked Joe, now interested. Dinner at the *Hyatt* was always a treat.

"Oh, it's just another boring function. Some travel company is presenting their sales awards. Actually, it's you I really want to talk to. I need your Western expertise."

Joe turned around to see Rachael coming over towards him. "Hold on a second," he said, "Rachael's here. I'm game, but I'll ask her what she thinks."

She nodded her head in answer to Joe's question before relieving Joe of the 'phone to have a daughter-to-father chat. Joe left them to it and returned to the bathroom to clean up.

He wondered what Arthur wanted to talk about this time. Arthur Downing was now a respected politician, having run in the last election and won one of the twelve seats in the Legislative Assembly, representing the smaller islands.

In fact, Arthur Downing was an important member of government who was responsible for the regulation of the thriving tourist industry. More importantly to Joe, Rachael's father and his own had been close friends and Joe respected him for the strong values that were now evident in his beautiful daughter.

After Rachael had hung up, she found Joe and said, "It starts in a couple of hours. Daddy wants us to meet him at the *Garden Loggia* in an hour and a half."

Chapter Three

The LeRices arrived at the *Hyatt Regency* slightly earlier than the arranged eight o'clock. With twenty minutes on their hands, they decided to make a detour to the *Britannia, a* golf-club bar, rather than fight their way through the hordes of hungry travel agents at the *Loggia.*

The club's balcony sat over a man-made lake that rippled with the gentle breeze, causing the moonbeams to dart to and fro like mischievous fairy children having escaped their mother's watchful eye.

It was being able to appreciate scenes like these that made the years of hard work seem worthwhile and although they remained silent, mutual thoughts of love and deep respect raced between them.

Pulling themselves away from this living landscape was hard, but hand-in-hand they strolled through the colonial surroundings and towards the *Loggia* for their rendezvous.

Their tranquility was broken as they entered the restaurant, a flustered maitre d' could only point them in the direction of their seats, too busy to escort them. Maintaining an air of grace during these functions was made difficult by excited people who were behaving as though they were in a fast food joint, rather than a respected, gourmet restaurant.

Joe and Rachael picked out a path through tamed, tropical foliage, past buzzing guests and over to an alcove where portly Arthur Downing and his wife, Elene, were seated.

"Good evening, Joe," Arthur greeted Joe, before kissing his

daughter. "I'd like you to sit next to me that is, if your wife doesn't mind?"

Rachael and her mother had hardly seen each other since she and Joe had moved into their new home and they were already locked in animated conversation.

"Sure," agreed Joe, sliding in beside Arthur.

"It's just that I've got a few questions I'd like to bounce off you," explained the politician.

"As long as it's nothing too complicated," laughed Joe. Talking was relegated to the back-burner whilst their glasses were filled with *Veuve Cliquot* by an attentive waiter, pleased to be away from the unquenchable travel-agents. Lips moistened, the foursome turned their attention to the menu and sifted through the options.

The three Caymanians, brought up on Cajun and Caribbean home cooking, eyed many of the unpronounceable dishes with suspicion but quickly tracked down the seafood section, especially the lobster. In a moment of nostalgia, Joe went European and selected the steak-au-poivre, medium-rare.

The waiter beamed with pride as he assured Arthur and his guests that all dishes were available. The local fisherman had obviously been out that day and there was nothing like Caymanian lobster to serve up a dish of national pride.

After they had ordered, Arthur turned to Joe who was expecting another debate that he and Arthur frequently got into. The two men had never really forged a classic, in-law relationship, but acted amicably towards each other, rather like business colleagues. They respected each other's backgrounds and occasionally, Arthur would seek Joe's opinion on subjects that he knew would go no further than the two of them.

"Joe, I know I don't have to say this, but this discussion finishes with the meal."

Joe nodded in agreement and braced himself for yet another round of politics.

"What's your position on legalized gambling?" Arthur commenced.

Knowing that all gambling in the Cayman Islands was illegal since the first constitution had been drawn up, Joe was caught off guard. He bought time with a question of his own.

"From a moral standpoint or a businessman's?"

"Both," countered Arthur.

"Are you talking about casinos, such as in Las Vegas and the Bahamas?"

"Probably." As ever, Arthur was playing the cagey diplomat, thought Joe.

"I'll start with the easy one first," said Joe. "From a businessman's point of view, a casino is said to be a foolproof way of making money."

"How's that?"

"It's the odds. The games that are played are cleverly designed to give the casinos the edge," explained Joe.

"In what way?" Arthur pressed.

"Take roulette. You've got zero to thirty-six, that's thirty-seven possible outcomes. If you win, you only get paid thirty-five to one. The very second you bet, the odds are against you."

"You're pretty knowledgeable on this, aren't you Joe?" Arthur observed. "Have you gambled before?"

"To a degree," replied Joe, "I joined a club when I was at university." He smirked at the irony of his statement.

"What was it like?" Arthur delved deeper.

"Exciting, especially when you hit that win and all the losses don't seem to matter. But losing money can be a real pain. I suppose all gamblers see themselves as winners. That's why casinos exist, to cater to all those winners. It's a bloody rip-off."

"Those are harsh words; perhaps I've hit a sensitive nerve?" prodded Arthur.

"Not as harsh as they could be," answered Joe, "but those days are over for me. It was just a bit of fun."

Joe refrained from elaborating, preferring to keep certain bad memories to himself.

"But you did have a free choice and it was legal?" Arthur said.

"That's true," agreed Joe.

"You can't tamper with democracy, Joe. People have died for free choice," stated Arthur, taking the moral high ground.

There was no argument to that. Getting back to the point, Joe probed, "Why the great interest?"

"Let's just say that the government is looking into various ways of raising capital," hinted Arthur.

"You mean there are going to be casinos here, in the Cayman Islands?" concluded Joe.

"Not exactly, at least not in the plural," explained Arthur. "I'm researching an offer that's been made by a group from the States to have the exclusive rights in the islands. There'd be only one casino."

"Well, Arthur, you asked my opinion, I'll give it to you," stated Joe, "you've got by without gambling until now, so why change?"

"Capital," stated Arthur, flatly. "There are a lot of things we've been planning to do and we simply don't have the resources."

"Money?" Joe simplified.

"If you like," accepted Arthur, "Look what happened to the school during Hurricane Gilbert last year. Do you know how much embarrassment that caused us? I mean, imagine a designated shelter losing its roof?"

"Can't you introduce a form of taxation instead?" asked Joe.

"And ruin the reputation of the islands? No way, an idea like that would be laughed out of the Assembly. Think of all that investment that might be lost if we impose tax."

"What about import duties, can you raise those?" offered Joe.

"I thought you'd be the last person to want an increase in import duties. You must pay a fortune on your building materials?" suggested Arthur.

"I do, but I'd be prepared to pay more if that meant keeping a casino out."

"I don't think that you're being objective, Joe," remarked Arthur frowning. "It was a bad idea to bring the subject up."

"You're the one not being objective, Arthur," retorted Joe. "You won't cream any more from the rich, because you're afraid of losing investment. So you'll be creaming from those who want to be rich, all those poor sods with stars in their eyes and gambling chips in their hands."

"Hold on, Joe. You've got to realize that I'm not familiar with the intricacies of gambling, but I'm doing my darndest to find out. I didn't say that a casino is coming; I merely said we were looking into the possibility of it. It wasn't my idea, I was asked to do the study by Executive Council, and that's exactly what I'm going to do."

"I just hope that you look at both sides of the coin," said Joe, cooling down hoping that he could drop the subject.

"Please hear me out, Joe" said Arthur, in a firm tone that briefly caught the attention of the two women, "If I felt that proposing new legislation would be detrimental to the country, don't you think I'd say so."

"I'm sure you would," agreed Joe.

"A dear friend of mine told me that when confronted by dilemma, there is only one thing that you can do," Arthur pontificated.

"Yes?" Joe prompted.

"To yourself be true."

Their eyes connected in a fleeting tribute to Joe's late father and this common ground defused the debate as starters were served.

After a sinfully rich dinner, the diners did penance by sitting through a standard dose of clichés after which, Arthur was called upon to present the awards.

Joe was left to mull over the implications of their discussion, retreating from any light family banter to the events that had given him such a rigid view on this subject.

During his college days, Joe, his flat mate Simon, and two other friends had joined a casino. Since the death of his mother, Joe had found himself fighting the kind of escapism that could be found in a bottle and the exciting atmosphere of a casino had seemed a natural progression. After several expensive forays, the eccentric but brilliant Simon had confronted Joe and mathematically proven that losing was inevitable.

Joe had just imparted some of his friend's words to Arthur along with his own experiences. Fear of losing his best friend had motivated Joe to drop his gambling, but he would never forget the addictive high that came with the winning wager. His two other friends were not so fortunate, and in a few months, they had lost every penny and dropped out from their studies.

Arthur resumed his seat and Joe approached the subject from a calmer angle, "How much time do you have before you finish your feasibility report?" he probed.

"About three months. Then I'll be meeting with the directors of the consortium to evaluate their final proposal, after which I submit my recommendations to Executive Council."

"But even if *ExCo* approve, it'll still have to go to vote in the Legislative Assembly?" inquired Joe.

"That's right. The whole thing could take a year before any new laws are passed."

Although the time frame comforted Joe, he knew that he had not heard the last of this. He felt powerless; after all, this was not his country and he didn't even have a vote. He would have to hope that Arthur would complete his study and arrive at a negative conclusion, but turning down instant millions might be too much to ask.

The restaurant was showing signs of emptying as the merry travel agents decided to take their chances of waking up with somebody they had never met before as they hunted the city-beat at one of the nearby nightclubs.

The quieter atmosphere was immediate relief to Arthur's indigestion and he expressed a desire to leave. Joe and Rachael stayed behind for another coffee while Arthur took Elene home.

"It sounded like you and Daddy got a little worked up?" Rachael began.

"It wasn't as bad as that," replied Joe. "He asked for my view on legalized gambling and I gave it to him, a little too bluntly perhaps."

"I don't think he knows much about it. We've never had it here although I've read that people can get rich overnight," she offered.

"That's true. I've never seen a poor bookie," mused Joe

"A bookie?" Rachael's quizzical look told Joe it was time to drop the subject.

"It doesn't matter, honey" said Joe, "it may never happen. Come on, let's go home."

After an afternoon of bliss, the evening left them driving home in silence. Rachael was Arthur's daughter, and that could neither be changed, nor compromised, so Joe decided not to rock the boat, and dropped the matter.

That night he lay awake thinking, chastising himself for being so idealistic, but try as hard as he might, he could not forget the destruction that he had so narrowly avoided. As the memories of his university days played themselves out in his mind, he felt himself remembering the incredible highs and lows that come with the life of a gambler. His pulse began to race and sleep eluded him. Mercifully, important thoughts about his current construction project delivered him from further torture and eventually, he drifted off to sleep at about 3.00 am.

Chapter Four

The four o'clock sun filtered softly through the reflective glass that comprised the outer walls of the Cayman Islands Government Administration Building. This centre of bureaucracy had swiftly been dubbed, *The Glass House* because of its resemblance to a huge mirror.

On the fourth floor of five, the weary shape that belonged to Arthur Downing sat uncomfortably in an executive chair. He was beginning to understand the feelings of a judge during a long trial as he weighed the pros and cons of the gambling proposal.

Holding onto the desk in front of him, he heaved his neglected body into an upright position and pushed his coastered chair backwards with his legs locking his knees. Raising his heavy arms and joining hands behind his balding head, he took a couple of deep breaths, which only made him more aware of how tired he really was. He moved slowly to the water dispenser and filled up a disposable cup. *Bloody things,* he thought as he tasted the warm mouthful.

Arthur had a right to be cynical. This confidential request to evaluate legalized gaming that had come down from ExCo was becoming a real Jekyll and Hyde beast. No wonder senior government had passed it on. This was certainly a complex issue and not for the faint-hearted. All the positive things that could be achieved with such vast sums of money warranted serious consideration.

So why was he apprehensive? What could go wrong? If the government fixed a high enough price for the sole gaming rights, then the current backlog of niggling problems could be cleared immediately.

That would also leave surplus money to address some of the real problems. They could commit cash to completing the Manse Road that had lain as a forgotten dirt-track for the last five years. A new school would be a popular addition to the list of short term achievements. What excellent popularity for the next elections in two years time? If ever a guaranteed second term was up for grabs, surely this would be the project to seal it? Alternatively, the government could reduce the fee for the sole rights in exchange for a percentage of the net profit? This would guarantee an income to government which would increase borrowing power with the banks, especially the Caribbean Development Bank to whom they were already in debt after building the new Gerrard Smith airport on Cayman Brac.

The options were becoming endless. It could even herald the dawn of a new era in the development of a solid infrastructure on Little Cayman. Poor Little Cayman. Although it was arguably the most beautiful of all the islands, it had no dock, no electricity grid, no industry and only about 30 people. That was on a good day when the population was swelled by the arrival of a few, millionaire fishermen anxious to subject themselves to the Spartan rigors of the *Southern Cross Club* and to enjoy the peaceful, empty beaches.

With all the obvious benefits, then why was he worried? Perhaps it had something to do with the contents of the information package that he had recently received from the Social Studies Research Department of the University of Duke, North Carolina. If, as suggested, anyone was stupid enough to lose everything they possessed, then surely it was their own fault? A result of free will nurtured in a democracy. It seemed like a good way to wheedle out those of weak character. Arthur felt confused. The conversation of several months ago with Joe seemed to justify his son-in-law's attitude. But that Joe LeRice could be such a testy individual and Arthur could never face the words, I *told you so,* from him. Here was a man whose mind was so closed, that daylight could never have brightened the darker recesses, but his own precious daughter loved Joe and he seemed to make her happy, so that was something and although Arthur chose not to like Joe, he could not help but respect him.

Arthur toyed with the notion that they could be dangling a carrot of self-destruction in front of their weaker citizens? What if it was his children that succumbed to the temptation? No, his children had more sense. Then it would be somebody else's children. Did that make it any better? But then what about freedom of choice? He had no right to say what people could do with their own money.

Arthur thought about some of his own friends. He envisaged them going through the motions that were documented in the research paper.

The prolonged absences, the habitual lying, loss of dignity, alcoholic tendencies, denial and possible stealing, not to mention legitimate commitments that could no longer be paid off. He put these scenarios in the category that they belonged; the extreme category. After all, a politician's job was to please the mainstream, and if the mainstream could have two cars in their garage, then it was mission accomplished. His dilemma was interrupted by the ringing of his private telephone. It had to be something important. It was Mike Ackroyd, one of the four members of *ExCo.*

"Arthur. It's Mike. How are you?"

"I'm struggling with that damned gambling report. No wonder *ExCo* passed it on. I still can't decide if it's win-win, lose-win or lose-lose"

"Come on Arthur," said Ackroyd condescendingly. "*ExCo* have enough on their plate, without added distractions. You're only doing a study, not building the Pillars of Hercules. Anyway, if the casino was to be approved, it would fall under your portfolio. We just happened to think that you would be the best man for the job."

"I'm sorry," apologized Arthur, "I'm just a little tired, that's all."

"I thought you'd breeze through it," said Ackroyd, sounding surprised at detecting anything other than excitement in his fellow politician's voice. "What was your final figure on the value of the package?"

"I'd estimate about one hundred and thirty million dollars. But it's not the money that's bothering me, Mike. It's the effect on our younger population." Arthur hoped that he was not beginning to sound like Joe LeRice.

"What do you mean?" Ackroyd pressed.

"Well, I'm not entirely convinced that introducing this legislation would be beneficial to the long term future of the islands. Honestly, I haven't decided what to recommend as yet."

"Have you thought what this government could achieve with one hundred and thirty million dollars? It would practically buy our seats for the next election."

"Seats are there to be won, Mike, not bought,' countered Arthur, secretly pleased that he was still able to sound idealistic.

"That's typical of you, Arthur," laughed Ackroyd, "but you are right, as usual. The directors of the consortium will be coming next week. Perhaps you can pick their brains a little before you give your final recommendation."

"Maybe you are right this time, Mike. I don't want to make a hasty decision without all the facts. But you do understand, don't you? We can't go around jeopardizing the future of our starry-eyed youth."

"Of course we can't. Let's hope it doesn't come to that. But you have to be objective and say what you think. After all, it's not as though we as a nation have had much experience of this kind of thing. I'll see you in the Legislative Assembly tomorrow."

They hung up. Arthur felt a little relieved thanks to the understanding of Mike Ackroyd. Although only in his forties, Mike had been in government now for eight years and was generally considered to be one of the more astute political figures in Cayman. A certain amount of respect was derived from the fact that he had a degree in business management from the prestigious University of California, Los Angeles. It was this academic success and a powerful drive that had propelled Mike Ackroyd from an ordinary Legislative Assembly member to Executive Council.

At the start of each new term of office, four of the twelve Assembly members would be elected by their colleagues to serve on this elite board. These four people were generally considered to be the most powerful members of the community, even more powerful than the Governor who was posted every four years from Britain. Cayman Islands Governors tend to remove themselves from politics and act as figureheads. A posting to the Cayman Islands by the Foreign Office is regarded as a reward for long service and usually occurs during the twilight of their diplomatic career.

One influential Caymanian politician is reported to have hit the nail on the head when asked his views on the Governor. He answered, "He may be the Governor, but I'm the Boss."

Arthur would have been justified in thinking that Mike Ackroyd had him to thank for his seat on Executive Council, but Arthur did not think like that. He saw Mike as the best man for the job and that was that. Ackroyd's heavy responsibilities jetted him all around the globe on behalf of the islands.

Arthur had compiled a long list of questions that he would put to the directors of the consortium. If they could not give him satisfactory answers then he would be forced to give a negative recommendation and then lobby the eleven other members of the Legislative Assembly to do the same when the issue became public and went to a vote.

There was nothing else he could do this evening. He locked the relevant papers away in his private safe and headed past his secretary's empty desk to the elevator. Perhaps he would have a pleasant evening tonight at Joe and Rachael's new house, he thought? If he didn't ask Joe LeRice's opinion on politics, he was sure to have a decent time. Failing that, at least he was sure of a good plate of food, they always did an excellent job with their cooking.

Somehow, he actually felt himself resenting their happiness. He could find no obvious explanation except that he was under a lot of strain at work. He cast aside his jealousy with the contempt that it deserved and strode out into the tropical humidity. The thick air hung around him like a mantle of discontent.

That night Joe soon became aware of Arthur's inner strife. As Rachael chatted with her mother, Joe took his father-in-law out onto the patio for a talk.

"What's wrong, Arthur? You don't seem to be yourself tonight. Anything I can help you with?" Joe asked.

"I appreciate your concern, Joe, but there's not much you can do."

"Is it that gambling thing again?" Over the last two months or so, Joe had thought of little else.

"Shit! I was hoping to leave my work in the office tonight," snapped Arthur.

"I didn't mean to pry, but I had hoped for an update." Joe interjected.

"I probably shouldn't have bothered you with it in the first place. It's my fault. Just forget I mentioned it," said Arthur, looking away as though there was something more important vying for his attention.

"If you've got a problem, I just wanted to help."

"How can you help, Joe? You're not even Caymanian."

"That doesn't mean I can't lend a sympathetic ear."

"What the hell. I might not agree with you, but sometimes it's good to have another point of view."

"If you don't like it, don't sanction it," finalized Joe. Privately, he had hoped that Arthur would arrive at this conclusion.

"Don't apply your simple solutions to a complex issue, Joe. Do you realize how much money the government could obtain for exclusive gaming rights?" Arthur paused. "It's over one hundred million dollars."

Joe's expression changed to one of disbelief. "That's an awful lot. I had no idea the market was that lucrative?"

"Now you know what I'm up against. I have to decide whether I have the right to make the peoples' mind up, one way or the other."

"They wouldn't have elected you if they didn't trust your judgment, Arthur. You've spent your whole life standing true. Why should this be any different?"

"But I still have to go one way or the other," reminded Arthur, trying to stamp conviction on his words. "I'll be meeting with four representatives on Wednesday next week. I suppose it will be the usual PR bullshit, fishing, island tour, you know the routine."

"Well, at least you'll enjoy that," said Joe.

"It sounds like the ladies are getting restless," Arthur changed the subject. "Let's eat, Joe. I'm famished."

After a hearty meal of local fish and imported vegetables, the family entered the sitting room together to enjoy some freshly ground coffee. The aroma wafted gently through the room aided by the rotating ceiling fans and the small talk carried on into the latter part of the evening. Arthur seemed more at ease and he settled down into his more jovial self, throwing his humorous anecdotes around with a skill befitting a politician. With another day beckoning, they parted shortly before midnight.

Chapter Five

A Cayman Airways Boeing 727 lifted off routinely on flight KX247 from the blistering heat of Miami International Airport. It banked to face due south and commenced its ascent to 32,000 feet. The five hundred miles to Grand Cayman would take about an hour depending on the prevailing winds.

At the first opportune moment, the captain turned off the no-smoking sign and, like sprinters hearing the gun, those with cigarettes at the ready lit up in unison, relaxing as the nicotine flowed to their brains. The first class compartment was no exception and three of the four representatives of the *Eastern Promise Inc.* gaming party followed suit, Luca Telesino being the only exception, but like the dutiful employee, he felt honored to be breathing the same air as his superiors and now he had the added advantage of being able to see it.

Next to him sat Kate Clementier, and a fiery bitch she was too, thought Telesino; he knew that idle talk was out of the question. This woman only opened her lips for business. He quickly turned his head to look out of the window to hide the lecherous smirk that had just crossed his face. A barrage from this super-confident woman was more than he felt able to cope with, so he turned his thoughts to the wife he had left back home. As his devious mind played out scenarios of how she could be cheating on him, it turned him on to think of the brutal beating that she would be letting herself in for if he was to find out. He resisted the temptation to pry as he heard Kate click open the burgundy briefcase she had chosen to match her Chanel outfit. Her profound, expressionless eyes focused through their hazel surround onto a mass of figures that comprised the cash flow projections for the proposed *Eastern Promise Casino, Grand Cayman.*

She felt at ease with these situations that were purely opportunities to manifest her relentless ambition. She was confident of a successful outcome in any venture that she was involved in. Where there was money, there were always men, and where there were men there were greed and weakness. She despised their simple needs. There was no man that she would ever respect. Her incestuous father had seen to that.

She was now in her early thirties and the success of this business deal would give her total freedom from the men that employed her and whom she secretly hated.

She tossed back her mane of auburn hair. It was a confident gesture and she knew it, as she pretended not to notice the desirous looks that she had just attracted. *Contemptuous scum,* she thought, reassured by the reaction that would have inspired the *Pied Piper of Hamlyn.*

Behind these two junior members sat the powerful founders of their profitable and diverse company, Alex Durant and Giovanni Medini. They had met ten years ago at a sales conference for self-help books and cassettes in Las Vegas. Sharing cocktails over a game of roulette, Durant had come up with the devious idea to modify the subliminal self-help messages to encourage gambling. Medini suggested that they find some financing for this idea and with the help of an eager Colombian investment cartel, they acquired the struggling *Eastern Promise Hotel and Casino* from the receivers for twenty five cents on the dollar.

As well as the pioneers of their subliminal casino, they were part-time money launderers hoping to hit the big-time. This trip would be the final step in their most ambitious plan to set themselves up as money launderers for the cash-heavy drug cartels, most of whom had expressed a desire to back their proposals. They dared not admit it, but this plan to set up in the Cayman Islands would enable them to make the transition from the relative underworld to the pinnacle of respectability and into the corridors of legitimate power, perhaps even controlling the destiny of nations.

Although these two men were both in their fifties, Medini was jealous of the more favorable treatment that Durant had received from the passage of his similar number of years. The only role that Medini felt entirely comfortable with these days was 'grandfather'. He refused to look in a mirror unless he had time to choose his most flattering angle, a task that was becoming ever harder. Even though his paunch could no longer be disguised by his expensive clothes, and his balding head could not be covered by the ridiculously long strands that grew out from above his right ear, he was still vain, and try as hard as he could, *Father Time* could not beat this stubbornness out of him.

On the other hand, Durant had developed an air of elegant maturity with his years. His thin face was creased with fine lines that enhanced a rigid bone-structure. His once jet-black shock of hair had now turned almost all silver and this emphasized the devilish glint in his shifty, blue eyes. He was a charming man to meet for the first time. Armed with his designer knowledge of classical music, fine wines and Renaissance art, he would operate as smoothly as oiled butter and consequently a trail of gullible women wallowed in his wide wake.

It was a wonderfully clear day. Even at this altitude, it was possible to make out the Cuban geography which they were now cruising over. Durant and Telesino guarded their views jealously as if they were original masterpieces recently purchased in a charged auction. They were especially surprised at the vast expanses of sand along which their straining eyes could make out none of the tell-tale signs of 'civilization', such as sprawling hotels and straight roads leading to them. Perhaps the Cubans were too busy with useful pursuits to be involved in non-productive, western decadence? Or perhaps they were just plain poor?

As the aircraft continued on its course, the light-blue, shallow water around the Cuban coastline deepened into a darker, colder blue that signified a final stretch of open water before they would reach their destination.

As the three men indulged themselves in their favorite drinks, Kate left her seat for the privacy of the bathroom. Safely locked inside, she took out her compact and pried the mirror out. In the little compartment that was revealed, a small plastic bag of white powder rested snugly. She put the mirror down at the side of the sink and gently emptied the contents of the bag onto the smooth, silvered surface, hoping that no unexpected air turbulence would disrupt the enjoyment of this small pleasure.

Seeing the powder before her lit up her eyes and hastened her preparations, as she removed a razor blade from her sunglasses case and slid it out from its cover. Then she expertly teased the mound of white dust into a straight line along the mirror, being careful to clean the blade before she replaced it. Then she lifted the make-up applicator from the compact and twisted off the head which exposed a hollow path through the stem. She referred to this toy as the 'successful woman's fun-kit', and smiled as she envisaged her patent application being turned down.

She put the tube into her nose and bent down over the drug. She was careful not to look in the bathroom mirror on the way down, sparing herself any self-pity that would have been inspired by her reflection. Quickly, she did her line, the initial dirtiness washed away by waves of euphoria. As she straightened up, she could now face her reflection, if only to remove any evidence that may have become visible.

She flushed her kit with water before packing it away. She was feeling pretty good as she pressed her face up to the glass to look for unlikely imperfections in her make-up. For good measure, she applied some blood-red lipstick to take the play away from her eyes.

Soon they would be landing, so she went back to her seat to enjoy the rest of her high. The guilty look on her face would have given her away to anyone knowing what to look for, but it was a chance she was prepared to take. She took up her seat and, with a scathing look of sexual superiority, averted Telesino's attention.

The plane started its descent and two illuminated cabin signs caused the fastening of seatbelts and the rapid puffing of burning cigarettes. The amnesty period was judged to be over with the patrolling of two watchful stewardesses.

The jet maneuvered into the headwind that would assist landing and a whirring noise indicated that the undercarriage had been lowered. The silver bird seemed to hang in the air like a seagull on thermals. Some of the first-time visitors to Grand Cayman suppressed rising landing fears by comparing the map of the island in the in-flight magazine to the view from their windows. From a distance, the island looked like a brown footprint in blue paint.

A pinpoint touchdown was followed by the roaring retro-action of the twin tail-turbines. The fuselage screamed bloody torture as the beast began to slow down. Passengers released their pent-up tensions with grins of victory. They had cheated death again. The craft taxied to the front of the new Owen Roberts International Airport. The structure looked clean and efficient, and the immigrants were soon standing in their respective lines. Due to the fact that knowledge of their plans was not yet public, the arriving American committee went through all the normal channels for visitors, keeping a low-key approach.

As soon as they cleared customs, they would be met by a certain Arthur Downing who held office over the tourism industry of the islands.

During the time that elapsed in which Kate had assembled her matching luggage, her associates had already regrouped on the other side of the Customs area. Her coolness had returned and she gave no hints to the officials that would warrant a detailed search of her belongings. Her air of aloofness implying true inconvenience helped her swiftly over this hurdle of bureaucracy. She was good and she knew it.

The foursome huddled for last words of encouragement from the two leaders with Medini's threatening in contrast to the suave eloquence of Durant. They all pledged resolve to the cause with false smiles through which they breathed the warm, Caymanian air.

"Mr. Medini?" inquired a soft voice.

"Yes, that's right," answered Medini spinning into the direction of the voice, "Are you Mr. Downing?"

An affirmative to that resulted in a rash of introductions followed by a hospitable hug from Kate, leaving Durant cringing behind his smile. Arthur arranged for their baggage to be sent on to their hotel and he offered to take them in his BMW.

Kate sat in the front, where she purred at anything that was remotely interesting, especially the alien sensation of driving on the left. Medini interrupted when he judged her to be adequately accepted. She got the message and fell silent.

Arthur drove through the outskirts of Georgetown and showed them some of the new office buildings that would probably cater to the ever-increasing hordes of bankers, insurers and their busy lawyers. The car turned right onto the famous *Seven Mile Beach* road. With hotels on the seaside and shops and restaurants on the other, they soon realized why this section of the island was referred to as *The Gold Coast*.

"Can you give me a ball-park figure on the price of this land, Mr. Downing?" asked Durant.

"Call me Arthur, please," insisted Arthur as he chanced a smile at Kate. She returned it.

"The beach is priced according to water frontage and the quality of the beach. Fine, sandy beach will go for about twelve thousand dollars a foot. All the lots are hotel sized. We re-zoned it about fifteen years ago," explained Arthur.

"That's not too bad," observed Medini. "But why are the hotels so small?"

"Safety. Geologists warned us that the underlying structure of the island would not be able to support skyscrapers so we decided to limit the number of storeys to five," Arthur stated, relishing his role as tour guide with such attractive company in the adjoining seat.

"Looking at it that way, it is fairly pricey," said Durant, "Because the higher you build, the more dynamic the return."

"Providing you can fill the place," added Arthur, "this is a small country."

As they passed a vacant ten-acre plot nestled between two hotels, Durant nudged Medini's attention toward the *For Sale* sign. They smiled.

The potential status of these guests meant that they were to be accommodated in the diplomatic suite of the *Grand Pavilion Hotel,* whose regal suite had been graced by Her Majesty, Queen Elizabeth II during her official state visit of 1983.

Their baggage had already arrived and been distributed accurately throughout their four rooms. Arthur saw them to their suites and arranged to meet them for dinner that night at the hotel's *Le Diplomat Restaurant* whose glowing international reputation was second to none.

Although tired from the seven hour journey from Las Vegas, three of the visitors were excited. This mild-mannered politician, Arthur Downing, may just prove to be their ticket to the top. Durant was the only skeptical one for he realized that Downing had not yet given any firm opinion on a single topic one way or the other. It was far too soon to make predictions and until they could sense his leaning, they could not judge which way he would fall.

Medini admonished Kate about trying to get too familiar too soon. He told her to rely more on her femininity and watch for any possible feedback. She was forced to agree and raged inside for having to take criticism. They separated to freshen up and settle into their rooms which would be their homes over the next few days.

Arthur paused at the front desk to make a couple of phone calls. The first was to his wife to inform her that he would be making his way home soon to change for dinner. The second was to Ackroyd to tell him that the guests had arrived at the hotel.

"What are they like?" asked Ackroyd.

"They seem very business-oriented, highly professional. The woman, Miss Clementier is very attractive..."

"You devil, Arthur," interrupted Ackroyd.

"Hold on, Mike. I've been happily married for thirty one years. Besides, I'm far too old for that kind of thing."

They both laughed and confirmed their plans for dinner with the visitors. Arthur was secretly relieved that his own wife and Ackroyd would be present. Although he had never met people from the gaming business before, these people were not the rough-around-the-edges people that he had expected. They did appear friendly enough albeit serious, so he decided to tread with caution.

That evening, dinner was apparently enjoyed by all. As the meal ran its course, the wine fueled the banter and the atmosphere gently transitioned from stiff small talk to informal relaxation. Arthur, his wife and Ackroyd had been treated to enthusiastic conversation on a variety of interesting topics. Durant particularly was on his best form as he charmed the others with his colorful, ironic stories of famous artists who were poor until they died.

Kate caught Arthur's eye a couple of times and she reacted with disarming smiles and fake coyness. The more-travelled Ackroyd was somewhat easier with the visitors and he acquitted himself honorably when the conversation turned to American professional sports, having once been a UCLA Bruin himself.

The following morning, Arthur was to attend his first meeting with them at ten o'clock. If all went well, there would be a fishing trip to Cayman Brac with the possibility of some snorkeling off the Cousteau-acclaimed, Bloody Bay ocean-wall.

Chapter Six

That night, the unpredictable Caribbean weather lived up to its reputation, as the stifling night became thicker, darker and heavier. The struggle to relieve this suffocating swell began with brilliant, blue flashes that gave split-seconds of total light followed by thunderous reports from colliding storm clouds.

At first, the huge raindrops fell to earth like swarms of over-laden honey bees, before appearing to merge together, forming sheets of water into which the dusty earth dissolved. It was a miracle if it was possible to see more than ten feet ahead. Of the few vehicles unfortunate enough to be still using the disappearing roads, some stood stationary, the drivers unable to cope with the ferocity of this storm.

An unfamiliar observer, conversant with Shakespeare, would have concluded that the natural order had been upset, usually the harbinger of dark forebodings. Those more familiar with regional weather patterns concluded that it was a heavier than usual tropical downpour. Whichever opinion was more appropriate, the disturbance ran its entire course during the night and the arrival of dawn was announced with a still air and a deathly-calm sea. Static boats looked as though they had been set in a huge tub of blue concrete.

Arthur had managed to get only a couple of hours of sleep and poor quality it was too. *Dreadful night,* he thought as he prepared for what should have been an eagerly anticipated day. As it was, he felt tired and lackluster but with the calm sea that followed such storms, it would be perfect weather for their fishing trip to Cayman Brac. He performed his morning routines with the usual faithful commitment ending with the customary goodbye kiss for his Elene. This time he stopped to savor the taste that he realized he had been taking for granted over the years. For a strange reason, he kept his eyes open and saw his own reflection in hers. This moment had taken many years to reoccur and its significance if any, did not register in Arthur's preoccupied mind. They embraced and he left carrying a bag that held his attire for the boat trip.

The four-mile drive to the visitor's hotel was made more interesting by the huge puddles that were trying to evaporate into the already humid air. Arthur found himself slowing down to negotiate these pools to protect the engine of this, his prized possession. Arriving at the hotel, he was informed that the guests were already in the conference room.

The heavy oak table had already been partially covered with their documents and the inviting aroma of fresh coffee pervaded through the air. Arthur accompanied his verbal greetings with nods of acknowledgement as he removed the relevant papers from his briefcase. Medini took the initiative and stood up. He began, "We have all been formally introduced to you, Mr. Downing, but I'll just take this moment to clarify our respective positions with you. I and Mr. Durant are co-owners and directors of *Eastern Promise Gaming Inc*. Miss Clementier here, is our executive manager." Medini paused and looked at Kate. She smiled on cue and Medini continued, "And Mr. Telesino is the general manager of our operation in Las Vegas and would be called upon to initially manage our proposed establishment for your island."

"Thank you," responded Arthur. "And now let's get down to business." Arthur was so relieved that this day had finally come and he wasted no time as he sought answers to their motivations. He decided on a moral tack, "As you know, gambling has always been prohibited in this country. This is the first time that we have had to address the question since our forefathers drew up the first legal code a couple of centuries ago." He stopped and scanned the faces of his listeners. "I accept that as time has progressed, so have our needs," he continued. "We do need all the trappings of modern society to be able to compete with advancing nations in the region. Therefore, we need the money to pay for them, but you'll have to convince me that your proposed establishment will not negatively influence the more impressionable members of our population." Arthur handed over the floor, quietly pleased that he had expressed himself so well.

Durant saw this as a challenge to his oratorical skills. He glanced at the other three as if to order silence. They needed no encouragement.

"Arthur," he started patronizingly, "You raise a valid point and I'm sure that you have researched your angles thoroughly. Gambling is one of the oldest, most exciting pastimes from which a lot of pleasure is derived. We leave it to the player to set his own level of moderation. People such as you would be able to appreciate our services for what they are; good, clean fun." He stopped to take a sip of coffee and let his last words sink in before resuming. "We would be lying if we said that not one member of your community could become overly-excited at this sudden injection of culture, but when a fresh wind blows, some of the weaker reeds are bound to break. It is inevitable, but that shouldn't spoil the enjoyment for everyone else. Also, don't forget that our marketing drive is not aimed primarily at your people, but at those holidaymakers who have brought enough money to have enjoyment in whatever they choose to do. Most of them will be American and European." Durant stopped and passed some papers to Arthur via Kate. She smiled again. The documents contained income projections.

Arthur rotated the papers to process the information and as the figures came into view, his jaw dropped. "How can you be so sure that you will do this kind of business?" he asked, visibly shocked.

"We know our business, Arthur," replied Durant. "We have already done preliminary studies and we are confident that an advertising drive out of Vegas would generate sufficient need for at least two charter flights per week."

"You sound pretty confident, I must say," remarked Arthur.

"We are." Durant smiled and added, "Take a look at the revised cash figure your government would earn, just by agreeing to accommodate us."

Kate leaned over and pointed out the relevant place in the document. Arthur got a tantalizing whiff of her perfume and instantly lost his concentration. He also realized that he was way out of his depth but too afraid to admit it. For two hundred million dollars, they could have bought the crown jewels. Money would be no object to his government but strangely, Arthur also sensed that there was more to this than met the eye and fell silent.

Durant changed his tones as he searched for reaction. Arthur seemed impervious. It was this lack of response that convinced Durant and Medini that alternative action was needed. They made eye contact as though calling a time-out.

The last points of the meeting were delivered, with Arthur promising to give the report his undivided attention and trying to sound as convincing as possible. This was a matter which should have been dealt with directly by Executive Council from the beginning, thought Arthur. When Ackroyd returned from the convention in Miami, he would pass this buck right back to him, he decided, feeling somewhat angry that such a massive decision had been kept from the people.

Whilst Arthur had another cup of coffee, the others returned to their rooms to prepare for an afternoon on the water.

As soon as they were behind closed doors, Medini vented his fury. "We blew it. He wasn't interested. He's just a trumped up pen-pusher, too afraid to commit himself. Why the hell was Arthur *fucking* Downing assigned to this? I'll guarantee that if he gets with his buddies in the Assembly, he'll turn them against us." Looking straight at Kate, he went on, "It's time for you now, Kate. I want you to use every trick in your dirty little book. He may not have contacted anyone yet, so there is still a chance to change his mind"

A gleam appeared in Kate's eyes as she relished her turn. These pathetic men had just wasted a morning pussy-footing around an issue that would have taken her a few minutes to resolve. It was time to strike while she had the upper hand, "Medini. The price just went up. I want half a mill' for pulling this one off. You've just made my job harder and now you pay for it. Take it or leave it."

"Don't push me, Kate," warned Medini, hardly surprised at this sudden turn of events. After all, she had learned from the masters and deep down, Medini and Durant expected nothing less. In fact, they exchanged glances as though they had prepared for this very moment. "Three hundred and seventy five grand. Maximum," he compromised quickly. "If I didn't need you, I would destroy you," he growled through clenched teeth, showing her his matching fist.

Her eyes flashed like a snarling leopard that had just tasted an accurate whip. Telesino cowered. He was like a fish out of water. He would have traded anything to be in his omniscient world back home.

Medini was right about one thing. Arthur had not yet given his opinion to anyone regarding his indecision as he had spent the last few minutes changing into his casuals. The group reconvened in the hotel lobby. The men's suits had been exchanged for shorts and t-shirts and of the three, only Durant managed to retain any dignity. His lithe form usually complimented most fashions, however diverse.

Kate kept her assets under wraps as she sported a knee-length beach shirt. Her face seethed with sensuality as she exuded the dark, mysterious qualities of her heroine, Mata Hari.

The hotel bus took them to the dock in George Town. Patiently waiting for his important cargo was Captain Hughes. He was not really a captain as such, but anyone who owns a boat in the Cayman Islands seems to use the title, perhaps as a cry back to the seafaring days of old. Captain Hughes and his single crew member, his eighteen year old son, welcomed the guests aboard the forty-foot cabin-cruiser. He had a special hello for Arthur with whom he had attended the Brac's only school over forty years ago.

Hughes punched the twin diesels into action and negotiated the tricky exit from the harbor with a skill that was natural and a courage that was furtively nipped from his hip flask. Once out into the deep, blue waters, he set an easterly course that would put them off Cayman Brac in about three and a half hours. He handed the helm over to his competent son and descended from the bridge to set up the huge fishing rods that hopefully would be able to withstand the anger of a hooked game fish. Hughes attached his favorite lures to the lines. Like many resourceful "Sons of the Soil" he was naturally intelligent and had designed these devices himself. His secret was that he would let them soak in rotting squid to impregnate them with a scent attractive to nobody except the intended victims.

The would-be fishermen watched the skill of the master with awe, amazed at his manual dexterity whilst captivated by his stories of the few that got away. He did not even need to look at what he was doing; such was his mastery of his craft.

With the lines now trolling behind the boat, Kate sidled up to the seated Arthur and took up the vacant chair beside him, expressing an interest in his opinion of the best way to react should they get a bite.

"Don't fight too much too early on," started Arthur paternally, happy that he could share his limited knowledge with someone who knew less. She had the added attraction of being exceptionally pretty and all men like to be in the company of pretty women. He continued, "Tease the beast and let it tire itself as much as you dare. Give it a lot of line while it panics. That way, it's less likely to break loose." Arthur was relishing the rapt attention of Kate who was hanging on his every word. "Then," he paused to enjoy the moment, "You start to pull it in. Bit by bit. If it feels strong, be patient."

She placed her hand on his firm, brown forearm and smiled, "Would you like a drink?" she offered, "I heard they've got some beer and champagne."

Arthur stood up and assumed the traditional role of gentleman as he went to fetch the refreshments. The younger Hughes admired Kate from the helm and hoped against hope that the hot sun would remind her that this was a perfect tanning opportunity.

Arthur returned from the galley bearing a cold beer for him and an apt champagne for the classy Kate. He only wished that he could impress her with a verdict on the vintage.

During the next hour, Arthur and Kate shared the cool, salty sea air, a couple of sandwiches each and some relaxed conversation. Their world was ever-shrinking and soon it seemed that only the two of them were left.

Seeing her chance, Kate made her move."It's about time I topped up the tan," she purred, standing up. This statement sent a shiver through the adolescent Bermuda-shorts that belonged to the astute, younger Hughes. His father was oblivious to the imminent unveiling of this work of art, sleeping off the effects of many bad nights.

With deliberate intent, Kate picked up the bottom of the shirt and lifted it up to her face, hiding behind the material for a brief moment. She could feel Arthur's stare warming her thighs as she heard the breath leave his body, the result of an instinctive reaction. The acting captain almost fell out of his perch. She slipped out of the cotton and smiled, assured in the knowledge that she had just revealed something special.

The scarlet bikini that she had chosen hugged her flat stomach and curved delicately around the luscious mound which had almost certainly been trimmed to fit inside. She folded the shirt and placed it on her seat, making sure that Arthur could get a decent rear view as she bent over. He did.

Arthur had forgotten that anything could look this good as he restrained himself from reaching out and touching her firm, rounded cheeks. There was definitely something happening in his shorts. He flushed with embarrassment. No one had noticed. Telesino, Medini and Durant seemed otherwise occupied with the rhythmic passage of the craft through the monotonous, blue monochrome.

Arthur stood up and quickly headed toward the small bathroom below. He was going to have to get some relief. If he stayed up there with that beautiful woman, he was probably going to end up insane or in jail. There was no doubt about it. She was divine. As he pulled the toilet door open toward him he heard Kate call his name. He turned only his head, keeping his bulging shorts away from her probing gaze. "Where are the drinks?" she asked, "I was just coming for a refill."

She eased over to Arthur and sensed his fear.

"Er...," he blundered, before managing, "Uh, let me show you." He pointed to the small refrigerator hoping that she would look too. She did, but only for a second. She turned back and faced him. He let his shame turn into lust as he reached out to pull her onto his hardness. He was surprised at her reaction. She grabbed his hand and thrust it into her own crotch. Then she turned her attention to his aching need as she deftly massaged him to a brutally swift climax. She wiped her hand on his shoulders pretending to ignore the look of total shame that had blended in awkwardly with his initial surprise.

"I'm sorry," he said, looking down forlornly at his hand that had come back too soon from paradise.

"It doesn't matter. Next time will be better."She kissed him lightly and took her drink out onto the deck. The whole scenario had only lasted a minute or two and nobody suspected anything until Kate winked at Durant who in turn whispered excitedly to Medini.

Perhaps this fishing trip was going to produce a bite after all?

A few minutes later a rather sheepish-looking Arthur ascended from the cabin. He resumed his seat and hoped that the rapidly-formed glacier of shame that had risen between him and Kate would melt, quickly. He did not have long to wait. Telesino suddenly broke the ice as he shouted with a mixture of disbelief and excitement, "I've got one! Quick! I've got one!"

This unwelcome noise and a contemptuous little kick from his helmsman son brought the elder Hughes back into the reality that up until now he had blissfully avoided. He shook his head and climbed out of his co-pilot's chair, hugging the stainless steel ladder as he clambered down to the main deck. This should have been a happy occasion and a chance to prove his vaunted hunting reputation. Then why did his brain disagree? He shook his head again before turning to show the best possible face that he could muster. *Bloody foreigners,* he thought, smiling.

He bent over Telesino to ensure that the latter was properly strapped in his seat for the imminent battle. The acrid stench of stale rum caused Telesino to hold his breath and smile weakly in thanks for this unwelcome attention. This was the kind of scum that he enjoyed taking to pieces in his Olympian heights back home.

"What sort of fish is it?" asked Kate, softly enough to let Arthur know that he was the only one she could have been talking to.

"It doesn't look like a blue marlin," replied Arthur relieved at this chance to renew his rapport. "It's too silvery for that. It could be a barra'."

"A barra'?" Kate's shades moved slightly as they mimicked her quizzical expression.

"A barracuda," clarified Arthur, suddenly feeling aloof and fatherly at having to explain this obvious abbreviation.

She leaned across him to get a better look. The delicate scent of her body triggered recently-activated glands. His brain rushed into a computational frenzy and fed the resulting sensations to all parts. He had to be crazy, but he had to have this woman. If a declaration of insanity was all that was required from him, then it would be a small price to pay for the privilege. And after that? After that implied that had taken place and it hadn't, yet. He would cross that bridge when he came to it.

The five and a half feet barracuda smiled vacantly as she watched the inept Telesino struggle with her cousin. She would soon be rich enough to be able to swim around her own private aquarium when this sad minnow, Arthur Downing was hooked. Incredibly, she found herself feeling somewhat sorry for him, and she quietly scolded herself for being so weak.

Although Captain Hughes still felt groggy, nature came to his aid with a burst of adrenalin that dispersed the haze clouding his vision. If he couldn't help to conquer this pathetic creature, it was surely time to hang up the tackle. He silently scorned the comical efforts of Telesino who was doing his best to translate the unusual dialect that these natives seem to fall into during moments of excitement.

Finally the mutually disliking teammates combined their equally strong hunting instincts and the beast was beaten. Whilst Hughes paid a snippet of gladiatorial tribute to his victim, Telesino despised its weakness as he gloated at the barracuda's apparent lack of stomach for combat.

Even by Hughes' standards, this barra' was a decent size. It was all of six feet long and close to eighty pounds in weight. Nothing really spectacular, but all these ignorant foreigners deserved, he judged.

The confused fish was hauled aboard, staying still and not betraying any sign of life with its two evil-looking eyes. Its mouth was partially open displaying a set of razor sharp teeth once revered by the ancients for their keenness.

A few minutes later, whilst Hughes was restoring Telesino's tackle, the latter edged over to the hanging fish. He went to prod it.

"Get away from it!" screamed Hughes.

Like lightning, the animal whipped its tail which gave impetus to its arching back. Its jaws twisted down towards Telesino's outstretched arm. He froze. He came face-to-face with a reflection of total hate. His expression turned to utter horror; then relief as his limb remained intact, except for a light graze.

Swiftly recovering his senses, he painted a layer of nonchalance over his exposed canvas of fear. As a child he was the sort of boy that would persecute a pet animal that had reacted in self-defense to his curiosity. If there had been nobody around he would have liked to beat it senseless with a suitable weapon and then watched in triumph as it died, vanquished by the superior adversary.

The overwhelming embarrassment that followed was tactfully averted by the silver-tongued Durant. "Are you alright? That must have been a shock. Sit down. I'll get you a drink." Whilst sounding concerned, Durant boiled angrily inside. There was no room for error. Unfortunately, evil was the essence of Telesino's job and he was good at it. He may even have been the best, but Durant still loathed his inferior intellect.

Arthur used this situation to comfort the apparently shocked Kate. She assured him of her composure and returned his overtures of concern with a tune of thanks.

The mood of the afternoon changed and the group made a unanimous decision to head back to Hog Sty Bay in George Town. This suited the amorously charged Arthur and by keeping his alcohol intake steady, he was successfully warding off any pangs of guilt. Hughes had a date with a full bottle. His son was bored and the other three men were anxious; it was Kate's success which they were anxious for.

Arthur gave his guests a brief history of Cayman Brac whose

famous, towering bluff had briefly come into their view. More at ease, he tried to impress them with the legends of hidden pirate treasure. It is said that the buccaneering Edward Teach, better known as *Blackbeard,* had made use of the labyrinth of caverns to deposit his ill-gotten gains. It is also rumored that he was robbed of the opportunity to make a withdrawal from this secretive bank. Be that as it may, the magical island of the bluff has steadfastly refused to divulge its contents to the few, still-active fortune-hunters.

The ozone-rich, sea air had cleared Hughes' head, and anxious to serve his master he pointed his faithful mistress homewards. Although he loathed these trips for pretentious guests of the government, the money was good and only one decent fish was all that was required. It was the so-called serious sport fishermen who worked him to death that really bothered him.

They disembarked just before sunset and after the mandatory photographs with their now definitely deceased prey, the part-time anglers took their seats in the waiting minibus for the short drive back to the hotel.

Hughes instructed his son to moor the boat off the beach about three miles north as his own day was over. Just across from the dock was the *Cayman Arms* and they were open, eager to embrace him.

During the ride back and in a bout of lucidity, Durant reminded his two male companions of the promise that they had made to the owner of the Texan bar about four blocks from their hotel. That night, the Running Rebels of the University of Nevada, Las Vegas were involved in an important collegiate basketball match and by virtue of one of the best satellite descrambling set-ups on the island, the game was being shown live.

No doubt sizzling, beef fajitas and free-flowing margueritas would help to absorb the entire evening.

Arthur turned down the invitation exactly as the cunning Durant had anticipated. In fact, Arthur was particularly delighted at the haste with which the three men prepared themselves and left. He watched their departure from his stool at the hotel bar. He left the last mouthful of the orange juice that he had been casually sipping and stood up, patting his pockets as though he had forgotten something. This little act was for the benefit of the bartender who would be able to, if necessary, justify his reason for going back in the direction of the suites. The bartender appeared to register this display of forgetfulness and satisfied, Arthur followed his mounting desire.

Padding like a panther after his prey, Arthur stalked up to the door of Kate's suite. His anxious, yet determined, knock telegraphed his mood clearly and his pulse began to quicken.

"Yes, who is it?" purred Kate, attempting to sound surprised.

"It's Arthur. I think I've forgotten something."

The door opened. Kate stood before him. No, he hadn't forgotten anything. He had just remembered. This was just like his dream and now the rehearsals were over, and he was truly grateful to *Destiny* for staying faithful to the script.

Chapter Seven

After what could be considered a successful day at the office by anyone's standards, Joe LeRice was pottering around in his fresh, new home.

He enjoyed his work as much as it was possible to enjoy a job. What he found especially appealing was that he could see the fruits of his labor. His company had built many houses and although a trip around the island would reassure him that he had been productive, he felt that it was time to move on.

The thought of bringing up children made him think about what it would be like to be a child in this place. He had never really given the matter much consideration; although he knew he would have to some time. Questions needed answering. Would his children have a happy young life? What were his responsibilities? Was it as easy as he had been led to believe?

Joe felt uneasy about traditional values that preached cold schooling with other equally unhappy children. He thought back to his boarding school days in England. How was it possible to rip a child away, only a few years from the womb, and stick it in a hell-hole, all in its best interests? He had learned to survive but the experience had left a bitter taste in his mouth. There was no way he was going to pack his kids off to school. They would learn at their own pace with sand between their toes, he concluded.

Today, his offer for a particular tract of land had been processed through a repetitive maze of legal jargon which although he understood, he hated. To him, it seemed that a lot of this corporate law was an endless and unnecessary game of *find the loophole*. Had these people never heard about the essence of the law? If they spent all day trying to catch each other out, then it was a pretty banal existence, he pondered. It appeared that a code of conduct once founded in spirit had needed to be translated into letter. The end result appeared to be a confused distortion possible only to be deciphered and manipulated by people with lots of initials after their names. Joe also felt angry at himself for not being able to do a thing about it.

Like most intelligent people he was a part-time pessimist but he had learned to repress any feelings of despair and imprison them in the deeper recesses of his searching mind. Occasionally a key would manifest itself that would unlock his darker thoughts like a particularly disturbing news report, perhaps about some senseless act of war in the name of some condoning god whose message had been twisted to justify such behavior. Failing that, it could be the effects of an environmental accident caused by desperation to keep up the almighty bottom line.

On the other hand, he knew that millions of people had dutifully accepted their lot on this hamster-wheel of a planet and he was grateful for his seemingly privileged existence. Although well-off, Joe did not consider himself wealthy, but he had worked hard for his house and had managed to put away a nest egg that would leave him and his family in relative comfort should hard times descend.

He remembered the time when he had sold a choice piece of land to the government for a proposed youth centre rather than bow to the dubious tactics of a supermarket group. Yes, he had still made a profit. He usually did, and although it wasn't as much as it might have been, he was satisfied. Anyway, the supermarket people could not have had much faith in their own venture. If they did, Joe was sure that their particularly cheap choice of building materials would have been upgraded to ensure the project's longevity. Perhaps they were planning to sell out during the trouble-free first two years? He would never know and he didn't care.

He looked over to Rachael, having nothing but admiration for her ability to be totally practical and objective about life. She appeared to view life from a different angle. Joe was convinced that she knew something that he didn't, because she seemed to derive more pleasure than him from simple situations.

Only last week, they had gone for a beach picnic and Rachael had seemed so at ease with her surroundings. She had brought no hidden expectations. She accepted the setting for what it was, a brief moment of freedom. It was a time to laugh, a happy time, whereas Joe had brought his fears with him. He imagined that this simple pleasure that he had striven so hard for could be taken away. It was this intense fear that prevented him from sharing his wife's calm. He looked at her serenity and realized that he was a part of it and suddenly, he felt useful. It was a start.

With the sounds of the crashing waves still flooding his senses, he managed to make out Rachael's voice calling his name from the telephone that she had just answered. "Joe. It's Mummy. Daddy's not home yet."

Joe admired the beautiful, unchanged way in which his wife referred to her parents. If he had referred to his parents as *Mummy* or *Daddy* at boarding school, he would have swiftly tasted the wrath of another soul darkened by jealousy.

"It's not surprising," he offered, "A morning meeting. An afternoon fishing and perhaps it's turned into an evening meal. All with business in mind."

Rachael relayed the sentiment. When her conversation had ended she replaced the handset on the wall and eased down the one step into the sunken living room. She didn't need a television or a magazine. She had her Joe; and he was sitting at the end of the Rattan sofa in one of those pensive moods that made him look attractively intellectual. She sat down beside him and turned her body so that her head lay on his lap and her feet dangled off the other end. He smiled.

"It's not like Daddy to be late," she began. "He usually calls."

Joe knew better than to question Rachael's intuition which was founded upon years of living under the same roof as the man.

"Perhaps the boat was late coming back?" was all that Joe felt able to offer. He spread the warm locks of her hair over his lap and softly ran them through his fingers. The day when he took such beauty for granted would be his last day on this earth.

"I hope he's alright," she said. The furrow that had just appeared on his wife's forehead looked so out of place that Joe tried to smooth it away with a gentle push from his thumb.

She adored the attention of this dreamer. If she had to draw up a list of adjectives that could be used to describe her relationship with Joe LeRice, 'mundane' would certainly not be one of them. After the early days, when Joe seemed to have sporadic drinking bouts, it had mellowed out happily and their relationship had become deeper. She did not always agree with him, but he had never let her down when the going got tough. Sometimes, this man had too much conscience for his own good. She remembered the time when he adamantly refused to sell a piece of his land to the highest bidder, ignoring the cruelty of this life that dictated the feathering of one's nest. She felt protective towards her husband, seeing herself as the guardian of his emotional fragility.

Her realistic outlook was in such peculiar opposition to Joe's idealistic approach that there had to be a more powerful, common bond between them. There was. It was that feeling that every human being is allowed to taste at least once in their lives, regardless of circumstance. It was that indefinable spiritual and chemical reaction that is simply referred to as love, and they had lots of it.

Rachael did not even try to analyze her feelings. She knew they existed and that was good enough for her. Anyway, why should she waste her time analyzing a feeling when she only had to open her eyes to see the real thing?

Their thoughts of mutual admiration were prevented from entering the physical realm by the unwelcome interference of the telephone. Rachael answered it. It was her mother again, telling her that Arthur had just arrived home, and there was no more cause for worry. Rachael remembered that she had a letter for Joe and she brought it out from her handbag before coming back. Joe noted a slight relief in the jaunty step that brought Rachael to him.

Joe took the letter and recognized the postmark as coming from the only place in England where he still had any ties, Humberside. It was from his old friend, Simon. Since leaving university, having gone separate ways, they had remained in touch, exchanging letters and cards on birthdays, Christmas and sometimes for no reason at all, except friendship.

Three years ago, Simon had become disillusioned with his position as an engineer in a national corporation and had set up his own electronics repair shop, called *The Computer Cabin*. He had also written that, although financially it had been the kiss of death, it left him time to play his guitar with his part-time band whenever he fancied.

Fondly, Joe remembered asking Simon to play his favorite songs and Simon could always oblige without so much as a glance at any music score.

Secretly, Simon harbored dreams of becoming a lead guitarist with a classical rock band, and although he was good enough, the spotlight had not yet shone upon on him so he still lived in hope.

Years ago, he and Joe had pledged that the first one to 'make it' would invite the other to his home for a holiday. Joe had just built his new home and felt he was as close to 'making it' as he ever would be. Joe had not forgotten the pledge or their mutual bond and had decided to make the first move. Simon had readily accepted Joe's invitation to come to the Cayman Islands and the letter said that November, later that year, would be perfect.

Joe set the letter down by the side of the sofa and reminisced a little over the old times.

"Simon says he can make it in November," said Joe, as though his friend would be doing him a favor.

"You sound happy about that, Joe," replied Rachael.

"It's been ...what, about eight years since I last saw him,"

"What's he like?" asked Rachael, "You've spoken about him, but you've never really said much."

"He's different. At least he was. I don't think he's the kind of person to change. I'd say he was a little eccentric, but he used to say the same about me. He's got a heart of pure gold, though."

"What does he look like?" asked Rachael.

"I can't say now. We've never sent photos. He lived in his leather jacket and he always had this long black hair. I probably wouldn't recognize him any other way. "

"He sounds like a real character. I bet you two were pretty dangerous," laughed Rachael.

"Actually, I was the dangerous one," said Joe. "Simon was brilliant with electronics. He was the one that kept me on the right track. He got a first-class degree from university."

Joe stopped as memories of those days materialized inside his mind. He saw Simon's room with wires everywhere, a BBC computer in the corner and his prized guitar always within reach.

"It'll be great to see him again," Joe went on, enthusiastically, "Do me a favor, remind me to buy his ticket and send it on to him."

Rachael was pleased to see Joe so happy. He had never wanted much, he seemed too busy giving. Their thoughts gradually converged until the world contained only the two of them.

Chapter Eight

The next day, a tentative question mark on Arthur's personal diary was swapped for a definite. Dolefully, he stared at the black book that occupied his thoughts and the centre of his desk. After all the recent events, it had become necessary for a final meeting with the *Eastern Promise Gaming Inc.* group.

It would be the ideal moment for him to finalize some last details regarding his recommendations to his fellow politicians. His mind had been made up and he had no choice but to advocate the sale of the exclusive gambling rights. Kate's charm had seen to that. He hadn't even bothered asking to see the photographs of his philandering. His choice had been fairly simple. Be exposed: or toe the line. There was nowhere to run to, so escape was out of the question. This was his home. Everybody knew him, and in such a small community there would be no rebuilding a life after such a fall from grace.

His friends and colleagues would not want to be seen in public with him. He would be a national laughing stock and even his own family couldn't be blamed for rejecting him. Since coming clean was out of the question, he would have to invent a whole new moral code. Now that he lived in a glass house, throwing stones was no longer an option. He would have to force himself to go against his own grain, and weave again the fibers of his belief structure, changing years of practicing as he had preached.

Perhaps, there were some positive aspects to his new path? If so, he had the rest of his life to find them, and to justify his existence.

Although he felt gutted by the truths revealed to him by his now twenty-twenty hindsight, he also felt betrayed because such pleasure that he had experienced with Kate had ended like this. He realized that this emotional isolation was part of the price that he would have to pay. He was afraid that he would never pay his debt in full.

Strangely, he felt no anger towards Kate. After all, he had got what he had wanted and so had she. It was simply more than he had bargained for. If only he had consulted the crystal ball of known experience? Now he had become just another statistic that gave more credence to the original consultation, had it been sought.

He buried his head in his hands and wept as quietly as he could without alerting his secretary to his distress. His emotional spectrum spanned from revenge to forgiveness, from love to hate and from despair to hope.

He wanted to punish and forgive himself in one sweeping judgment, but it was not possible. A crime had been committed; a sentence would have to be served.

He reached over his pen holder and picked up a glass cat that had been a keepsake from his daughter's teenage years. As the fluorescent light fell upon its transparency, it appeared to come alive and struggle from its now unworthy captor.

He hoisted himself up and slipped the memento into the inside pocket of his sports jacket. An aching in his neck reminded him of his droopy posture and his attempt to straighten himself was thwarted by his shameful burden. He gave up and shuffled to the door, pausing to taste a salty tear on his lip. A wipe with his soggy handkerchief satisfied him that it was safe to leave, all signs of grief now hidden under his practiced political facade.

"I'm going to that meeting now, Janine," Arthur stated, "I'll be in the conference hall of the Grand Pavilion. Don't disturb me unless it's absolutely necessary." He was quietly surprised at his level of assertiveness. Was it a glimmer of hope on the emotional horizon?

"Yes. Mr. Downing, I understand," responded Janine, paying attention to her boss's uncharacteristically curt tone.

"Oh, and if Mr. Ackroyd calls, tell him that I'm on my way and that I'll meet him there," added Arthur, turning to leave.

A little spring of contrived confidence showed in Arthurs' steps as he walked towards the elevator. This was going to be a difficult meeting but it would soon be over and if he could disguise his decision as a well-thought-out strategy, he would have no problems with his fellow politicians in the Legislative Assembly, especially those that had followed his voting stance during past issues.

The fifteen minutes that it normally took for the trip to the conference hall was one of those peculiar journeys where all traffic laws are faithfully abided by, but trying to remember any details is impossible.

Arthur's conscious mind regained control as he tried to negotiate a tricky parking maneuver between a huge Lincoln Continental and a faceless import. Without thinking, he judged the owners by their machines and gave a little more space to the larger vehicle.

He took a deep breath before climbing out of his car. He hoped that he would not have to face further humiliation from the Americans and as he prepared to enter the meeting room, his heart pounded. Arthur noticed that the room appeared to be a lot smaller than he recalled; but then again so was his choice. The impolite clouds of cigarette smoke affirmed this conclusion.

The four envoys from Las Vegas had arrived early in an

enthusiastic mood. They were shuffling papers between each other at the end of the table and dispensed with any formal greetings to Arthur. They had no reason to respect him now that they owned him. He could not resist a glance at Kate who showed no acknowledgement. Durant was smiling, tapping his fingers on the wooden table in time to one of his favorite classical melodies.

Telesino looked relieved. He had felt awkward during this trip, not having the control that he had become accustomed to. He knew that he would have to return soon to run the new casino but at least it would be on his terms. Medini was anxious to get to the end of matters in hand and he beckoned Arthur to a seat, strategically selected at the bottom end of the table.

Arthur, hoping that Ackroyd would not show up and see him squirm, was soon to be disappointed. Ackroyd had just returned to the island after one of his state duties that carried him all over the political world. He had just come back from Miami where he had attended a one day import-export meeting. Arthur welcomed Ackroyd who grabbed his outstretched hand warmly and shook it firmly. Arthur held on to the handshake a little longer, as though drawing courage from Ackroyd's confidence.

"Sorry I'm late. How's it looking?" Ackroyd whispered to Arthur.

"Not bad," replied Arthur, "I think they've got some excellent propositions that we should seriously consider, especially the initial cash payment. It looks like you might get your school after all."

"Let's not be hasty, shall we?" warned Ackroyd quietly, before greeting the guests. He sat next to Arthur, but below him in the table's hierarchy. After coffee had been poured, Ackroyd commenced, "I hope that you have enjoyed your visit to our islands. As you know, I've been away in Miami yesterday, so I haven't had an opportunity to discuss any further details with Arthur, but I will in due course."

"We have been highly impressed with Arthur's professional approach to our offer," said Durant, shooting Arthur a cold look. He continued, "Early this morning, we finalized what we consider to be a most generous package. I hope that Arthur does not think I am being presumptive, but I feel the contents will meet with your approval."

Durant handed a folder to Kate who in turn passed it on to Arthur. He let her put it down in front of him before he touched it. He opened it and scanned the first page with a blank face. He sat back in his chair feeling for its support and said, "Any negative thoughts that I may have had can be allayed. As a nation, we can only benefit from such a massive cash injection, therefore paving the way for a brighter future for us all."

Durant began to experience paternal feelings toward this 'son' who was saying exactly what he wanted to hear.

Arthur went on, "I also have here a cash flow projection, the revenue from which will support many of our long term ventures." He handed the document to Ackroyd who took Arthur's respected word and set it down, promising a full review after the conference. More coffee and cigarettes accompanied the following light talk. Any pervading tension had vanished, and all the actors had dutifully played their parts and now relaxed. To those in the know, rave reviews flashed back and forth with eye contact. The die was cast and the seal had to be set. Only bureaucracy stood between *Eastern Promise Gaming Inc.* and its final goal. Once the twelve-man Legislative Assembly had put the issue to what should be a successful vote, planning approval would be sought and granted for their new casino.

A round of hand shaking was followed by a round of drinks at the hotel bar. The only exception to the bottle of Moët & Chandon was Arthur who greedily grabbed at an atypical, neat, over proof rum. Without pausing to squeeze the lime, he jumped the toast and gulped.

Angry at Arthur's lack of respect for it, the rum punched him in his chest and knocked the wind out of him. He sat down immediately to recover his breath, sucking air in over his burning tongue as the evaporating alcohol filled his lungs. He coughed drily and his eyes watered.

He ordered another to accompany the toast that Durant was about to propose. "To the pioneers of this memorable venture and most of all, to the Cayman Islands."

They drank. Kate's tasted sweetest. Her money had been well and truly earned. She couldn't wait to get back home and gain her independence from these animals.

The Americans brought the proceedings to a close with the announcement that their reservations for the next flight back to the mainland had been confirmed and that they would have to depart soon. To maintain the facade of *entente cordiale,* Arthur offered to drive them to the airport. Medini and Durant combined in refusing this offer.

The only favor they required from him was that he keep his part of the sordid bargain. Durant slyly cornered him out of Ackroyd's earshot and hissed, "Remember, you're the one with most to lose. Don't fuck up." His face was fierce. Arthur's grip tightened on his empty glass.

Durant spun to bid Ackroyd farewell, rapidly changing his face like a master of disguise. The suave Durant, ugly Medini and shallow

Telesino made their last journey to the rooms that had housed them during this interesting episode. Kate remained behind and sat between Ackroyd and Arthur. She finished her drink and put it down closer to Ackroyd. He jumped at the chance of pleasuring such an attractive woman and picked it up, offering to refill it. She mused briefly before requesting half a glass.

With Ackroyd at the bar, Kate turned to Arthur, "I'm sorry that it had to be you. This thing is bigger than both of us. I had no choice." Arthur felt that he was going to stammer something but the lump in his throat quashed this notion. Kate opened the palm of her hand in a calming gesture and continued, "If it means anything to you, I enjoyed you. You made me feel good."

Incredibly, part of Arthur leapt with elation at this news. It was the part that exists within all men anxious to know if in pleasing themselves, they had satisfied their partners. The rest of him felt numb, overcome by the totality of this powerful emotion.

Quickly, he rummaged in the inside pocket of his jacket and pulled out the little glass cat. He pressed it into her soft palm and closed her fingers around it saying, "I shouldn't give you this but I hope it brings you some of the happiness that I've always associated it with."

A tiny fleck of remorse appeared in her eyes as she opened her hand to admire it. She slipped it into her Gucci handbag and rose to accept the drink from the returning Ackroyd. She took a single sip and put it down on a coaster. *"Au revoir,"* she said softly, reverting to the tongue of her descent. She rippled her fingers as a last farewell gesture and left.

Arthur had forgiven her. If it hadn't been Kate, it would have been somebody else. In a morbid way, he was glad that it was Kate.

Ackroyd broke the silence, "So, Arthur, you've made your mind up? Do you honestly think that this will mark a new era in the future development of the country?"

"Yes, it probably will," answered Arthur, "we can discuss the entire scheme late this afternoon if you like. I'm sure that I can convince you to see my point of view."

"As long as this country can prosper and we can guide it, then I can see my vote cast in favor of this motion," said Ackroyd. "This afternoon is perfect for me. Tomorrow, I'm off to Montreal to the official opening of that new tourism office."

"The price of politics," offered Arthur.

"These official duties are beginning to take their toll," complained Ackroyd. "I'm exhausted. After the next elections, I'll be passing these chores on. The novelty soon wears off."

Arthur hoped that he would not be elected next time around. He would put up a half-hearted campaign effort and then fade away into obscurity. The Americans had surely taken the pound of flesh that they had conspired for? He had nothing left to give in the service of his country.

They parted until the afternoon when Ackroyd would come to Arthur's office to review the draft paper that would be submitted before the Assembly. Arthur would spend the next few days setting the ball in motion for the topic to be aired publicly.

Arthur called his wife and told her that he would not be joining her for lunch. Today was Thursday and the *Cracked Conch* restaurant was serving his favorite conch chowder.

He called the restaurant and placed his usual take-out order. "Yes Mr. Downing. It will be ready immediately," came the lively reply, happy at the custom of one of the islands' most respected figures. Arthur arrived there in a matter of minutes.

The food was ready as promised and he sensibly declined the offer of a drink. That would be all he needed, to be stopped by the police for erratic driving and failing a breath test. His self-esteem was low enough; he didn't want it joined by his public opinion. Gutter press would have a field day. He made a determined effort to concentrate on his driving, fending off the attentions of the two large rums and his hunger which was being titillated by the wafting chowder. He reduced the fan-speed of his air-conditioning to lessen this agony as he carved a way through central George Town.

Arriving at *The Glass House*, he parked in the closest available spot to the entrance. Clutching his food with one hand, he pushed the heavy door with a combination of two of his remaining limbs. He smiled at the receptionists, who were sniggering as this awkward picture, and entered the lift. In the enclosed space he was tempted to open his lunch but the thought only lasted a few seconds as did the ride. The doors slid back and he stepped out, ignoring Janine who was about to give him his messages. "Not now, Janine. Not unless it's pressing."

Her silence assured him it wasn't and he continued into his office followed by the delightful aroma. Life still had a few pleasures to offer, he thought, as he wrestled with a packet of salted crackers. It was still hot and it tasted so good. He emptied the container in a time short of desperation and glanced back into it a couple of times in the off chance that he had missed a tiny morsel. He sat back in his chair and ran his tongue around all those oral hiding places that hold special fascination for us as children. There it was! A scrap of conch was nestling between his upper lip and gum. Using his tongue, he created a vacuum and sucked it down onto his front teeth where he crunched it, hoping to break open any pockets of flavor. He was glad that he hadn't bought two helpings because if one portion had made him feel this hungry, two would have left him famished.

He grinned at the absurdity of this thought as he threw the evidence of his lunch into the wastepaper basket. He licked at his fingers before summoning Janine on the intercom. She appeared, holding several pink slips that were his telephone messages.

"Mmm. Smells good. Conch chowder?" Any seafood was worth talking about. Arthur's bashful silence confirmed her suspicions. She couldn't help noticing that he had left his friendly side at home, so she went on, "There's nothing urgent but Mr. LeRice asked if you could call him when it's convenient to you."

"Thanks, Janine," said Arthur, grateful for her efficiency.

She handed him the notes and left. He leafed through them and arranged them with the least important one at the top. He went through all but one of the list and rewarded himself with a cup of water to moisten his dry throat. Dialing Joe's number, he noticed an unfamiliar feeling come over him. He had never felt this uneasy with Joe before. Arthur decided that although Joe seemed to be right, he would never have to know. He struggled to bury the underlying guilt as Joe's voice filled the earpiece, "Joe LeRice."

"Hello Joe, it's Arthur. Janine told me you'd called."

"Yeah. How did your meetings go?" asked Joe.

"A lot better than I had expected. They had more to offer than I thought, so I'm still giving the matter serious consideration but don't be surprised if I give the go-ahead."

"That's a turn up," said Joe, sounding somewhat deflated. He backed off and asked about the fishing trip using it as an excuse to change the subject.

"You know these big city people," condescended Arthur, "they haven't a clue how to behave on boats."

"True," agreed Joe, having been one of them a long time ago.

"Anyway, getting back to business, you can follow the proposal in the press. There's going to be a debate in the Assembly, followed by a vote."

"I'll make a point of it," commented Joe, mystified by his father-in law's overly formal tone. He decided that this was not a good time to extend an invitation for dinner and rang off politely.

Arthur was pleased at his handling of this tricky moment and he busied himself about preparing the documents necessary to set the wheels of politics in motion.

Chapter Nine

After several eerily calm weeks, the news broke. Was it possible? A casino would be coming to Grand Cayman? The island divided itself into the usual three factions. Good idea, bad news and don't care. Insatiable press fed greedily on the scraps of information, but most of the politicians kept their cards close to their chests. This was the biggest issue since independence from Britain had been discussed and rejected over twenty years ago. The churches were up in arms; the business folk licked their lips. Foreigners who years ago, had invested in the innocence of these islands, threw their hands up in despair and began to look for other places that didn't have the same kind of snares that they had tried so hard to leave in the first place.

For every one prepared to leave, there were a dozen eyeing up the possibilities, anxious to share their knowledge of the real world with the baffled islanders who were amazed at this rush of concern.

Speculation of the outcome was rife, but whatever the result, it was going to be close. Pressure of not being 'with it' laid heavily on some politicians and calls for wisdom reverberated in the ears of others. Two of them had even publicly changed their minds. The nation tuned in eagerly to the Assembly debate that was broadcast on local radio. Observers were forecasting a hung vote, but it was just not possible to be sure one way or the other.

Joe LeRice was taken by surprise at the passion that Arthur had begun to show toward the issue. He had not seen or spoken to Arthur since the visit of the Americans and his untrained eye did not see through this avoidance.

Joe found himself in an unusual situation. After all the years that he had spent trying to gain acceptance as the husband of Arthur's only daughter, now he felt helpless, blood exchanged for water in his veins. Not surprisingly, Arthur's family, including Rachael, had rallied around him under the traditional banner of unconditional trust.

Exclusion from his own wife was a cause for Joe's concern. In her eyes, Arthur could do no wrong in her eyes and Joe had no right to interfere in the matter. He accepted her judgment but that did not prevent him from sensing tension in her. He had decided to ride the storm out on a silent platform of availability.

That night, on the eve of the vote, Rachael called him from Arthur's to tell him that she would be late coming home from work. He decided to fix dinner more from a need to occupy his time than necessity. He made an effort to time the meal's readiness with his wife's arrival, spending a particularly long time preparing the vegetables. The therapeutic crunch of slicing through crisp onions and peppers helped to allay his anxiety. With all the ingredients now simmering away, Joe laid the table, settling on a single candle as the centerpiece. It was these little gestures that his wife appreciated and now was probably as good a time as any to reach out.

In the half-hour remaining before Rachael's return, he felt that a bottle of white wine would be an ideal complement to the home-made, beef stew. He turned the cooker off before leaving and climbed into his Ford Mustang. The powerful five litre engine roared into life as though aware of the importance of the mission. Joe stuck the automatic gearbox into *Drive* and did just that to the nearest restaurant about a mile away. His haste made him freely agree to pay the full tariff for the litre of chilled Chablis. He would have preferred a red, but Rachael invariably chose white regardless of the main course.

He arrived home fifteen minutes before Rachael whom he met with a hug. She smiled but with a pleading look. Joe didn't press her but simply poured her a glass of wine and escorted her to the table. He lit the candle and they began to eat. She seemed reluctant or unable to unwind as she half-heartedly picked at Joe's savory offering. He watched the candle flame throw light on her face exposing vulnerability. She glanced up at him and quickly looked away. Her first attempt to speak was crushed in her throat. She tried again,

"Joe. I'm sorry. It's my father. He's depressed and unhappy. We can't get a word out of him. Mummy's desperate. He won't talk and he's drinking much more than usual."

"It's alright," soothed Joe. He stood up and went over to her. He cradled her head in his arms and pulled her to him. She began to sob. Gently, he raised her up and held her. Joe looked up to the heavens for inspiration as her shaking body spilled out its frustration. She became heavy, her legs barely able to support her.

Joe teased her face upwards and kissed a moist cheek. He walked her slowly to the bedroom and lay with her, needing her touch as much as she needed his. She slept, and Joe soon followed her.

Next morning Joe woke first and slipped out to the kitchen. While the coffee percolated, he cleared the table, still strewn with last night's unfinished meal. Like a butterfly leaving its cocoon, Rachael emerged from the bedroom.

"Feel better?" he asked.

"Lots," She looked it.

"I know you can probably handle this situation, but do you want to talk about it?" Joe probed.

He poured her a coffee and sat down beside her in the living room.

"We think it's this damned casino thing. Daddy's so wrapped up in it. The pressure is getting him down. He won't admit to it but he says it has nothing to do with how he feels."

"He's been pushing it pretty hard," said Joe, "maybe too hard."

"It's not like him. He's always been able to talk about work at home. Now he refuses to. He can't sleep and he won't see the doctor any more. We're all so worried for him. He says that his chest feels like it's exploding." Rachael's voice broke as she shared her fears.

"They're voting today in the Assembly, aren't they?" said Joe.

Rachael nodded. Joe continued, "Perhaps when it's all over, he'll feel a lot better. I can't say that I agree with him but whatever the outcome, I hope that he can get back to normal. I have no idea why, but I know he's been avoiding me."

"He's got nothing against you, Joe. He respects your opinion but he knows you disagree with him. I guess he was just cutting out the chance of conflict?" Rachael concluded.

"He should know me better than that," retorted Joe, a little piqued. He checked himself and changed tone. "Tell him that if I can help, I will, even if it's only an afternoon fishing or something else that'll help him ease up."

"I'll try," promised Rachael, sounding pleased at having tackled this matter that was straining their lives.

"When I married you, I married your problems too, you know," said Joe, smiling.

"You too, Joe LeRice," replied Rachael affectionately.

Arthur Downing had spent another harrowing night of sleeplessness, and his brain racked. He felt as though the last few weeks had been ridden out on a sea of nausea and at last the final day had arrived. He had almost fulfilled his part of the unfair bargain and he could do no more. He had campaigned as ardently as possible for the success of the proposal, holding meetings and chairing debates. The telephone had rarely been from his hand.

In some corners he was being touted as a man of great political foresight about to take the nation to higher peaks of greatness and in others he was branded a Judas, who was about to sell the soul of his trusting people for the almighty dollar.

The whole sordid business had taken its toll, and the stress made him afraid to try and sleep, for fear that his heart would simply give up. This frustrated him and only widened this vicious circle of despair, so much so that he had contemplated medical help.

He had become grateful for exhaustion for it was the only way to get relief. If he had been lucky, two hours of unbroken sleep was a godsend. Then he would wake up frightened, expecting to see his corpse lying there as his soul left it. Heaven or Hell, it didn't matter anymore. Hell couldn't be worse than this. It wasn't dying that he was afraid of, only the pain that he associated with it.

He was the first member of the Legislative Assembly to arrive that morning. He took his customary seat and waited. One by one the other delegates arrived, until at ten o'clock, Ackroyd strode in confidently, making up the twelve.

Voices droned, papers rustled and eyes darted. The Sergeant-at-Arms and the Speaker were the coolest people in the room. Theirs was not the choice.

The Sergeant slammed the door shut, shocking everyone into silence. The charged air crackled with the Speaker's formalities. Ears pricked.

"Honorable Members, I draw your attention to the matters discussed in motion C.I.G. number 1147." A brief silence followed. None of them needed reminding as to what that number referred to. They had argued about nothing else during the last few weeks. No one exercised their right to make any further comment. The talking was over and it was time for some to climb down from their fences.

"Will those Honorable members in favor of the aforementioned motion raise their right hands?"

Time froze. The beating in Arthur's chest threatened to tear it open. It was unbearable. He looked to his left. On the front row, Solomon Fairbanks and Ben Mayotte slowly raised their hands together. Arthur had been counting on them. He didn't have to look directly behind. The sudden cooling in his neck told him that Ackroyd's raised palm was now blocking his sunlight.

Arthur's peripheral vision showed one other vote from the left. It couldn't be? In the second row, a surprise! Brigitte Okie from *ExCo* had come in from the cold. By now, Arthur was shaking uncontrollably. As he turned his head to the right he hesitated and noticed the Speaker mentally adding up the total. Shit! He thought as he inhaled deeply. Only the solitary support of Chris McLeod stood out from a line of blank looking faces. He spun around again to reconfirm. That was only five votes. It would be a defeat. Suddenly his own hand shot up and Arthur was mad at himself for such negligence, but it was still only six, dammit! A draw. A tie. Deadlock. Failure. A hung vote was not enough to secure new legislation. He cringed as he imagined the impending scandal that would destroy his reputation.

"Those against?"

Arthur buried his head in his hands. He had given his all. Somehow, he felt relieved; he could not sink any further.

"The ayes outnumber the nays. By a count of six to five I pronounce the motion duly carried."

Arthur opened his eyes. A sledgehammer blow smote at the foundations of his disbelief. Countless emotions invaded the exposed core. Someone had abstained! Who was it?

He didn't know nor did he care. A guardian angel had stayed the hand of his executioner. He almost passed out with sheer relief. He sat through the remaining proceedings remaining silent. His work was done. That was all that mattered.

When the session was over, he called his wife who could hardly make sense of his garbled ecstasy. She was more pleased than him, maybe a little peace and quiet would return to their strained marriage?

The victorious six arranged an impromptu celebratory lunch. Two hours quickly passed by, helped by three bottles of champagne. Arthur headed back to his office to put in a token appearance.

He greeted Janine with a hug that would have shamed a grizzly bear before waltzing into his office. He sat down and savored the moment, allowing himself the luxury of overlooking the dubious motivation of his triumph. By anyone's standards it had been a gritty performance and the effort that he had put in had only served to strengthen the saying that success was the reward of hard work.

He looked down. Lying on his desk were three letters, one of which was marked confidential and unopened. He picked it up and scrutinized the smudged post mark. Los ...something or other. No, it was Las...Las Vegas. He tore it open and read.

Chapter Ten

That same evening, Joe and Rachael conspired to spring a surprise visit on Arthur and Elene. With Rachael holding a colorful bouquet of flowers arranged in a faux-crystal vase, Joe drove slowly along the pebbled drive up to the stucco-walled house. They laughed, it was impossible to sneak up in silence with the incessant crunching of the smooth stones under the heavy wheels of Joe's Mustang. Joe parked alongside Arthur's black BMW and Rachael leapt out towards the front door. Joe set the flowers down out of sight and Rachael rang the bell. *Bing Bong.*

After about thirty seconds, Joe remarked, "That's odd. There's no hiding from that racket in there."

Rachael frowned. Joe was right. It wasn't a quiet doorbell. A second ring was followed by another silence, before Rachael's concern prompted Joe to go around to the back of the house. He looked about to see if any lights could give clues to their whereabouts; they had to be in because Elene's car was also parked at the front. Joe allowed himself a laugh. During his more buoyant moments, Arthur had been known to enjoy a practical joke of his own. He grinned as he imagined Arthur doing especially well this time to involve the typically-demure Elene. On the other hand, perhaps they were in bed, he thought? He hoped that their visit would not be disturbing anything.

A dim light peeped out from the master bedroom window. It was probably the light to the adjoining bathroom, he thought. He went back to the front where he reassured Rachael that everything was under control and scrabbled for a handful of pebbles. Returning to the rear, he used his sense of feel to discard the larger stones, not wanting to sour what was supposed to be a social call with a smashed window pane.

Thankfully, he missed the first time. He changed to a softer underarm throw for the second attempt. Crack! Joe felt like a juvenile delinquent suffering from acute boredom. He heard the missile thud to the soft ground and he waited. Silence. Two more throws and still nothing. The joke was over. Joe called out loudly to Arthur. There was no reply. By now Rachael had joined him.

"Joe, something's wrong. I know it." She gripped his arm and her trembling rippled through his taut sinews.

"I'm going back to break in through one of the downstairs windows," declared Joe, "it's better than battering the door down."

He returned to the front as it was better illuminated by the little light that the miserly quarter-moon had to offer. He found a window with the top catch already unfastened. He removed his right shoe and lined up the bottom of the pane for a blow from the heel before turning his head away. He grimaced as he swung. Fortunately he felt no stinging from wayward slivers as the glass fragmented. Then he struck the shoe against the wall to dislodge any wayward shards. He flicked the bottom catch, pushed the frame up and hoisted himself inside. His first movement was toward the front door where he let Rachael in.

Before she could utter a word, he had turned already and opened the hallway door. He flew up the stairs and raced across the landing to the bedroom. His suspicions about the bathroom had been correct but he could never have predicted what he was about to find.

He checked and whirled around to restrain Rachael who had just entered the bedroom.

"Oh God! No, Daddy!" she screamed. Refusing to believe her

eyes, she surged toward the bathroom. A rush of adrenalin gave her unnatural strength as she brushed Joe aside with ridiculous ease. Reeling, Joe fought for balance before going in after her. Lying on the floor was Arthur, half naked, his eyes rolling listlessly in their sockets. His ashen face resembled a death mask and his limbs hung loosely about, incapable of responding to the faint signals that came from his dying brain.

Kneeling beside him in a trance was Elene. She was holding his left hand as she rocked to and fro gently, her glazed stare boring into the cold, tiled wall.

About a foot away from Arthur's right hand laid a discarded, brown, plastic bottle. The white lid that may have once belonged to it was half buried in the blue mat at the base of the sink. Joe picked up the bottle. He read the label out loud, "Pheno...Phenobarbitone 100mg... two times a day. Thirty tablets." They quickly agreed that there were about eighteen tablets left give or take the odd one that had slipped through their shaky fingers whilst they tried to count them.

"Call the ambulance, Rachael," said Joe grimly as he clung on to his composure, "ask for paramedic help." His determined voice forced her into reality and she hurried to deliver her precious message.

Joe pulled Arthur's left hand free from Elene who was completely oblivious to her surroundings. The faint, irregular pulse gave impetus to Joe's cause. He managed to shift Arthur's mass onto its side as he had remembered from somewhere, magazine or television, he wasn't too sure which. He allowed himself a passing commendation for checking that Arthur had not swallowed his tongue and then he grabbed a large towel to spread over the man's cooling body. He draped a bathrobe over Elene's shoulders electing to leave her in that state of trauma. If he shocked her back to reality, he would have to face the possible hysteria that might follow, he thought. A task far beyond his boy-scout experience.

Rachael reappeared, "They're on their way. It should take about five minutes." She knelt down between her parents and united them with her touch. Joe went downstairs and opened the front door. He stood in the doorway willing the medics on.

The ambulance tore up the driveway spitting out pebbles violently on either side. One man got out whilst the driver turned the vehicle around for speedier loading of the patients.

"Upstairs, quickly," hissed Joe urgently, showing the way. The driver followed. The two experienced paramedics began to assess Arthur's predicament.

"Pulse irregular and weakening."

"Airway clear."

"How many pills did you say he had?"

"No more than twelve," Joe answered immediately.

"I hope we're not too late. That's technically fatal. If he's strong he might make it,"

"Glucose-saline drip." One of them prepared the clear, plastic drip bag whilst the other tapped at a vein in Arthur's wrist to enlarge it before inserting the needle.

"What about Mummy?" asked Rachael.

"Coax her downstairs into the ambulance and stay with her," the head paramedic ordered.

Rachael and Joe took a side each and carefully lifted her. Elene reacted as though she had heard because she did not resist in any way, but her face was completely devoid of any expression.

The paramedic who drove came down with them and helped seat Elene comfortably. Rachael stayed with her and Joe was drafted into helping carry the stretcher upstairs. A minute or two later Arthur was in the ambulance and hooked up to a portable electrocardiograph. As they were leaving Arthur's house Joe looked back catching a glimpse of the once colorful flowers now radiating an ominous hue of icy-blue.

The blaring siren and the flashing light carved a passage towards the hospital. The combination of the fearful din and the realization of somebody's plight made most drivers pull over to speed the life savers on their way.

The imminent failing of Arthur's vital signs was accompanied by a bleeping sound from the monitor.

"Shit! He's going into cardiac arrest. I'm going to try CPR," said the paramedic sitting by Arthur as he began to knead at his heart, reminding it of the implications. Obstinately it refused to comply and revealed its intentions by modifying the bleeping to a continuous tone.

"For God's sake, do something!" screamed Rachael.

"Move away from the stretcher!" insisted the 'medic. "Don't touch it!"

He flicked the charging switch on the defibrillator and smeared jelly on the contacts. Arthur's bare torso saved valuable seconds.

Whump! The device discharged itself in a fraction of a second right into Arthur's pallid chest. He jerked violently before slumping back, his eyes opening for a moment grotesquely revealing only the whites.

Although the movement was enforced, it gave a glimmer of hope, which the persistent monotonous tone dispelled immediately.

"Again! Do it again!" urged Joe, anticipating the man's action.

Whump! Another convulsion.

"Sweet Jesus, please!" Rachael was crying.

Arthur's failing heart, no longer able to resist the powerful demands made on it, flickered into a feeble activity, begging more of the attention that had revived it.

The driver sighed with relief as he pulled into the emergency forecourt. His radio plea for assistance had been met with laudable haste and a doctor and his team of nurses warmed swiftly to their task. With Arthur now in capable hands, Elene was shepherded inside and intravenously administered pethidine carried her into a world of swirling white clouds.

Joe held Rachael as she watched her sick parents being wheeled away. They waited, with Joe shunning a seat in favor of pacing up and down. Every time he saw someone resembling a doctor, he accosted them for updated knowledge of the situation. At last, a man appeared and introduced himself as Dr. Thompson.

"Mrs. Downing has been severely traumatized. She's under sedation now and will be until at least tomorrow. We are confident that she will regain her faculties over time with proper psychiatric care and mild sedation. She'll need all the support you can give her."

"And Mr. Downing?" pressed Joe.

"We've pumped him out and the evidence suggests that all the barbiturates had not fully dissolved. This may have saved his life. I won't make any promises but I am hopeful. Until such time as I see fit, I'll keep him on the critical list."

"Thank you, Doctor. Thank you." said Joe, squeezing Dr. Thompson's hand. "It's going to be alright, Rachael. I promise you." Joe sat down beside her and put his arm around her; sensing her tension, he pulled her closer.

"Waiting here isn't going to do any good, sweetheart. Why don't we go back to your parents' place and fetch them some things. You know? Pajamas, nighties, toothbrushes, those kinds of things."

Joe telephoned for a taxi and it arrived a few minutes later. The journey to Arthur's house was shrouded in silent fears. Having arrived, Joe slipped the driver a ten dollar note and hurried away before the word 'change' could be mentioned. Efficiently, Rachael set about getting her mother's necessities together; her favorite nighties with lots of matching knickers, her toiletries, not forgetting her preferred perfume and other niceties that Rachael herself would have appreciated had the roles been reversed.

Joe, on the other hand, had to think a little harder. He made up a mental list in his mind and worked his way through it methodically. When Joe saw that Rachael had included Elene's handbag in her list, he asked, "What about your father's wallet, Rachael?"

"You'd better get it, to be on the safe side," came the reply.

Joe looked around for a jacket or a pair of trousers that it may have been left in. The trousers that were draped over the bed yielded nothing and with no jacket in sight, he slid back the louvered door to the clothes closet. A gap between two jackets suggested that one of them had been hung up recently. He delved into the pockets eventually pulling out the wallet. There was a piece of paper wedged awkwardly in it, too large to fit inside. He removed it and saw that it was a letter, inside which rested a worn newspaper-clipping. Curiosity took over and he read the letter:

"Mr. Downing,

For God's sake, don't let *Eastern Promise* into your islands. I have just read in our local press of the historic campaign to bring gambling to your country and of your association with them. You could not be tied up with a bigger bunch of crooked, murdering bastards if you tried. I know they killed my brother who was a desperate gambler, but unfortunately I cannot prove it.

Have they fooled you so much that you can't see through them? Any money that you get from letting them in will be a poor substitute for the damage they will cause to your country. There will be other victims, but this time, they will be your people and you put them there. Think again!

A friend."

Shaking, Joe managed to unfold the clipping without ripping it. He read:

"Body found in refuse tip. The body of a man was discovered during the early hours of yesterday morning in a garbage disposal area. A police spokesman implied that it may have been a gangland revenge-killing. Police pathologist, Theo Travis, stated that the head had suffered a severe blow with a blunt instrument. He added that a hand had sustained a gash indicating a considerable loss of blood, although this is not believed to be related directly with the cause of death. The dead man was named as... ...of Las Vegas."

The area of the text where the man's name appeared had been crudely torn away giving no immediate clues to the victim's identity.

"Oh, Jesus." murmured Joe.

"What did you say, Joe?" asked Rachael, still busily packing.

Er... Nothing, just thinking out loud," said Joe, hoping that he had disguised the quivering in his throat. This letter was incredible, he thought, and it seemed certain that this had to be linked to Arthur's desperate attempt at suicide. Why should Arthur react so strongly to something that came out of the blue, something so vague and anonymous? He could have easily tossed it away; that would have been the obvious thing to do, unless Arthur had experienced their tactics, and therefore had good reason to believe the letter was genuine?

There and then, he decided not to tell Rachael or anyone for that matter. Her parents would need all the support that she could give them and this revelation could prove to be more of a hindrance. He hoped that he was making the right decision as he folded the papers up and concealed them in an unused compartment of his own leather wallet.

Rachael double-checked that none of her parents' essentials had been overlooked before leaving the bathroom. One last look threatened to bring back her horror so she swiftly backed out and closed the door.

As they left the house, Joe picked up the vase of flowers and dumped them in the dustbin, disgusted in his new knowledge that the triumph they would have been used to glorify was apparently rooted in evil.

With Joe's car now loaded, they drove back to the hospital. Dr. Thompson stopped them in the corridor that led to the emergency ward.

His grave face shot pangs of dread into Joe and Rachael. He took them to one side and clasped Rachael's hands in his.

"It's Mr. Downing. I'm so sorry. He just couldn't hang on. His respiratory system failed and he went into cardiac arrest. We were unable to revive him. He died about fifteen minutes ago."

Rachael turned to Joe and sobbed into his chest.

"Why, Joe, why?" she wept.

Joe stayed silent as Rachael grieved. Why would someone as loved as her father try and take his own life? Why didn't he say anything?

Joe felt strangely distant. His father-in-law had never really accepted him. Their relationship had been superficial and Joe did not feel comfortable feigning a display of grief, so he just decided to be as supportive as possible to the living as they prepared to bury their dead.

Joe went over to the doctor and had a quiet word in his ear. Dr. Thompson nodded and left, only to reappear a few minutes later with a small bottle of pills that would help them sleep that night.

Joe asked if he and Rachael could see Elene. They were led to her room and the sight of Elene resting allowed Rachael to see some hope at the end of this ordeal. They sat with her for an hour before Joe managed to coax Rachael home. He could not help but admire the courage that she was showing.

Chapter Eleven

A week had passed since Arthur's death, the verdict, suicide. The whole country reeled in shock and mourned. Flags flew at half-mast and it was considered fitting that Arthur be buried on his beloved Cayman Brac alongside two generations of his family.

The close-knit community always shared occasions of bereavement and hundreds had made the journey from Grand Cayman to the Brac. Cayman Airways promised to provide as many additional flights as needed and cancelled several international round trips to service the need of their grieving nation.

In addition, nearly all the one and a half thousand inhabitants of Cayman Brac had showed up to pay last respects to their son who had so faithfully represented them during his political career.

The church managed to house those nearest and dearest, with the remaining islanders forming a solemn guard-of-honor to the final resting place. Arthur's coffin lay open, his waxen face more reluctant than resigned, as his grieving family filed past for a last look.

Joe and Mike Ackroyd led the pallbearers on Arthur's final pilgrimage. After the pastor's spiritual blessing, Ackroyd added a few words of his own, "I know Arthur will be sorely missed by us. In all my life, I have never known anyone more selfless or conscientious. If he could be accused of anything, it would be that he cared too much. I am sure that I speak for all of us, present or not, in offering our heartfelt condolences to the grieving family."

Joe put his arm around Elene to soften the impact of the painful tribute. Ackroyd looked towards Elene as he continued the panegyric, "I would like you to know that the nation as a whole shares your deep sorrow and we will always be here for you, should you need assistance of any kind, material or spiritual."

On behalf of Rachael and Elene, Joe acknowledged Ackroyd's words with a nod. Elene had not once been able to raise her eyes through her black veil during the proceedings as she clung to her strong daughter.

The mourners dispersed. Whilst Rachael put on a courageous front to thank the pastor for a touching service, Joe went back to Arthur's grave and waded through the mountains of flowers that surrounded it. All that was left of his father-in-law was a wooden box and angry emotions piled high as the discarded bouquets.

He spoke softly, "No goodbyes, Arthur. I think you really fucked up. I promise to look after Elene and Rachael." Joe suddenly felt as though his soul had been exposed to an invisible wind and with the prickling sensation still in the back of his neck and running down his arms like electricity, he turned away wondering if he had finally connected with Arthur.

Two days later, they were still on Cayman Brac. The morning sky looked like a solid block of tinted blue perspex. There was not a cloud in sight. The air was still and the heat persisted.

Rachael was adamant about keeping a protective eye on Elene, who felt compelled to spend hours upon hours by Arthur's grave, talking to him, praying for him, loving him and weeping for herself.

Rachael discerned that Elene could become overwhelmed by grief, so she decided to act, confronting Joe, "Joe. It's Mummy. She can't go on like this. It's killing her."

"I know, but I feel so powerless," said Joe. "I'm worried for you too."

"I'll make it, Joe. At least I think I will. I admit there's times when I feel like breaking down, but then I look at Mummy and I know she needs me."

Joe held his wife tightly, humbled by her gritty determination, and declared, "There's no way we can leave her alone right now. It's going to be a long time before she'll get over this, if ever at all. We're going to have to look after her. I think she should move in with us. God knows, there's plenty of room."

"Do you really mean that, Joe?" Rachael's face lit up with pride. "There's a flight back to Grand Cayman this evening," she said, "I'll try and coax Mummy to come back with us."

Eventually, Elene was persuaded and the three of them shared a last hour with Arthur before leaving. Joe took advantage of this opportunity to spend some time by his own father's memorial. He drew courage from the thought that two old friends were re-united somewhere else, possibly somewhere better.

They arrived back on the main island just after eight o'clock that evening. They were met by an uncomfortable humidity and hordes of hungry mosquitoes. Without wasting any time, Joe hailed a taxi and they went straight home electing not to stop at Elene's on the way.

After a snack, Elene took some of the sedatives that she was fast becoming dependent on and Rachael sat by her bedside until she was certain that her mother had succumbed to the chemically-induced sleep.

Joe went into his study and closed the door firmly. The room was full of a grayness that made him aware of his own uncertainty. Turning on his desk lamp, he scanned the walls, searching for inspirational patterns in the shadows that were cast. He reached into his wallet and removed Arthur's letter and the clipping. He wondered if he had done the right thing by not informing anyone of its contents.

After all, it would not bring Arthur back and there was no hard evidence of any wrongdoing, just an angry man's opinion. No, Joe was certain that Arthur had experienced something so shameful that this letter was merely a tipping point.

Joe glanced at the digital clock on his desk. Perfectly-formed numbers said nine-fourteen p.m. It was time to do some math. As far as he remembered, Nevada was next to California and if the times were the same, Vegas was on Pacific Time, three hours earlier than Cayman time. That would mean it was after six p.m. in Vegas, but Joe was pretty confident that if anyone did not work regular office hours, it would be a police pathologist, such was the nature of the job. Anyway, it was the only lead he had, so there was no other choice.

He picked up the telephone and dialed 119 for the Cayman Islands international operator.

"Good evening, International Operator. Can I help you?" a confident voice gushed. Joe recognized the peculiar accent immediately. A small community always breeds familiarity. The voice sounded eastern Caribbean, possibly Barbadian, and smacked of a good education. This lady had connected many of his business calls in the past. He had always associated a matronly face with her, purely because of that assertive tone and her unfailing efficiency.

"Good evening, Operator. I need information for Las Vegas, Nevada," requested Joe.

"Please hold the line while I connect you to their local operator," said the voice, "Area code for Las Vegas is 702," she added, saving Joe a little more work.

After three faint rings, the Las Vegas operator answered in a curt tone cultivated from many years of dealing with curt people.

"What name please?"

"Er...Las Vegas Police Department," said Joe taken aback at her directness. A click was followed by a recorded female voice singing, "The number you require is..."

Joe jotted the number down and waited for the information to be repeated to check that he had heard right the first time. He had. He stayed on the line and the Cayman Islands Operator came back on.

"Do you want me to connect you, sir?"

"Yes please, do you need the number?" asked Joe. Before he had finished speaking, he heard her connecting his call. *She's good*, he thought.

"Las Vegas Police Department," the answer came.

"Good after...evening," replied Joe, realizing that Vegas had hit evening too. "Can you put me through to Pathology, please?"

"Who do you want in Pathology?"

Joe looked at the name in the article and said, "Theo Travis, please."

An internal phone rang a couple of times before a man answered, "Pathology, Doctor Kelly speaking."

"Hello Doctor Kelly, is it possible to talk to Theo Travis?" inquired Joe.

"You're just a little late. Dr Travis retired a month ago."

"I'm sorry. I had no idea. The switchboard put me through."

"Welcome to bureaucracy, where the right hand knows what the left is doing," Kelly answered, his tone tainted with sarcasm.

"I'm calling from the Cayman Islands, I wonder if you can help me."

"Does the fact that you're calling from the Cayman Islands oblige me to?" drawled Kelly.

This was a miserable son of a bitch, thought Joe. He decided to press on. "It's very important; I need to ask him about a man who was murdered..." Joe's receiver filled with laughter.

"Which one?" exclaimed the pathologist, feigning surprise. "There have been twenty this month already. There were forty-two last month," he added drily.

"He was dumped in a garbage disposal area," offered Joe, "He had a knock on the head."

"Well that narrows it down to a few. Got anything else?"

Joe scanned his cutting. "Yes, his hand was cut too."

"Oh, yeah, I think I remember that one."

"Could you tell me his name, please?" pleaded Joe.

"No, not until..."

"What, not until what?" Joe regretted interrupting, and apologized immediately. Kelly held the key and pissing him off might lock this door.

"What I was about to say, was, no, I couldn't tell you anything *until* I've looked in the file. It'll take a few minutes."

"Do you mind if I hold?" petitioned Joe.

"If you're paying for this call, mister, you can do what you like. The information is public. You could get it from the newspapers."

"I'd prefer it first hand, that way you get the facts," said Joe, playing to Kelly's ego.

"Hold on then..." Joe clung to his sweaty handset.

A couple of minutes later, Kelly's voice came back on the line. "You still there? Higgins, W. D. of Las Vegas." He stated without giving Joe the time to answer.

"Yeah, I'm here," answered Joe, a little relieved. The last two minutes had seemed like ten.

"Thank you. Thank you very much," said Joe. "Do you have a next-of-kin for him?"

"He was identified by his brother, Bro- Wait a minute! I can't give you that information."

"Why not?"

"It's not public. We're not supposed to. Is there anything else? I've a stiff on the slab that's just crying out for my attention." Kelly sounded bored with this game and he hung up, cutting Joe off in the middle of his thanks. At least Joe now knew that the man who wrote the letter was called Higgins. He also knew that his first name started with a 'B'. It was a start.

Joe dialed the Cayman switchboard again and requested the operator that had just put him through to Las Vegas. After a short pause, she came on the line.

"Yes sir, what can I do for you this time?"

"I need information again," Joe declared.

"Las Vegas?" asked the operator.

"Please."

She obliged. Joe hoped that there were not too many Higgins' in Las Vegas.

"What name please?"

"Higgins, Mr. B. Higgins." Joe was ready for her this time.

"Do you have an address?" she countered quickly.

"No. I'm sorry, I don't," Joe felt as though he had just played a bad card, and regretted it.

"Listen, Sir. I have two screens full of the name Higgins, about eighteen of which have the first initial B. Two of the eighteen are ex-directory. So which one is it?"

"All of them please."

"One inquiry, one number. I have lots of other calls to deal with, sir."

She activated the recording that gave Joe the number for the first B. Higgins and he scribbled it down. After the second repetition of the number, the connection was automatically terminated and the Cayman Islands Operator came back on the line.

"Not very helpful was she?" said Joe. "Perhaps if she knew how important this call is, she may have sung a different tune."

"Life or death?" asked the operator, lightly.

"Important enough for me to beg if I have to," said Joe.

"I doubt that will be necessary, sir. I don't know who you are, but I've dealt with you before. My experience tells me not to question your sincerity. I'm going to stick my neck out for you. I'll try a clearance code and compile the list for you. After that you're on your own. Give me an hour or so and I'll get back to you."

"Thank you," blurted Joe, "By the way, what's your name?"

"Operator number fourteen," came the reply.

"I understand," said Joe, "Thanks, number fourteen."

At ten-thirty, Cayman time, Operator number fourteen called back with the list as promised. She hadn't managed to obtain the two unlisted numbers but Joe accepted that it was way beyond her call of duty and hoped that the law of probability would hold true.

She wished him luck and recommended that he dial direct to keep as low a profile as possible. After dialing the first ten numbers, Joe was beginning to run out of hope and excuses as he drew a series of blanks from unanswered calls or people who hung up before he could even apologize for disturbing them. He was about to classify the eleventh call as yet another unanswered one when he heard a woman pick up and repeat the number he had just dialed.

"Is Mr. Higgins in?" asked Joe.

"Hold on, please," came the response. Joe heard the dull thud of the handset being set down on a hard surface. He pressed the receiver close to his ear and he barely heard the woman call, "Brogan, it's for you."

Fear and excitement vied for first place in Joe's heart, the combination forcing him to perspire profusely. He swapped hands with the receiver allowing him to wipe his sweaty right on his trouser leg before changing back. Then he heard a rattling sound before a tired voice crackled in his ear.

"Brogan Higgins."

"Mr. Higgins. I'm calling from the Caribbean. Perhaps you can help me?"

"What? Who are you?"

"I *was* Mr. Downing's son-in-law. He killed himself a week ago."

"Who's Mr. Downing?" the reply came instantly.

"The politician whom you sent the letter to." Joe challenged him.

"What letter? Listen, I don't know what you're talking about. I don't know any politicians in the Cayman Islands."

'How did you know I was calling from the Cayman Islands, Mr. Higgins? I only said I was calling from the Caribbean."

"It was a slip. I don't know...a guess. What do you want, anyway?" asked Higgins, now appearing somewhat annoyed.

"Do you know how easy you were to track down? What if Arthur Downing had grassed you to *Eastern Promise*? Do you think they'd be calling you to ask for your coffin size? Get real, Mr. Higgins."

"Alright, alright. What do you want?" Higgins surrendered, hoping that the inconvenience of this awkward call would soon be over.

"Help."

"Help for what?"

"To stop *Eastern Promise* coming to our islands. Isn't that what you want too?" Joe heard laughter, "What's your problem?"

"Do you have any idea what you're saying, Mr..?"

"LeRice, Joe LeRice."

"Yes, Mr. LeRice," repeated Higgins, "because if you did, you wouldn't be calling me."

"Come on, Higgins. You know you're involved, or else you would have put up more of a struggle when it came to denying the letter. Let's face it, you've lost someone and you're angry, but when it comes to doing anything about it, are you going to dry up? There's a word for that."

"And there's a word for people who go rushing in where they don't have a hope."

"Have you lost hope, or what?" Joe pressed.

"Maybe. If you had any sense, you would too."

"I suppose I'm just plain dumb, then," said Joe, his tone laced with contempt.

"I'm not sure I can help you, Mr. LeRice, at least not as much as I'd like to."

"Could you meet with me," said Joe, his tone more earnest. "I don't know anyone in Vegas and if I was to come over, I'd need help."

"Yeah, but don't come over here like a bull in a china shop, or you'll be busted up pretty quick."

"I had no intention of that," retorted Joe.

"I'm prepared to meet with you, Mr. LeRice, but don't get your hopes up."

Joe's triumph was interrupted by Brogan who added, "I'm asking you get rid of the letter. It was written in a moment of anger. I just glimpsed the thousands of lives that will be destroyed by those bastards if they come to your country."

"I'll bring it with me," replied Joe. "You can be the one to get rid of it."

"It's up to you."

"You'll be seeing me. Count on it."

Joe's ecstasy was choked by guilt. He had to get his priorities in perspective. He hadn't shed a single tear over Arthur, and even if he did find out what pushed the man to suicide, what gave him the right to gallivant around like some vigilante? Was his life so boring that he needed excitement? Or was it from a genuine sense of right? He carried these unsettling thoughts with him as he slid into bed beside Rachael. She was sleeping, but had pushed one leg into his side so he would have to move her gently to get in.

As soon as Joe touched her, she stirred, and wrapped herself around him. His body did not soften and she felt as though she was gripping a board.

"What's wrong, Joe?" asked Rachael, sensing his tension.

"Rachael, darling. I'm going to ask you to be stronger than you've ever been."

"What is it, Joe, what's wrong?"

"It's your father. I think he felt he had no choice but to kill himself."

"How do you know?" Rachael tensed up, her eyes wide open.

"You're telling me this now?" she said confused.

"Hold on, honey," soothed Joe, "there's no proof. I have a hunch, that's all. It wouldn't stand for anything in a court of law. All I have is a letter to your father and a newspaper clipping."

"Show me." demanded Rachael, and Joe did so. "Why didn't you go to the police?" she frowned.

"I thought about it, and perhaps I was wrong, but there's nothing to go on except the opinion of an angry man," explained Joe. "I believe your father was forced into a corner he felt he couldn't fight his way out of. He may have been bribed or threatened, we'll never know. I just didn't want you and Elene to get dragged through all kinds of nasty gossip especially when there was no way to bring your father back."

Joe stopped and he and Rachael looked into each other's eyes knowing that this was one of those rare moments when something, however implausible, had to be done to prevent wrong from triumphing over right. No more words needed to pass between them and Rachael nodded assent, her eyes now glinting with a fiery determination.

"You know they're coming here," Joe continued. "They've got to be stopped."

"How?" asked Rachael, channeling her anger.

"I don't have a clue," admitted Joe, "but I know that I have to meet this Higgins fellow."

"What if it's dangerous? Does that mean I lose you too? Why Joe? Isn't one death enough?" Rachael flung her arms around her husband.

"Darling, I won't be taking any risks," Joe tried to reassure her. "I'm taking a flight out tomorrow. Don't worry. I'll be ok. Your mother needs you now more than ever before. She's depending on you."

"What about you, Joe? Where will you be when I need you?"

"There's no choice, I have no choice," murmured Joe, shaking his head.

"Perhaps it was all a mistake. Perhaps Daddy was unhappy."

"Do you really believe that?" said Joe, looking her in the eye.

"No, not really," she answered, looking away. "But losing you would be too much. How do you think I've managed so far?"

"Don't think I'm running out on you. I'll be back soon, I promise."

That night they made love with a passion that suggested it would be some time before they would be together like this. Joe lay awake afterwards, unable to sleep, haunted by visions of failure that churned around his mind. He stole out from the bedroom into the kitchen and took one of Elene's pills, crunching it up for a quicker reaction. He washed the powder down with some water before going back to bed and within ten minutes he had joined Elene in a strange, peaceful world where not even dreams can escape.

Chapter Twelve

It was five in the morning, and Joe's alarm clock reminded him that he was expected on the red-eye flight in two hours time. He was glad that his alarm clock had worked because the sedative had left him feeling hung over and exhausted. He felt as though he had been on a journey, but for the life of him, he could not remember where.

He nuzzled up to his wife before thinking about getting up. She was warm and a lingering hint of Givenchy that mingled with her natural femininity made him question his decision to leave. She gave more strength to this argument by moaning softly as she shook off her slumber, wrapping her arms around him. He felt himself become aroused and wished there was no reason to resist; except that he may miss his plane. He decided that this moment, and many just like it, would spur him home.

Reluctantly, he moved away, and it was time to test the myth that a cold shower could dispose of an erection. Rachael, thwarted in an effort to have her man, went to the kitchen to make breakfast. At least her Joe would leave on a full stomach. In no time at all, eggs were scrambling, bacon was sizzling and bread was toasting. A fresh pot of coffee completed the early-morning aroma.

Still clothed in his bath-towel, and with no evidence of an erection, Joe packed a medium-sized suitcase with several changes of casual clothes along with a couple of his favorite suits, the grey one and the navy-blue. He managed to squeeze a second pair of shoes into the case before struggling to close the lid over the two plastic lips.

Joe climbed into his favorite pair of Levis before following his nose to the kitchen. He slid up behind Rachael and looked over her shoulder as she prepared the food. He kissed her neck and was reminded that there was a better scent than breakfast.

They sat down together. Rachael watched Joe as he swiftly worked his way through the plate. Wondering what to say, she hardly touched her own food. "Joe, are you sure you know what you're doing?" was as good a start as any.

"Not really, but I'm going to try and find a reason why we should refuse these people a business license to operate here. I'm looking for anything, previous convictions, frauds, you know, things like that? If I can get some hard evidence, we might have a case. If nothing's done, we lose."

"Yes, and if they find out, you could be in trouble. If they're as nasty as you think they are, there's no limit to what they'll do."

"I'll be careful," promised Joe, "if things don't work out, I'll come straight home. Now remember, don't give any clues away as to where I am. Don't call me. I'll try and call you every day to let you know how things are. You're going to have enough on your plate with your mother."

"I'm still on leave for the next three weeks, so I'll be keeping a good eye on Mummy." She paused and thought, before saying, "Three weeks. That's far too much. I hope it doesn't take that long before you come back, Joe."

"I hope so too, darling. I shouldn't think I'll be away that long."

"You'd better not be. Don't forget that your friend from England is supposed to be visiting you next month," reminded Rachael.

"Shit, you're right. To tell you the truth, I'd completely forgotten about Simon," admitted Joe. "That's an extra incentive right there."

Joe left the table and went back to the bedroom where he picked out a white, cotton t-shirt and the denim jacket which up until now, he had never worn in the heat of the Caribbean. The mid-October evenings of Las Vegas would be a little cooler so it might be useful, if only for the two decent-sized inside pockets into which his travel documents would fit snugly. Joe rubbed a towel through his moist, brown hair before brushing it. He stopped to watch a couple of strands fall to the white, tiled floor and sighed. He patted his crown to make sure that he couldn't feel his scalp and was hardly re-assured by the result.

Rachael looked in on Elene and seeing that her mother was still fast asleep, she closed the door gingerly behind her. Rachael hoped that her mother wouldn't wake up to an empty house while she was out driving Joe to the airport, so to be on the safe side, she left a couple of pills out on the kitchen worktop with a note explaining where she had gone. She took the bottle with her, blindly refusing to analyze her reasoning.

Joe arrived in good time for his flight and checked in: His ticket had already been prepared since his phone call the night before. He had only purchased a return ticket to Miami, calculating that no-one would be able to check his intended destination should they have access to local records. He would buy his ticket to Vegas once he had got to Miami. The less people that knew what he was doing, the better, he thought.

The tannoy announced, "Would passengers for flight number KX048 to Miami, please prepare for boarding."

Joe turned to Rachael. "This is it, sweetheart. Wish me luck." She looked deeply into his soul through his eyes and gave him a final reason for not going. He wanted to heed it, but he forced himself to smile saying, "I'll call you, tonight."

"Don't you dare forget, Joe? I'll be sitting by the phone." She too managed a weak grin before they shared a last hug. A little tear rolled from the corner of Rachael's eye and was lost in the dark blue, denim collar of Joe's jacket.

"I love you, Rachael." whispered Joe. Rachael answered by squeezing him more tightly to her.

Joe rushed through the metal-detector doorway and then had his passport stamped before joining the queue of people that were shuffling towards the boarding gate.

Twenty minutes later, the 727 was airborne and heading due north. As soon as the plane had leveled out, the two stewardesses began to serve breakfast. They worked fast, because this flight was only an hour long and they would have to clean up as well. When he saw what was on offer, Joe was glad that he had already eaten, but gratefully, he accepted a cup of steaming, black coffee. Memories of Arthur flashed through Joe's mind. By now, Joe was in no doubt whatsoever that Arthur had hit a rough patch with those *Eastern Promise* people.

Shit breeds shit, thought Joe, wondering what sordid choice they had given Arthur. Sex, drugs, bribery or violence were probably part of their game-plan, he concluded. He hoped that any threats of violence were not aimed at Rachael. If so, then he knew he would be able to resort to violence if necessary. The thought filled him with horror.

He surmised that Higgins' letter must have arrived too late to stop Arthur from voting against the gambling motion but the contents of it must have made him aware of the damage that he had done. Joe reckoned that he understood why Arthur had decided to kill himself. Arthur was certainly a proud man, and maybe he had been overcome by guilt, but Joe still felt remorse in the knowledge that Arthur had been unable to talk to anyone. Perhaps his secret was so terrible that he felt justified in suicide? Maybe he did it to protect his family? Joe decided to leave his conjecture at that until he had some firm evidence to go on.

The aircraft landed and Joe wasted no time in clearing U.S. Immigration and Customs. At the Flight Information Desk he was informed that an Eastern Airlines flight would be leaving for Vegas in just over an hour, stopping at St. Louis, Missouri. He bought his ticket and was pleased to see the clerk misspell his name. He did not point it out, glad at the help to shroud any details of his mission.

The Eastern Airlines jet was half-empty and Joe took up a window seat in a row that was unoccupied. He slipped his briefcase under the seat in front of him and began to leaf through the in-flight magazine.

There wasn't a single worthwhile article hidden within the shiny pages, but there were lots of pouting women and classically manufactured men, probably paid by unscrupulous merchants to help unload their overpriced trinkets and toys, thought Joe.

When the plane landed in St. Louis, Joe disembarked to stretch his cramped legs. He took his briefcase with him, and soon he had the distinction of being able to say that he had set foot in St. Louis, if only the airport terminal, which looked like lots of other airport terminals.

When it was time to re-embark, Joe found himself in yet another queue with the people that were joining the flight for the first time. When he went back to his seat, he found a young girl sitting in his place. At least she looked like a young girl; it was difficult to tell under all that caked-on make-up that she had obviously struggled with that morning. Her tousled, blonde-streaked locks hung limply around her peeked face. A girlishly-pretty, snub nose fought for daylight and a closer look at her hair revealed the darker roots that she had subdued in her quest for greater sexuality. Joe eased himself into the seat next to her, his choice severely reduced by the amount of new passengers.

"Hello," said Joe, "That was my seat."

She said nothing.

"But if you prefer the window," he continued, "It's yours." He smiled at her. She ignored him completely and kept her gaze fixed firmly on the window. Joe noticed that she was tensed up as though she was trying to withdraw her whole body into itself. Her hands shook whenever she moved them away from her body, her emaciated limbs unable to give her full control of them.

She reached into her battered handbag and pulled out a bottle of pills. She tried to open it and seemed to lose hope along with her temper. The bottle fell to the floor. She threw her head back onto her chair as though she had given up.

Joe bent down and retrieved the bottle of pills. Before giving them to her, he pressed down hard on the child-proof cap and twisted it loose. He couldn't help but think that the lid had done its job when he handed the pills back. He got a good look at her face. She couldn't have been more than fourteen. "Here, you dropped these," he said. She had pretty, blue eyes, but they were surrounded by a harsh border of thick, black eye-liner.

She snatched the medicine from him and murmured muffled thanks.

She emptied the remaining four pills into her hand and chased two of them around her palm before trapping them. She dropped them, one by one, into the bottle and they rattled as they bounced around, hinting that she would soon need a refill. She made a point of leaving the lid off as she stashed the container into the only compartment of her bag that didn't have a broken zipper. After popping the other two pills and swallowing in one deft motion, she dropped the bag on the floor in front of her.

Joe couldn't help but notice the painfully-thin, stockinged legs that stuck out from her scarlet mini-skirt like a couple of cheap matchsticks.

A middle-aged man had taken the remaining place on the row and nodded in acknowledgement to Joe's welcoming expression.

"Heading for Vegas?" asked the man.

"I hope so, or else I'm on the wrong plane," laughed Joe, making light talk.

"Business or pleasure?"

"A little bit of both, time permitting. I'm visiting an old friend," Joe lied. "What about you?"

"I live there, I'm in real estate," and before Joe could say another word, the man had pulled out his business card and went into his sales pitch, blabbing something about no job being too tough and his unique ability to accept a reduced commission 'for the sake of the deal'. Joe took the card and was glad that he hadn't mentioned his own property company. The last thing he wanted was some common ground with this smooth-talking wheeler-dealer.

When the drinks trolley came near, Joe ducked out of the conversation and back into the magazine which he decided was the lesser of two evils. Present company suggested such was Joe's luck, if this had been a bar, he would have ended up next to the drunk.

The girl by the window was asked what she wanted to drink. She replied gruffly, "Bloody Mary. On the rocks."

"Sorry. Tea, coffee or fruit juice?" answered the air-hostess.

"Virgin Mary, then," she compromised, remembering the vodka in her handbag. The stewardess obliged and passed the spicy tomato-juice over before stating, "Two dollars, fifty cents, please."

The girl's face dropped. "Ya gotta be kiddin'. I ain't got a nickel. Keep ya fuckin' drink." She went to pass it back.

Joe stopped her trembling hand and said, "I'll get this. It's no big deal."

The girl took the drink and coldly turned away.

"I'll have one of those as well, please," said Joe handing over a five-dollar note. The girl looked at him. Joe met her stare with one of his own.

"Thanks, but I charge more than just a drink," she said huskily.

"Oh?" said Joe, wondering if he had heard right.

The girl picked up her bag and began to rummage around inside it looking for the vodka with which she planned to defile her drink.

Joe sensed himself being nudged by the man sitting on his left. He turned quickly and said, "Yes, what is it?"

The man sat as far back in his seat as he could and strained against the firm cushions of his headrest. When he was sure that the girl would not be able to see him beyond Joe, he touched his lips with his finger as though to demand silent attention. He shook his head and said softly, "Junkie slut. Don't mess. She's all strung out."

"Thanks for the advice, buddy," said Joe, with more than a hint of contempt.

The row fell into total silence. This became too much for the real estate man who, robbed of the privilege of hearing the sound of his own voice, left to find another seat.

"Want some?" asked the girl, holding out a small bottle of vodka.

"No thanks, it's a little early for me, but thanks for the offer," replied Joe. She looked desperate and Joe felt sorry for her.

"Are you from St. Louis?" he asked.

"I was," she answered, "at least up until today."

"So you're moving to Vegas? Got anybody there?"

She laughed, "Mister, you sure got a lot to learn. Isn't it obvious? I'm looking for tricks. You know, a lady of dubious reputation." She cackled, as the last title had obviously held some humorous value for her.

On the other hand, Joe thought it was quite brave of her to admit it. "You're young, aren't you?"

"I'm as old as you want me to be. Besides, the way I see it, I ain't got much choice," she explained.

"What about your parents? Don't they care?"

"What's it to you?"

"Nothing, it's just a little sad," said Joe.

"My tricks don't tell me that it's sad."

"You've got the wrong idea," said Joe, "I wasn't trying to pick you up or anything."

She laughed, "I know, I was just playing you up."

Joe sighed with relief.

The girl looked up and went on, "My folks drink. Dad beats us. My mom's jumping into bed with men when he's at work. That is, when her black eyes have healed."

"I'm sorry," said Joe, a little embarrassed, but he knew that he had asked for it.

"Don't be, it's a hard life. You just gotta go day to day. Normal people like you would never understand." Her upper-lip visibly stiffened.

"How are you going to make it in Vegas?" asked Joe.

"I'll get by. I usually do. If I can't make it on my own, I'll have to get a pimp."

Joe was finding her honesty strangely refreshing and had decided that he wanted to help her a little, even if it only meant giving her enough money for a decent meal. "Listen, what's your name?"

"Bobby," she answered, and a little grin mellowed her drawn features.

"I'm Joe; it's nice to meet you, Bobby." Joe offered his hand and Bobby hesitated before shaking it. She held Joe's hand for a little longer than the shake and he felt coldness in her grip.

"You're not American, are you, Joe?" said Bobby. "You sure have a weird accent. Joe laughed.

"I'm originally from England, but I live in the Cayman Islands now." Joe didn't feel threatened by telling her this.

"Where's that?" asked Bobby, intrigued by this strangely sweet soul.

"The Cayman Islands? It's a group of three islands in the Caribbean. There's Grand Cayman, Cayman Brac and Little Cayman."

"Which one's yours?"

"If you put it like that, Grand Cayman, but I have a soft spot for the Brac. It's homely, and the people are kind, but lots of them have to work on Grand Cayman because there are more jobs, but it's all pretty peaceful. At least it is now."

"I bet it's real nice, Joe. You're a lucky guy." Bobby's voice sounded dreamy and it matched her face. Her mind had just flown her to an imagined paradise built from snippets of media memory, and she was suddenly walking along a deserted beach, feeling the salty sea air blowing away the past. Joe sensed true emotion behind her tough face and was angered at his own apparent smugness.

"I'm sorry, Bobby, I didn't mean to sound so selfish," he apologized, patting her hand as though to bring her back from the trance.

She turned the palm of her hand up to meet Joe's. They gripped each other instinctively and Joe looked directly into her eyes. They were unfathomable. He sensed her effortlessly enter his spirit as though using a key that he had entrusted to her eons ago. She feigned an attempt to pull away, happy at Joe's different touch. It was the first time in ages that she had been touched by a man who had no intention of hitting her or putting her through all those bizarre routines that she was getting good at, or so she was told.

"I don't need your sympathy, Joe," she said, regaining her composure, "I'm pretty tough, you know."

"I can see that. Listen, I'm starving. I'm getting something to eat after we land. If you need a lift downtown and you're feeling hungry, you're welcome to come along. No catches, I promise."

"I'll think about it," replied Bobby, a little taken aback at this offer of something for nothing. "No catches, you sure?" she checked.

"As sure as I'll ever be," said Joe, as he wondered what he had gotten himself into.

"It might be a deal," said Bobby, cagily. She dug in her bag and brought out a yellow-stained handkerchief that had once been white; a long time ago. She dabbed the corner of her moist left eye with it, being careful not to dislodge any of the mascara that she had plastered on that morning.

They found it easy to talk to one another. Their totally opposing backgrounds made sure they had nothing in common that would bore the other. Every time one of them spoke, it was about something that the other had no experience or inkling of. Joe was sure of his honorable intentions but could not help but wonder what Rachael would say if she knew that her husband was taking a whore under his wing. Joe concluded that if she was the kind of person who wouldn't understand, then he probably wouldn't have married her in the first place. He felt re-assured by this affirmation and chatted away happily with his 'adopted daughter'.

The plane began to approach McCarran International Airport, Las Vegas. Through the window, it was just possible to make out Lake Mead, home to the famous Hoover Dam. Bobby seemed a lot less wound up now and Joe thought she looked more like an excited schoolgirl on a daytrip to the zoo, than a hooker getting ready to prowl a concrete jungle.

After they had landed, Bobby followed Joe to the baggage carousel, cementing her plan to take Joe up on his offer. They made their way through blinking and flashing ranks of one-armed bandits and down an escalator.

Joe's suitcase was soon on its way. He grabbed it and turned to Bobby. "What does yours look like?"

She laughed raucously. "What's the matter with you?" he asked, baffled.

"It's black, made of plastic and..." Joe began to look out for it, "...and it's right here," she chuckled.

"Where?" Joe couldn't see anything.

"In my hand, where else?" She held up her handbag towards Joe and said, "This is it Joe, this is all I've got." She wasn't laughing any more. Joe's foot was still in his mouth, so he pointed to the way out and began to walk. Bobby followed.

By the exit, they found a row of courtesy phones. Joe quickly scanned for what accommodation was available. It seemed that everything was focused around *The Strip*. He found the Yellow Pages by the public telephones and chose a motel that advertised itself as being on Fremont Street and only five minutes drive from The Strip.

Bobby suggested that they take a limo because it was cheaper, but Joe settled for a taxi that was available now, rather than wait for a limo which would stay put until it had enough passengers to make the journey worthwhile.

The driver flicked a switch which opened the boot and meant that he would not have to get out and help Joe with his suitcase. Having seen the caliber of his passengers, he decided that a contemptuous approach was best suited to the 'the little slut and her 'trick'. The sordid conclusion that he had jumped to was only affirmed by Joe's request to go to one of the cheaper, sleazier motels. Thirty minutes later, after driving through what appeared to be a predominantly residential side of town; they were at the Golden Palace Motel. The driver accepted Joe's tip-less fare without even looking at him and flicked the boot switch again. The passengers got out and Bobby waited outside while Joe went into the run-down reception area.

Joe booked his room and was pleased at the chance to stretch out on a bed. He promised Bobby that they would go out to eat soon but he told her he felt travel-weary and would take a few minutes off his feet.

Whilst Joe melded into the contours of the soft bed, Bobby turned the television on and sat on the floor in front of it flicking aimlessly through the channels. A few minutes later, Joe's exhaustion caught up with his tired body, and he fell asleep. Two hours later, he awoke to find himself alone. He looked at his watch. It was four pm. Vegas time. Bobby must have grown tired of waiting, and she was probably up to tricks by now, he thought.

He began to unpack his suitcase. He thought about what he was going to say to Higgins. He went to take out his wallet to check that he still had Higgins' telephone number.

"Oh shit! The fuckin' bitch," he shouted loudly, as he furiously kicked the wall. His wallet had gone, and Bobby with it!

"Bastard LeRice. Good fucking Samaritan!" he roared. He tore off his jacket and threw it against the wall, anger and disgust giving it added impetus.

How could he have been so narrow-minded? He cursed. Living in the Cayman Islands had certainly softened him up. If he was going to get anywhere in this tough place, he had better sharpen his act up, pronto.

The damage had not been too severe. Only a few hundred dollars in cash, a drivers license and two credit cards which he would now have to report stolen. They could be replaced pretty quickly and then he could draw cash on them. But how embarrassing! What could he say? He played it out in his mind.

"I was with this whore in my motel room and I fell asleep. When I woke up, my wallet had gone."

The only answer to that could be, "Serves you bloody well right! You got rolled." Joe winced. He grabbed the telephone directory and looked through the Higgins'. He recognized Brogan's number and felt a little better. At least his mission had not been compromised. Then he called information and obtained the local numbers to the credit card companies' offices. His first call was being diverted to the relevant department when he heard a knock on the door followed by a chirpy voice, "Room service."

He hung up quickly before he had given any details about his loss. What was going on? He hadn't ordered anything and besides, motels didn't have room service, did they? He heard another knock. He went over to the door and yanked it open. There was Bobby, eyes glazed and holding a paper bag from a fast-food restaurant.

"I hope you like cheeseburgers, Joe," she grinned. Joe grabbed her arm and pulled her inside. He closed the door and turned to face her.

"What the bloody hell do you think you're playing at?" he demanded.

She looked shocked.

"I thought you were hungry so I went out to get some food." She explained, as she delved into her bag and pulled out Joe's wallet.

"You were asleep. I didn't want to wake you." She handed the wallet over. Joe leafed through the cash; it was fifty dollars short. He was more relieved than anything now, but he still confronted her, "Pretty expensive cheeseburgers, eh? Where's the change?"

"You know how it is, Joe?" said Bobby, wistfully.

"How what is?"

"My pills ran out and I had to get a hit. I couldn't stop myself."

"What hit? What are you talking about?"

"Coke, Joe. I'm hooked. The pills I take. They're supposed to help me, but I ran out."

"You'll have to get some more then, won't you?" urged Joe.

"With what?"

Joe realized what he had just implied. The girl would have to go out on the streets to get laid by some punter so she could get some money to get some drugs that would keep her off other drugs. A compromise was necessary.

"I'll help you get some pills. But no more taking without asking, is that fair?"

"Fair, but they won't give me the pills without a note."

"Then we get you a note. What's the problem?" said Joe.

"Doctors cost money."

"Look, Bobby. I said I'd help," said Joe, a little irked. "And I suppose you need somewhere to stay tonight?" he complained, immediately regretting his apparent coldness.

"I'll be alright." rasped Bobby. "The streets are my home. Forget the pills and the doctors, Joe. I'm only in your way." She went to the door. "Thanks though, you know you're alright." She began to open the door.

"Bobby, Stop!" Joe called her back, "If I was alright, do you think I'd just let you walk out like that. Come back here, now." Joe dumped the fast-food in the garbage can. "Come on, let's go and find some real food."

Bobby relented and they found a little Chinese restaurant a couple of blocks away, near a mall. Joe couldn't help thinking that it was Bobby's first decent meal in days, as she packed away two enormous platefuls of chicken chow mein. She had a little too much wine, but it would help her to sleep and keep her out of mischief, so Joe didn't say a word about it.

On the way back to the motel, Joe took Bobby on a little detour to a clothing shop where he gave her two hundred dollars. "Pick out some clothes," he told her.

"Are you sure?" She knew better than to look a gift horse in the mouth and said with a wink, "Come to think of it, I do need some new panties."

Joe waited outside whilst Bobby made her choices. She came out half-an-hour later armed with two shopping bags. "Thanks, Joe," she gushed. "I don't even know how to repay you." She set her new bags down and brought a receipt and change out of her handbag. She gave them to Joe.

"Ta, Bobby. You're learning," said Joe, slipping back into some English slang.

"Joe? What does *Ta* mean?"

"It means thanks."

They went back to the motel and Joe let Bobby have the choice of one of the two beds. Bobby was so tired that she fell asleep without so much as a thought about a bath, somewhat to Joe's annoyance.

Rachael was beginning to get a little worried. It was nearly midnight on Grand Cayman. The phone stood silent and then she would imagine that she heard it ringing. She would rush back into the living room only to be disappointed. "Come on, Joe," she whispered time and time again, willing him to call.

Elene had been very quiet, but she was beginning to show signs of improvement. She had got so wrapped up in a sentimental television movie that it caused her to miss a dose of tranquilizers. After, the film however, her loneliness became apparent and she felt forced to take some. It was a start though, Rachael observed.

Suddenly, the phone did ring. Rachael rushed to it and nearly dropped the receiver on the floor in her fraught haste to answer.

"Joe," she said, her voice quivering. She hadn't even waited for a voice on the other end.

"AT&T, Las Vegas. I have a collect call for a Rachael LeRice."

"Speaking."

"Will you accept the charges?"

"Certainly."

"Go ahead then."

The operator clicked off the line and paved the way for Joe who was calling from the motel. "Rachael, it's me, I'm so sorry. I fell asleep and then I went out to eat."

"Are you alright? Is anything wrong?"

"No. Everything's ok, sweetheart. I'm in a motel. The journey was a little tiring, but apart from that I'm alright." He paused, "This place is the pits. I miss you already."

"Then come home." Rachael knew there was no harm in trying.

"I wish, but no can do. Not yet anyway," said Joe.

"Promise me you'll call sooner tomorrow," implored Rachael,

"Tonight was awful. I thought something had happened to you."

"I promise. I should be over this jet-lag by then. Any messages? You know, business?" asked Joe.

"No. Nothing important. I checked with your secretary. She said you had received a check for an interim payment on the Anderson job. She was going to deposit it. Otherwise there's nothing urgent, but she said she'd let me know if there was."

"There shouldn't be any problems. The men have got enough work on now for the next few weeks, with that other house up at Cayman Kai. Did my secretary ask you where I was?"

"Yes, she did. I told her that you were visiting old friends in England."

"Good girl," said Joe affectionately. "So, I'll be calling you tomorrow, then. Earlier, I hope."

"There's no 'hope' about it Joe LeRice, if you know what's good for you."

The conversation stopped and they realized that the silence that followed reminded them of the times when they looked at each other when the talking was over. Now there were nearly three thousand miles between them and talk was all they had.

"I love you, Rachael."

"I love you too, Joe." Rachael held on until she heard Joe say goodbye. She hung up after holding the phone to her breast.

"Was that your wife, Joe?" came a soft voice. Joe turned to see Bobby, stretching out from her nap.

"Yes, it was." Joe sounded vacant, lost in thought.

"Is she pretty?" quizzed Bobby. Joe took out a photograph from his wallet and handed it to her. She had already seen it, but pretended she hadn't.

"Her name's Rachael. I think she's pretty, but there's more to it than that," explained Joe, suddenly feeling alone.

"She's beautiful, Joe. But she's also very lucky."

"Why's that?" Joe was intrigued.

"Well, to have someone like you."

"I've always thought it was the other way round." Joe laughed.

"That's just like you, Joe. You're far too easy. I don't know what you're doing here, but you don't belong. Vegas is tough, you'd better wise up or you'll get burned. I could have easily stolen your wallet and not come back."

"But you didn't, did you?" Joe reminded her.

"Don't miss the point. You need someone to look after you while you're here." Bobby flashed a smile.

"And just who do you have in mind?" Joe already knew the

answer to that question.

"Yours truly, Bobby Verrill, at your service." She bowed playfully and then looked earnestly at Joe to show him that she meant it. Then she added, "By the way, what *are* you doing in Vegas?"

"It's like I said before, I'm mixing business with pleasure." Joe wondered where the pleasure would come in.

"I still think you need some help," hinted Bobby.

"I'll need to think about it, Bobby. I can't rely on you if you're up to tricks and snorting coke."

"If I can get some pills then I won't need to go on the streets, and if I don't need to go on the streets, then no tricks. Easy."

Bobby hoped it would be that straightforward.

"It's getting late," said Joe, "I've got a busy day tomorrow. I've got to make some calls and then check out some places. We'll make a move first thing in the morning."

"I don't feel tired anymore," said Bobby, refreshed after her nap.

"You will when you've had a shower," said Joe. Bobby's face wrinkled with displeasure.

"Come on, Bobby. Those clothes are filthy. Your hair could use a wash, too." She was in no position to argue and she sidled into the bathroom. It was a full hour before she emerged with a towel around her body and one around her head. Her face, without its painted mask, actually looked like that of a sixteen year old girl and she looked happier.

"Where are your clothes?" asked Joe. She fetched them and dumped them on her bed. Joe went over and picked them up. They stank. Bobby watched him intently.

Joe then rammed the racy clothes into the garbage along with the fast food.

"That was my favorite skirt," moaned Bobby.

"You're right," agreed Joe. "Was."

Her protests stopped immediately. Joe took a shower and made sure that Bobby didn't see him take his wallet along. When he finished, he was pleased to see an angelic peace on Bobby's face. She was enjoying a dream, the dream that she had experienced many times before and now it was real. She belonged. Joe pulled the blanket up to her shoulders and nodded his head as he looked at her. Gone was the angry barrier of suspicion that she had learned to hide behind, at least it was gone until tomorrow. To Joe, she was just a young girl who had got tough. It wasn't her fault, but the poor girl had probably missed her entire youth. Joe slid into his own bed and turned the light off.

Chapter Thirteen

"Wake up, Joe. I thought you said you had a busy day lined up."

"Wha...What time is it?" grumbled Joe.

"It's after nine," said Bobby. "If you want to keep me off the streets, you'd better get me to the doctor's. My hands are beginning to shake. That's always a sign."

Joe sat up in his bed, and looked at Bobby. She had made him a cup of instant coffee using the sachets provided in the room; he eased it from her unsteady hands and thanked her. She was wearing her new clothes and Joe said, "Stand back; let's have a look at you, then."

Bobby moved away from the bed and twirled around. She looked a lot healthier in the pair of black jeans that covered her thin legs. Her little bottom cheeks could not quite fill out the space provided, but the trouser legs were a perfect length, stopping just above her pale ankles. She had chosen a white, cotton blouse which contrasted nicely with the jeans. A token, red belt broke up the harsh transition from white to black.

"Very nice," judged Joe, "better than you had on yesterday."

"Thanks, Joe. Thanks for everything. I've never met anyone like you before."

"That's funny, I was about to say the same about you."

They both laughed, the joke achieving in seconds what hours of conversation could not.

Joe picked up the Yellow Pages and thumbed through the list of doctors. After a few attempts, he found one that would be available to see Bobby that morning. Joe explained that she was his niece and that he would pay for the consultation and the prescription.

The receptionist insisted on taking his credit card number there and then. Joe did not argue but after he had hung up, he warned Bobby to make sure that she checked the bill before signing a receipt.

"No problem, Joe. I'll ask them about everything." She seemed to relish Joe's trust. He noticed, but remained silent. Then he gave her some money for the taxi and some food.

The taxi pulled up outside the rooms of the motel and honked its horn. "Here, take the key," said Joe, "You'll probably get back before me. Now remember, no…"

"I know, no tricks," Bobby chuckled, as she closed the door behind her. Joe believed her.

Turning his attention to matters in hand, he dialed Higgins' number. Mrs. Higgins answered and informed Joe that her husband had gone to work at the store. She gave Joe the address and he had to ask her to repeat it. East, West, North and South, boulevards, avenues, places and such, that were made harder to understand by a smattering of numbers and decipherable only by those in the know; it was enough to put off any budding explorer. Joe hoped that he wouldn't be there long enough to be in the know.

Encouraged by the knowledge that he could call on Brogan Higgins at any time of the working day, Joe decided to arrange some more money because Bobby's extra needs had drained almost all of his cash. Soon, he was changed and walking in the direction of what looked like the denser part of the city, turning left off Fremont Street and onto Maryland Parkway. He stopped at a small, quiet diner for some breakfast. A fat grill-chef came over to take Joe's order. Joe noticed the thick, yellow grease that had congealed around the gold rings on the cook's stubby fingers.

"See the game last night?" bubbled the cook enthusiastically.

"What game?" asked Joe, thinking that it was a strange opening line.

"The Rams against the 'Niners."

"I must have missed it," replied Joe.

"Oh man, it was great. Fourth and inches on the thirty and a bomb from Montana saved the day. I was sweatin'. I had a Dime on the 'Niners. "

He saw that Joe was baffled by this conversation and he looked into his pad, pencil at the ready.

"Just a coffee, please." said Joe. The man stood still for a moment as though expecting Joe to say something else. He scratched at the beard that had been grown to conceal the true size of his bloated face.

"Is that it?"

"Yes, that's it," echoed Joe, concluding that this man was the nervous owner of an ailing business.

Joe paid the man and left half of the drink, preferring to leave to his imagination what delights he would have found in the bottom of his cup, had he finished it. The cook, engrossed in the form page of the newspaper, didn't even see Joe leave.

Joe found a bank that advertised services on the credit cards that he held. He requested an advance of a thousand dollars. He was glad that he still had his passport with him, because the teller insisted on formal identification. After a phone call and a sneaky look at Joe as he waited, she began to fill out the forms with familiar ease. She had seen it all before. Gamblers, all their cash spent, having to milk their credit cards for as much as they could get, leaving just enough for one last withdrawal, which would enable them to make the minimum payment for the bill at the end of the month. She also realized that if it wasn't for this type of person, she could easily be out of a job.

Joe elected to hail a taxi and meet with Higgins. He gave the driver the slip of paper on which the address was written. The driver assessed the information in a split-second, leaving Joe to admire the skill of this accomplished code-breaker.

They took a right and drove into the heart of the city. Joe assumed that he must have been on *The Strip.* The bright, desert sun was forced to compete with a thrashing, neon sea that heaved and swelled along each street, enticing punters to be swept through the doorways below it. The people going in were eager to assume the smiles that those coming out had left inside.

Was this the proverbial Mecca to where he would have made his final pilgrimage? Joe thought. On huge bill-boards were ageless, so-called celebrities who would have happily exchanged their own faces for the ones advertised. Joe wondered how much of their exorbitant fees went back across the table from where it came. Maybe they were immune? Yes, that was it, like cooks who didn't taste their own food.

Joe sensed an unusual level of bitterness rising in him due to the fact that these *Eastern Promise* people had gone beyond their station to force a dubious agenda. In doing so, they had castrated an unsuspecting democratic nation, removing its right to sow the seeds of its own destiny. If Arthur had gone against them, as he may well have done in different circumstances, they would have lost the vote, something they could clearly not accept. This inability to accept was the common link between them and Joe, and he refused to accept that his adopted country had been given no choice.

Although, he had been brought up in the system and still belonged to it, it didn't mean that he had to dance to its every beat. He regularly questioned its composition and its priorities. In fact, the more he thought about it, the more he became convinced that so-called democracies were thinly-veiled dictatorships where all people vote for a few and the few become corrupt serving themselves, not the people who put them in power. After all, he surmised it would be a hell of a lot cheaper to buy off a few politicians rather than an entire nation. It was no wonder that elected politicians shied away from the referendum.

Joe had no politics. Not since the age of eighteen when he and fellow pupils were driven to the local polling station in the public school's minibus and told that the school was depending on them for its support and that meant only one choice. Vote to the right. Joe had considered going to the left in protest, but when he saw the opposition who disagreed for the sake of it, he dropped the subject completely. He had never voted, refusing to condone a system that would never truly represent the will of the people.

By now, Joe had lost track of where he was. They passed a casino calling itself *The Gold Coast* and a sign that said Flamingo Road, but it meant nothing. Joe's poor sense of direction had evaporated minutes ago amidst the sheer, pulsing energy of *The Strip*. The car stopped. "Four-fifty," demanded the driver, hand out-stretched. Joe got out, gave him five and walked away, knowing that he shouldn't expect any change unless he asked for it.

Joe looked around and found himself on a row of jewelry stores. Across the road were a couple of pawnbrokers. Joe imagined all kinds of scenarios arising out of this peculiar set-up. He looked at his address again and realized that 'the store' was, in fact, The Store and he was right outside of it.

He went inside, cautiously at first, but then he saw several smiling faces on the other side of the counter and he walked over to the closest one. It belonged to a thin, mustachioed man who stooped in subservience, probably weighed down by the ungainly, gold watch that hung loosely around his narrow wrist.

"Yes, sir? Can I help you?"

"I was looking for..."

"Well, there's no charge for looking this week," interrupted the salesman. Then he guffawed at his own joke.

Joe grinned weakly.

The salesman continued, "Welcome to The Store. What you see are all original works by a world-famous designer, captured in eighteen and fourteen carat gold and complimented with precious and semi-precious stones. All of our diamonds are at least VVS quality and the pieces come with a certificate of authenticity."

The red-faced salesman paused to draw breath and a first reaction from his prospective 'sale'.

"I'm looking for Mr. Higgins," explained Joe, pleased to have switched off this monotonous tape-recorder.

"Oh," said the salesman, deflated. "He's in the back. I'll call him." He left.

A good-looking man of medium height and build came out from the back and walked around the counters to the sales floor. A pair of heavy-rimmed glasses rested on top of a head of thick, black hair and a friendly smile lay on his lips. He looked to be in his late forties.

"Mr. Higgins?" inquired Joe. The man pulled his glasses onto his nose and squinted as if to inspect the newcomer.

"That's me. Who wants to know?" said Brogan.

"I'm Joe LeRice," said Joe, "From the Cayman Islands."

Brogan's face dropped. "You'd better come in the back, Mr. LeRice."

Joe followed and Brogan ushered him into a tiny office and squeezed behind his desk before offering his guest a seat.

"I was hoping this wouldn't happen," said Brogan.

"What do you mean?" said Joe.

"I'm having a hard enough time losing my brother without some private eye from the middle of nowhere poking around."

"But you said on the phone that you would at least talk to me," insisted Joe.

"I know I did. But I'm not very happy about it. Well, you're here now, so what can I do for you?"

Joe paused, relieved to have finally got his chance to speak to Higgins. He started slowly, "I need to find a way to stop *Eastern Promise* from getting established on Grand Cayman. If I can dig some dirt on their top executives, then there may be a case in favor of blocking their application for a business license."

"What, in particular do you intend finding out?" asked Brogan.

"I'm not really sure," confessed Joe, "Previous criminal records, or present dishonest activities, drugs, bribes, you know?"

"Yes, I do know," stated Brogan firmly, "And I also know that as soon as they suspect that you're digging around, they'll be digging your grave. You are either so naive, or..." Brogan stopped.

"Or what?" prompted Joe.

"Dumb." Brogan was shaking his head.

"Listen to me, Higgins," fumed Joe, his lips pursed with conviction, "These bastards kill your brother, force my wife's father into suicide and God knows what else, and you lie down and take it. You remind me of a bloody ostrich with its head in the sand and its arse in the air."

"You really are serious, aren't you?" Brogan almost toyed with the improbable notion of liking this mad fool.

"I hope so, but I'm also frightened," admitted Joe, "afraid of what will happen if I try and do something, and afraid of the consequences if I don't."

Joe reached into his pocket and pulled out Brogan's letter to Arthur. "Mr. Higgins..."

"What's with all this Mr. Higgins crap? Call me Brogan."

"Alright Brogan, call me Joe," said Joe, returning the sentiment, "I know you care. You were so easy to trace from your letter to my father-in-law. You took a chance and you know it. If Arthur Downing had been totally sucked in, then he would have handed you over, and they would have come looking for you. True?"

"I suppose so," agreed Brogan, "When I wrote it, I was so angry. I had just read in the papers that they were coming to your islands. I felt I had to do something. After I'd sent it and cooled down, I regretted it. I was also afraid for the same reason as you."

"They are vicious, conniving bastards," said Joe, glad that he now had someone else who agreed with him.

"That's only half the story," declared Brogan, "I'm convinced that they're up to something in their casino, like brainwashing, doping or something."

"That's pretty scary, why do you think that?"

"It's just a hunch. My brother hinted at it before he died."

"You mean he told you?"

"Not exactly, he left a message on my answering machine. It was the last I heard of him," explained Brogan.

"Do you still have the message?" Joe asked.

"I do, it was all I had left, but there's nothing on it that you could use. He doesn't name the place, but he does mention thought-control."

"What made your brother think he was being controlled?" asked Joe.

"I don't know, but over the last few years, he seemed to change. He began to shut everybody out."

Brogan too had changed over the last few minutes as he seemed more willing to co-operate. He went on, "He kept going back to the same damned place. It was the *Eastern Promise* all the time. Gamblers are usually superstitious. If they have a bad run of luck in one place, they usually move on to another."

"So your brother may have seen something to convince him that he had been brainwashed," deduced Joe.

"I hope so," said Brogan, "otherwise this whole angle is useless."

"Do you mind if I listen to it?" asked Joe.

"Not at all, Joe, but like I said, there's nothing to go on."

"Do you have it with you?" Joe pressed.

"You kiddin'. It's at home, buried in some trunk. I'll get it for you, tomorrow. "

"No chance today, then?" asked Joe, frowning hopefully.

"I'm sorry, Joe. I live on the outskirts of town. It would take me nearly two hours to find it and bring it back. Besides, I keep harping on at my employees that they only get an hour for lunch."

"I understand," accepted Joe, "Tomorrow then?"

"Tomorrow," consented Brogan.

"In the meantime, do you know where the courts offices are?"

"I do, but I'd advise you not to go," recommended Brogan.

There was a knock on the door and it opened. The salesman whom Joe had first met poked his head into view and looked at Brogan.

"It's ok Chris, what is it?" asked Brogan, implying that it was safe to talk shop in front of Joe.

"There's a Japanese guy out there," Chris gushed with excitement. "Gold Rolex, top of the line camera, the works. He's loaded. I'm trying to get him on the two-carat solitaire. He really likes it, but I can't quite close him. I told him I was coming in the back to get a better price. I need a turnover."

"Wait here, Joe," said Brogan, knowing that a turnover required him to help Chris close the sale. "I'll be back in a minute."

Five minutes later, Brogan returned with a smile on his face and a platinum American Express card in his hand. He gave it to an assistant for processing and turned to Joe, smiling.

"Flattery gets you everywhere. Now, where were we?"

"You were going to tell me why I shouldn't go looking in the court records. Why?"

Brogan was still a little flustered, having obviously worked hard to close a big sale. He sat down.

"These people have their hands in everything. I'd put money on the fact that they'd know about more about you before you could pin anything on them. I'm sorry Joe, but I live here. I know how these people operate."

"What about if I checked the past newspapers?" suggested Joe.

"Fine, if you've got a couple of years free. Face it; you don't really have any clues to go on. I think you're barking up the wrong tree. If you want to fight fire, you've got to use fire."

"You mean I should just burn their place down?" said Joe, looking mystified. Brogan laughed. He was beginning to endear himself to this stupid, brave fool.

"No, I mean if they play dirty, then you should too.

Joe looked at Brogan hard, and saw that he wasn't joking.

Brogan continued, "This is an urban jungle. There are laws, unwritten laws that are obeyed. We know our place.

"Speak for yourself, I know my place and these bastards are trying to ruin it," said Joe, making it clear that he was willing to go it alone.

Brogan shook his head and rose from his chair, "Come back tomorrow and we'll listen to the tape. This is a tough place, Joe."

"I know," muttered Joe, "I've met your salesmen." They laughed. Brogan showed Joe out, before they shook hands firmly.

Joe was aware that he still hadn't so much as glimpsed the infamous *Eastern Promise Hotel and Casino*. Until he had formulated a plan, he reasoned, it made no sense to be seen in the area in order to maintain the element of surprise. Why he needed the element of surprise, he had no idea; it just seemed the logical thing to do. He walked towards the city, refreshed in the knowledge that he now had a vague idea of directions; very vague. He awkwardly crossed a massive freeway and a block later, he was back on The Strip, otherwise known as Las Vegas Boulevard. At the junction, four huge casinos sprung out of the ground all around him. He turned left and carried on. Lights flashed, the streets were alive, charged with a mysterious energy. Symbols and words of wealth bombarded his mind, *lucky this, golden that, big bonanza, silver dollar.*

Joe leaned out to hail the first passing taxi, its horn blared as it drove straight by. He was a little luckier with the next one. It stopped, allowing him to scramble in.

"You look lost, sir," declared the driver.

"I am, I think." Joe agreed.

"All these casinos, it's enough to make anybody confused. I was the same when I moved here about ten years ago. These *Strip* casinos, they're all the same."

"Why's that?" Joe hadn't realized that he had forgotten to tell the driver where he wanted to go.

"They don't seem to change. They get a good location and they think that's enough. I could show you a place that you wouldn't believe. It's real close."

"I was hoping that you would take me back to my motel." Joe recalled his purpose.

"Which one you at?"

"Golden Palace," said Joe, a little embarrassed at having to repeat the ridiculously inappropriate name.

"Great, it's on the way," enthused the driver.

After five minutes of driving around completely unfamiliar territory, the driver pulled up outside a large hotel and casino.

"Have you got a minute? Come on, I'll show you round. It's the best place in town."

Reluctantly, Joe got out of the cab and looked over at the foyer of the building. In large, golden, oriental letters, it proclaimed, *Eastern Promise Hotel and Casino.*

"Shit," hissed Joe. This, he did not need. He decided to feign illness, as he put his hands on the side of the taxi and buried his head in them.

"What's your problem?" asked the driver, his voice devoid of all compassion.

"I feel dizzy, I think I'm going to faint," Joe fibbed.

"I'd better get you inside, quickly," urged the man.

Joe realized that this would be a bad move and knew that he would have to wriggle a little harder to stop ending up in the one place where it mattered. He stood up and said, "I feel a little better now? A few deep breaths and I should be ok."

"That's good. Now perhaps we can go in and look around," insisted the driver. Joe became suspicious. Dragging people into casinos was surely not part of the man's job description? Play time now over, Joe turned to the driver, "Listen, you asshole, I don't want to go in this fucking casino, so bugger off and go find some other sucker. I don't give a shit if your uncle owns this place."

"Suit yourself; I was just trying to help." The driver got back in his taxi and screeching tires left rubber on the parking lot next to Joe. He began to walk away hastily, and somewhat bewildered at this strange encounter.

Taking taxis was beginning to become an inconvenience, but hiring a car was out of the question because driving on the right-hand side of packed inner-city streets appeared far too daunting a transition from the small left-hand system in the Cayman Islands. His other option was to find somewhere to stay in the heart of the city. That would probably mean taking a hotel room in one of the many casinos or a more expensive motel with a central location, and gambling facilities.

Joe found himself thinking about Bobby. He wasn't looking after her because he felt obliged to, nor was he motivated sexually, but she certainly made life more tolerable in this place. He waved a cab down and asked to be driven back to the motel. On the way back, he scanned the streets for landmarks so that he would be able to walk into town on his own. The trouble was that to his woeful sense of direction, all the landmarks looked the same. When he arrived, Joe estimated that he was well over an hour's walk away.

The curtains to his room were still closed and he knocked on the door. Bobby had already returned and she let him in. There was an orange smear around her lips and the offending slice of pizza was in her free hand. Her welcome was garbled with the food that filled her mouth. Once she had swallowed, she brought the box over to Joe.

"Want some?" she asked.

"Yeah, thanks," said Joe, his hunger magnified by the inviting aroma. "Looks like I got here just in time," he noted, taking one of the two remaining pieces.

"I'm a growing girl, you know."

'Girl', was right, thought Joe and thought it was good to hear it come from her own lips, however inadvertent.

"So how did you get on at the doctor's?"

"Not too bad. I got the pills and he gave me the address of some therapists. The worst part was when they took some tests. I hate the sight of blood, it's bad enough seeing the needle. They said they would send the results here. I gave them this address." She handed Joe the bill. He looked at the bottom line and judged it as reasonable, before putting it down.

"Why did they give you blood tests?" he queried.

"I dunno. The doctor said I looked a little pale. He said I hadn't been eating properly. He was right." Joe didn't doubt it.

"So you'll be alright then?" he added.

"'Far as I know." Bobby took a pack of cigarettes out of her bag and went outside to have one. Joe joined her. They sat down on the front step of the room. She offered him one. He was almost tempted to take it but he said, "I'd better not. I gave it up about ten years ago."

"It hasn't always been easy for you, Joe, has it?" Bobby shot him a sideways glance as she blew out a cloud of blue smoke. She was checking to see if she hadn't overstepped her mark. Joe watched the smoke as it was picked up by a puff of desert wind and carried off towards the city.

He looked lost in reflection. "What makes you say that?"

"I dunno, it was just a notion."

"You're probably right. When I was a kid, I spent most of the time away at school. Then both my parents died…"

"I'm sorry, Joe," sympathized Bobby.

"Don't be, it was a long time ago," said Joe gathering himself, "I feel as though I hardly knew them. I still wonder what it would be like if things had been different."

"Yeah, me too," said Bobby, as she joined Joe on the painful journey into the past.

Joe resumed, "I nearly lost it when I went to college. I used to drink a lot, fooling myself that all students were supposed to party their brains out." Joe paused for a moment as he searched for a reason. "Looking back, there must have been an awful lot of unhappy students. We just seemed to get wrapped up in everything. We were just kids."

"When did you change?" asked Bobby, hoping that he might impart a pearl of profound wisdom.

"I don't think I really changed," Joe admitted, "I just understood. That made all the difference. Also, if it wasn't for my wife, I might not have made it."

"Was it that bad?" asked Bobby.

"It could have been. In the early days of our marriage, I think she liked me because I was a lot of fun. After we got married, she became a lot more responsible. I suppose I just followed suit, but it wasn't so easy."

"You haven't said anything about kids, Joe. You got any?"

"I'm working on it," he smirked, "I mean we're working on it."

"I'd like to have a couple of kids," interjected Bobby, "one day when things start to work out for me."

Joe turned to face her. She knew what he was thinking. "I mean later, lots later," she explained, lighting another cigarette from the first one."I can see it now," she resumed enthusiastically, "We'd have a little wooden house somewhere in the country. I'd be out feeding the animals and my kids would be helping me. A girl and a boy. We'd have the girl first, then the boy. My husband would come home from work and I'd have a load of good home cooking on the table for him...Yeah, I can see it now." The fleeting glimpse into her impossible dream abruptly vanished and her voice ebbed into an awkward silence. Joe put his arm around her as if holding the broken pieces of her soul together.

"Will it always be this hard?" she murmured softly.

Joe didn't know the answer to that question and before he could admit it, Bobby seemed to recover her control.

"What are you really doing in Vegas, Joe?"

Joe dropped his arm as he sensed that Bobby's quick mood change signaled her return to independence. "You're sure as hell not seeing a friend," she laughed, her left eye squinting mischievously.

"Did you read the letter in my wallet?" guessed Joe.

"I had a look at it," confessed Bobby nonchalantly, "But I didn't pay much attention to it. I had other things on my mind."

"What do you remember from it?"

"Not much, something to do with gambling. It didn't turn me on. Like I said, I wasn't interested. I did read the little newspaper bit." She dismissed the subject and tossed away her cigarette. Joe trod it into the ground before following her into the room. She had already turned the television on and was about to sit back to watch it when Joe walked over and switched it off.

"It's time for us to talk, Bobby." Joe paused and tried to put his best serious face on. Bobby did not even flinch. Joe continued, "Things are about to heat up. It might get dangerous and I can't take responsibility for you."

"You mean action? I can hardly wait," smiled Bobby, as she toyed with Joe. He frowned at her and she went on, "I don't mind heat, Joe. I've lived with it all my life."

Anyway, she had nowhere else to go and nobody to take an interest in her. She didn't care what Joe was doing as long as he didn't discard her.

"There's no way that I can get you involved in what I'm doing."

"You robbin' a bank, or what?" taunted Bobby, "Cos you ain't no cop."

Joe was getting a little irked by her flippancy but maybe she would change her tune if he told her what was really going on.

"There's a casino in town-"

"I've seen lots," interrupted Bobby.

"Give me a chance, will you?" frowned Joe. Bobby shut up. Joe carried on, "The owners are going to build one in the Cayman Islands. My wife's dad was a politician. I think they blackmailed him."

Joe stopped as he remembered Arthur.

"Why did they blackmail him?" asked Bobby, now interested.

"To get him to vote for a law that would allow gambling. Gambling has always been illegal there," he explained.

"You said he 'was' a politician. Why? What happened?"

"He committed suicide after he had voted for them. I can only suppose the guilt got to him."

"So you're gonna ride to the rescue, just like you rescued me?"

The sarcasm in Bobby's voice was not intended to hurt, but it did. Joe became a little reticent.

"Something like that, but I've got to stop them."

"You got a piece?" Bobby tested Joe.

"A piece of what?" He failed.

"A gun. You know, to shoot people with."

She formed a pistol with her index and middle fingers and pointed it at Joe, her thumb cocked.

"Cut out the games, Bobby. I'm serious."

"That's what I'm afraid of. You ain't got a chance, Joe. You couldn't swat a fly, even if you wanted to. Bang!" She released her thumb. "This is a tough town, like most of 'em. The type of people that I think you're dealing with doesn't fuck around when it comes to making money."

Joe had heard eerily similar lines earlier that day from Brogan Higgins. He was beginning to feel a little out of his depth.

"What do you want, Joe?"

"Information. I need information without anyone knowing that I'm getting it," explained Joe.

"Then it's simple. We steal it."

"Steal? We?" Joe didn't know which of the two words sounded more ridiculous.

"Yes, we." Bobby was adamant. "Joe, I want you to answer a couple of my questions. Deal?"

"Alright." Joe gave in.

"What am I?" Her eyes blazed with intensity.

"A girl?" Joe was being polite and Bobby wasn't fooled.

"What am I, Joe?" Her voice became louder.

"A hooker," answered Joe, ashamed to use the word.

"Right, and who do hookers hang out with?" she pressed.

"Crooks, thugs, pimps. . . "

"Very good, Joe," Bobby patronized, "So it would be a fair bet to say that I know pretty well how these folk operate?"

"I suppose so." Joe admired the way she had manipulated him to see her point of view.

"And you need all the help you can get?" She didn't wait for an answer to that question. "It's settled then, Joe. Where you go, I go."

Joe gave in and spent the next half-hour explaining how he had got in touch with Brogan and what had happened during their meeting earlier that day.

"Can I come with you tomorrow?" asked Bobby.

"I don't see why not, if you don't mind walking."

"Why are we walking? What's wrong with a cab?"

"Some driver tried to get me into a casino today. He was pretty pushy about the whole thing."

"A set-up," said Bobby, nodding her head.

"A what?"

"A set-up. We used to do that in St. Louis. We'd find tricks and bring them to bars and restaurants and get them to spend their money."

"What for?" asked Joe.

"All sorts of reasons," explained Bobby. "Some girls would get a cut, others owed the owners and some were just plain frightened."

"The casino he took me to was the same one that's coming to Cayman."

"Did he get you inside?"

"No way," said Joe almost proudly. "He didn't seem frightened, though. I'd say he was more aggressive. "

"It's the same thing. He probably owes them and they've put him to work. It's no big deal. 'Happens all the time. We can take a cab and if we get hassled, we just bite back. Leave it to me," Bobby declared poking her thumb into her bony chest.

"You're pretty confident, aren't you," said Joe.

"I learned in a tough school."

Joe was beginning to see Bobby in a different light. It seemed impossible, but he sensed that he would have to trust her judgment. He decided to let her budding maturity wait until tomorrow to blossom and took her out to watch a movie. When they returned, Joe called Rachael. She sounded a lot happier when she answered. "Hi Joe, honey, is everything alright?"

"So far, so good. I met with Mr. Higgins today; he seems pretty cooperative so far. How's your Mom?"

"A lot better. I took her out for a picnic today. We went to our favorite spot on North Side."

"Where? Sand Pointe?"

"Right, she loved it. Oh, I've got some news for you. It's about the casino."

"What? What is it?" urged Joe.

"I stopped in at my office today, to make sure everything was alright and I found out that *Eastern Promise* have already submitted a planning application for their building. You know what that means?"

"What?"

"It means they've already got a piece of land under contract," explained Rachael.

"Where?"

"I won't be able to find out right now, but I'll keep working on it," she promised.

"Be careful," Joe cautioned. "Don't let anyone know what you're doing. It's dangerous enough without you getting involved."

"It's not a real problem; their documents have to come through our department anyway. The information will probably become public soon enough. I don't think it can help us."

"We'll see," said Joe.

After they had hung up, Joe was feeling somewhat disconcerted by this turn of events. He was amazed at the speed with which *Eastern Promise* were progressing. Either they had the world's fastest design architects, or else they had drawn their plans up well in advance. Something wasn't quite right.

Chapter Fourteen

The next morning, Joe and Bobby took a cab to *The Store.* The driver appeared on the level and took them straight there without so much as a, "Good morning."

Once inside Chris the salesman took them into the back to Brogan's office. On seeing Bobby, Brogan gave Joe a strange look, as if to ask what he was doing with a girl half his age. Bobby sensed this and wished that she had a little make-up on to hide behind. Joe introduced Bobby as a friend and she remained silent.

Brogan explained that he had made a copy of the tape as he handed it over. He also explained that he was hanging on to the original because, however morbid, it was the last memory that he had of his brother.

They had the tape. Now they had to listen to it. Joe was aware of what Brogan had said about it being useless, but he wanted to make that decision for himself.

"Have you got a cassette player here?" asked Joe.

"The only one I've got is the one that plays music for the shop," answered Brogan.

"That's no problem," said Joe, "We'll just buy one."

"If you go left out of here, left again, and up two blocks, you'll come to *Bernstein's.* They'll have one."

Joe thanked Brogan and motioned Bobby to get up to leave. She stayed silent and stood up.

"I'm sorry I can't do more for you," Brogan apologized as they were leaving.

"You've done all you can," said Joe. They left. When they were outside, Bobby turned to Joe and held his arm. "I don't think he gives you much chance, Joe."

"That may be the case, but at least he's done what he said he would."

"I didn't mean that he wasn't rooting for you, I think he is, but he knows what could happen if you make a mistake. We all do, except you."

"What about you, Bobby, what do you think?" Joe stopped walking and stared coldly at her.

"I'm rooting for you, Joe, all the way."

"Why?"

"Because I owe you, is that what you think?" she snapped. "If I thought that, I'd have screwed you ages ago." She stopped and appeared to grapple for words that could express what she felt. Exact words were elusive, but she tried anyway. "I'm not sure what it is. You're just...different. I thought about not coming back, but something made me, even when I was high."

Joe wilted under her honesty, she went on, "You made me believe in myself, you accepted me, that's all I know. I don't care about your money, I do care about you. Deep down, you're one of us."

"What's one of us?" asked Joe, confused but fascinated.

"There are only two kinds of people, Joe," she began to explain, pausing briefly to make sure she had his attention. "Those that sit back and just take all the shit and those that don't."

"What's the difference?" Joe entreated.

"The difference is, those that take it live in their own fake world and swear that they're happy. Well, we live in the same world and we know we're not. If there's a god up there, I bet he's just shaking his head.

"Do you believe in God, Bobby?" asked Joe, as he turned to walk on ahead.

"I dunno," offered Bobby, as she caught up with him. "They used to stick it to us at school but I never really had a big enough donation to get saved. That's saying nothing about what clothes we had to wear. Funny thing was, they said they weren't important, but they didn't talk about much else. I was always ashamed when they stuck the plate under my nose."

She stopped and a wry smile caused her cheeks to dimple slightly. Then she said, "What about you? Do you believe in God?"

Joe realized he had laid himself wide open for that one, so he took a deep breath as if to imply that he would try and do justice to the question.

"I change my mind a few times every day," he vacillated. "When I'm up, and things are going well, I guess I don't really think about it that much, but when I'm down, I need someone to blame, and who better to blame than the all-powerful one." Joe realized that he was incapable of explaining the life force that had sustained him since birth but he continued awkwardly, "But, if I had to answer your question with one word, I'd have to say, *Yes.*"

"Me too, Joe," agreed Bobby, nodding slowly, "but I ain't got much hope for my chances when it's time to look in the Big Black Book. But, I guess it's easier when you know you're in trouble, rather than get it as a surprise."

Once again, Bobby's candor refreshed Joe's soul as he decided that if there was indeed a God, he would have to have a special place in His heart for this little broken angel.

"Come on, Confucius, let's go and buy this machine," said Joe.

They found *Bernstein's* and had a look around. All their moves up and down the counters were mirrored by an attentive employee. Joe spotted a basic cassette player for fifty dollars and pointed it out to Bobby. Unsolicited, the employee, moved his ladder over to the region where they were pointing and began to ascend it.

Joe turned his back to the man and began to count out fifty dollars.

"Give me the money and wait for me outside," Bobby whispered.

"Why?"

"Trust me, Joe," she hissed with a wink.

"No games?"

"No games, I promise."

Bemused, Joe gave Bobby the money and left. He wondered what surprise this little firecracker had in store for him. Minutes later, Bobby emerged, a triumphant glow on her face. She had a small carrier bag in one hand and some money in the other. She gave Joe the cash, it was fifteen dollars. Then she winked at him again.

"Just like I said, Joe. You're too easy. He was in a mood to bargain, at least he was when I told him I was gonna go somewhere else."

Joe held out a five-dollar bill. "Here, you little shark, you'd better go back in and bargain for some batteries to put in the thing."

"They're already inside," she beamed, "I talked him into leaving them in after he tested it." She was grinning from ear to ear, glad at this chance to prove her worth in Joe's eyes.

"Right then, let's get a bite to eat and have a listen to the tape," suggested Joe.

"Food sounds like a good idea," agreed Bobby. "By the way, Joe, who's Confucius?"

They walked on past *Bernstein's* and turned left at the next block, coming up to Sahara Avenue. They by-passed a couple of fast-food places in favor of somewhere a little more leisurely. On the other side of the street they picked out *Bennigan's Joint* which looked as though it did a decent brunch. The seating arrangement looked conducive to quiet conversation and Bobby darted over to a free table in the corner. She sat on the first seat and shuffled over it towards the one by the wall, snatching the menu on the way. She had already made her mind up as Joe took his seat.

Bobby removed the tape-recorder from its box and put it on the table in front of Joe. He saw the waitress coming over, so he put it down on the seat beside him. Bobby ordered and Joe, too nervous to think about food, asked for the same. After she had left, Joe slipped the cassette out of his pocket and after checking that the tape was rewound, he put it into the machine and pressed 'play'. He put the whirring device on the table between them, their necks craning ever closer bringing them a few inches apart.

After the useless, red-plastic portion had silently run by, they strained their ears in readiness, hoping for enlightenment. They heard a hissing and then a shaking voice, "Brogan. The bastards got me. It was a set-up. Some kind of thought-control. I never had a chance. I love you. Tell Penny..."

A click followed and then nothing.

Joe stopped the tape and sat back. He looked through Bobby, lost in thought. He rewound it and played it again. This time he looked into Bobby's face as they listened again.

"Pretty desperate stuff?" said Joe, after it had finished.

Bobby nodded pensively, before saying, "A set-up. It's not so bad if you never know. Sounds like he just found out."

Joe fumbled around in his pocket, bringing out his pen. He took one of the restaurant's white paper napkins and folded it in half to give it more thickness and protect the wooden table from reproducing his writing.

"Ok, Bobby. Play the first few words and then press 'Pause' to give me time to jot them down. Then press 'Pause' again and it'll play the next bit. Got that?"

"Shit, I hope so," replied Bobby wondering why Joe had such difficulty remembering what she could already repeat by heart. It took Joe three pauses and two rewinds before he was satisfied that he had got the transcript verbatim. He took a fresh napkin and prepared his final draft. The waitress interrupted their sleuthing as she served their food and drinks. Joe shoved the tape-recorder out of sight under his chair before wading into a pile of eggs, toast and pancakes. He glanced at Bobby and saw that she was tucking in heartily and he grinned before joining her.

Bobby licked her knife clean before raising her head for the first time since seeing her full plate. Joe passed her a paper serviette, "There's egg on your chin, Bobby," he observed. She looked down for it, only to be outpaced by its retreat. Joe laughed. It was the oldest trick in the book.

Bobby crumpled up the napkin and threw it at him. They drew a couple of condescending stares from people on high barstools and they laughed a little more.

"Let's get out of here," said Joe, "we've got a few questions to ask Brogan Higgins."

Joe paid the bill and was about to leave, when Bobby reminded him that the tape-recorder was still under his seat. He gave her a wry look before fishing it out.

Bobby confidently guided them back to *The Store* a shorter way than when they had come. When they arrived, Joe managed to talk Brogan into sparing some of his time to shed a little more light on the circumstances surrounding his brother's death.

"Did your brother always gamble?" Joe began.

Brogan thought back a long way and remembered the days when his brother, William, was just a regular person. "No, he didn't. He used to live up in Utah before. There's not much gambling there. It's a pretty strict place. You know, home of the Mormons."

"How long had he been living in Vegas before he started gambling?" asked Joe.

"Well, according to his wife, Penny, it started about two or three years after they moved here."

"We think he may have been tricked into going to the *Eastern Promise*," surmised Joe. "Perhaps he won at first and got hooked, or he was brainwashed into coming back."

"Or both," Bobby interjected. This statement made them stop and think. Brogan flashed a fleeting glance of acceptance at Joe's sidekick, respecting her tough, American street smarts..

Brogan resumed the discussion, "So how would they brainwash him without him knowing it until the end?"

"I've thought about that," claimed Joe, "The way your brother spoke, it didn't sound as though he had much idea, so up until he figured it out, it would have to have been something unseen and unknown."

"Like what?" Brogan asked.

"Well, you know those tapes that you get to help you stop smoking, lose weight, that kind of thing?" said Joe. "They're supposed to have hidden messages in them"

"You mean subliminals?" answered Brogan.

"That's it," recalled Joe, "Apparently there was a bit of a stink about them a few years ago.

"Yeah, I remember," said Brogan. "They put messages in movies telling people that they were thirsty and then they flashed the name of the drink that they wanted them to buy."

"Right," interrupted Joe, "But the messages flashed by so quickly that no-one could remember having seen them."

"But that was on a screen and they were looking at it," Brogan pointed out.

"Yeah, although the tapes they have today are for listening to, it's the same concept, and the message gets to your brain through your ears. I've heard they do it in supermarkets; they play tapes with buying messages hidden under the music."

"Isn't that illegal?" queried Brogan.

"Hell, I don't know," conceded Joe. "You'd think it would be."

"Anyway, even if it was, a few dollars across the right palms would buy a blind eye," said Brogan, "Or a deaf ear, if you like."

"On the other hand, they might be putting something in the drinks," suggested Joe. He added 'or both' before Bobby could and they all exchanged smiles.

Joe continued, "I read this book once, about some people that brainwashed a whole town by a combination of subliminal audio messages and something they had put in the water supply."

Brogan brought them back to reality, "Let's face it, even if you know, there's not much you can do about it, is there?"

Joe picked up on Brogan's use of the word *you* and sensing that he might be losing a valuable ally, he quickly spoke, emphasizing the word *we*.

"If we can prove it, then perhaps the press would be interested," he prodded hopefully. "Sometimes they're up to feeling brave, especially when it comes to plotting someone's downfall."

"How can you prove it?" inquired Brogan, doggedly refusing to be drafted onto the *we* team.

"If the message is hidden in the music which would make sense, then we can go inside the casino and take a tape recording. I think I remember enough from my electronics degree to slip a recorder into my pocket and switch it on. Then we can have a good listen to the tape, perhaps even speed it up or slow it down and see if there's anything there."

Joe was beginning to like the sound of his own idea, and Bobby was absolutely rapt by these developments, as she secretly hoped that Joe would let her play a part.

Joe wanted to bounce a couple of ideas off Brogan so he continued, "It sounds to me as though your brother might have seen something to make him suggest 'thought-control'. If he had known before, I'm hope I'm right in saying that he would have stopped going?"

"Probably," agreed Brogan, "not even he could have been that stupid."

"Another thing that's bothering me," said Joe, "is why would he say, 'Tell Penny' something or other, when he could have told her himself?"

"Not unless he felt sure that he wouldn't get a chance. He always was a fiery, little bastard," said Brogan, with fond recollection.

"So he found out, called you, went back and that was the end," speculated Joe.

Brogan said nothing. Joe decided it prudent to change the

subject at that point.

"Ok, it's settled," Joe announced. "We get one of those micro-recorders and we go to the casino."

Bobby was already out of her seat. She was looking forward to going to *Bernstein's* again. A plan was forming in her devious mind. Joe and Bobby headed to the door. As Joe was about to follow Bobby out, Brogan called to Joe; he stopped and faced Brogan.

"Good luck, Joe," he whispered. Joe's serious wink pulled half a smile onto his determined face. He hurried after Bobby who was already on her way out of *The Store.* They knew where they were going and they didn't speak until they reached *Bernstein's.*

"We don't need the tape recorder any more, do we Joe?"

"I suppose not," he replied.

"How about you let me try for a trade?" Bobby pleaded.

"Go ahead then," agreed Joe. "I'll wait outside." He already knew the rules to this game. Bobby made sure the first machine was neatly packed before slipping through the door. Joe was imagining the look of despair on the salesman's face. The poor man was probably thinking that his recent Waterloo was about to become unconditional surrender.

Minutes later, Bobby emerged triumphantly and said, "He'll take it back and another twenty dollars buys us a miniature recorder. You should see it. The tapes it plays are tiny. It's just like sexy panties, the smaller they are, the more they cost."

Laughing, Joe fished out the cash and gave it to her. When she returned, Bobby insisted on holding the little package for which she had fought so hard as though it were a trophy to her loyalty.

"Perfect, Bobby. Well done," Joe congratulated her.

"What now, Joe? Are we walking back, or shall we take a cab?"

"Walking?" echoed Joe.

"Yeah, we came south this morning, then west. We've just come north, so if we go a few more blocks north and turn east, we'll be pretty close. I'd say about forty-five minutes walk."

"How did you know all that?" asked Joe, totally baffled.

"I stayed awake when we came here," she laughed. "It's natural; I've only ever lived in cities."

"What do you want to do, Bobby?"

"Shit, I don't care. If I was feeling lazy, I'd say cab, but I'm not, strangely enough. This is the first time in months that I've felt strong like this."

"Let's see how good you really are, Bobby. We'll walk."

They kept on walking until they came to a junction. They turned right onto Charleston Boulevard.

"About four or five blocks and we should be back on Fremont," said Bobby. She led Joe under the same freeway that he had crossed the day before, before announcing that she knew a short cut. They turned up the appropriately named Casino Centre Boulevard.

"Stop," said Joe abruptly, "Is that what I think it is?"

"What are you looking at?" asked Bobby as Joe looked towards an impressive-looking, municipal building that loomed up across the road.

"Look, Bobby. It's the County Courthouse. I wonder if we should give it a try?" He remembered Brogan's warning and added, "Maybe we should keep it as a last resort?"

"It's only a short walk from the motel," said Bobby.

"I'll have to take your word for that." Joe was only following. He had never found directions easy. The block after the courthouse proved Bobby to be a true bloodhound. They were on Fremont Street, albeit the busy section. They had to wait several times to cross but soon they would be back at the motel. They stopped at the little mall and Joe picked up a couple of cold beers while Bobby chose a couple of sandwiches for later.

Back at base, Joe informed Bobby that he would be going alone to *The Eastern Promise*. This news was not accepted graciously and Joe tried several excuses to dissuade his eager friend. She thwarted Joe's two main arguments of age and dress code by insisting that he would have to get her some new clothes and that, given an extra hour or two, she could make herself look twenty-one.

Again, Joe was forced to give in. He offered token resistance because secretly, he was glad to have his tenacious, little friend alongside him.

"What are you wearing tonight, Joe?" she asked.

"Why?"

"I want us to match," she laughed. She had already taken for granted that Joe was going to give in again and hand over some money for more clothes.

"I'll probably go with my grey suit," he stated, "Because it's got a big inside pocket."

Joe took out the grey suit from the wardrobe and laid it on his bed. Then he took the tape-recorder from its box and tested the fit.

"Perfect," he judged.

Bobby went to the door and opened it. "I'll see you soon," see sang cheerily.

"Why, where are you going?" asked Joe.

"To get my clothes, where do you think?" answered Bobby.

She closed the door behind her and Joe realized that she hadn't asked him for any money. He grabbed his wallet and dashed out after her. He looked across the road, but she was nowhere to be seen. The wind caught the room door and blew it back. Joe turned and there was Bobby, hand held out.

"I knew you wouldn't forget me," she smiled.

Joe didn't think twice about giving her some cash, her heart was in the right place and she had shown real loyalty. As he watched her jaunt off toward the mall, he thought about how much his new friend had grown on him and he found himself really liking her, happy that he could show her some generosity that had evidently been lacking in her short life.

Joe didn't have to sell everything he owned to come up with a tidy sum, and he never really thought of himself as a millionaire. He just knew that he had enough and that was all that mattered. He waited until Bobby disappeared from view, before going back into the room.

It was getting well into the afternoon and Joe felt that a nap would recharge him for the night's activities. He lay down, feeling as calm as he ever had since this mission of madness had begun. Sleep wrapped him in her sweet embrace and in an instant, he was back on his recliner in Grand Cayman.

Chapter Fifteen

Joe awoke to hear the shower running in the bathroom. He washed down one of the now soggy sandwiches with a warm beer as he waited. He was feeling confident about taking the recording, since there was not much that could possibly go wrong. After testing the machine a couple of times to make sure it was working properly, and, he slipped it back into his jacket pocket, satisfied it would do the job.

"Hi, Joe," said Bobby, coming out of the bathroom. "Ready for the big night?"

"It's hardly a 'big night', but I'm ready," he replied. He took a couple of towels before locking himself in the bathroom. He had not shaved since arriving in Vegas and he looked at himself in the mirror. The growth gave him a rugged look which he decided, however irritating and clichéd would not look out of place in the tough gambling city.

It was about eight-thirty in the evening. The places were probably beginning to fill up, he thought. Any additional camouflage was always appreciated. He was also happy that he had never met any of the *Eastern Promise* people during their time in Cayman.

An idea came to him. He would ask Rachael to send him a copy of the Caymanian newspaper that contained a photograph of the Americans. After the news became public, he recalled that there were a few issues that carried references to them, at least one of which was bound to include photographs.

He knew the information would take a day or two to arrive, but it would give him some idea of who he was up against.

When he had finished his shower, Joe came out to be met by Bobby who looked naturally beautiful in a silky, cream blouse and an ochre, ankle-length skirt.

Joe whistled playfully at her and she glanced at him from her seductively made-up eyes. It seemed that she had assumed her new role with ease. Secretly, she wished that Joe would notice her as a woman, but she didn't want to spoil what she had. Not yet, anyway.

Joe, bare-chested, fetched a white shirt from the wardrobe. The travel-wrinkles were still in it, but it was nothing his jacket wouldn't hide. He took out his red tie, folded it and put it into the free inside pocket of his jacket, should any dress code demand it. Bobby watched his every move, admiring his firm features that rippled with his unconscious movements.

It was a strange feeling for Bobby who had not seen a man the way she viewed Joe. To her, men were a pretty brutal lot who seemed hell-bent on self-satisfaction. Joe was different, she wanted to please him and that would please her. It wasn't until now that this feeling had begun to create moistness in her sexual desert. She looked away from Joe and took out her new hairbrush from her equally new, brown handbag. She walked over to the mirror and brushed her downy hair. It fell around her shoulders like layers of fresh snow.

"Ready then, Bobby?" asked Joe.

"Yeah, I guess," she sighed; now knowing that she would have preferred to stay in that night with him.

When Joe called Rachael and asked for the newspapers, Bobby was a little jealous at the devotion that coated the conversation. Joe told Rachael the address to send the newspapers to. Bobby hated Joe's declaration of love for his wife at the end of the call.

While Joe telephoned for a taxi, Bobby went outside for a smoke and a think. She had barely reached half-way down her cigarette, when the taxi pulled up outside. Joe locked the room and followed Bobby into the car.

"*Eastern Promise*, please?" requested Joe confidently, and happy that he was going there of his own accord.

The desert sun, unable to endure the pace set by the twenty-four hour neon, had taken the rest of the day off. The city was more alive than ever with displays that seemed to steal parts of the night as they surged across their darkened mountings. The surplus energy overflowed into the eager gamblers who rushed about, spoiled for choice.

Bobby and Joe gaped in awe, almost forgetting the reason behind their outing. The taxi-driver sat smugly as though the whole atmosphere belonged to him and he was allowing his passengers a taste of his own town. It was fares like this, at this particular time, which earned him the biggest tips, his passengers mesmerized by the hypnotic effects of The Strip at night. Joe was to be no exception. *Eastern Promise* was only a couple of blocks off *The Strip* and when it came to pay the fare, he was still suffering from the side-effects of the trip.

"Good luck," said the driver, eagerly accepting Joe's tip-heavy cash. He gave Joe a card in case they would need a ride back. They went through the reception and down a plush carpeted hallway. One-armed bandits formed a guard of honor as the two friends followed the sign that said, 'Gaming Room'. The walk seemed to take an eternity as oriental-shaped dollar signs danced deceptively on the wallpaper and appeared to reflect from passing people's eyes.

They turned right and came face to face with another battalion of beckoning bandits. They had stopped and were working out the best way to carve a path through the opposing ranks of machines, when a beaming lady, weighed down by a satchel of silver dollars asked if they would like to buy some.

Joe politely refused the offer of feeding her pets and headed towards the clouds of smoke that would reveal puffing punters crowding an exciting game. Joe could see why this place was called *Eastern Promise.* As a builder he was well aware of the effort needed to achieve such authentic decor and this place would have cost an absolute fortune. Brilliantly-colored, velvet drapes hung from marbled walls and imitation minarets sprung from above them, calling the faithful to play.

Bobby held onto Joe as they walked, pleased to be this close to him. Joe sensed her touch and felt protective towards her.

"Unreal," exclaimed Bobby.

"In every way," agreed Joe.

Bobby gripped Joe tightly and whispered, "The tape. Is it on?"

"Shit, I forgot," said Joe.

They were standing behind a Blackjack table. Joe pointed out that the music sounded clearer now than when they were by the machines. "So we're just gonna stand here for an hour or so?" asked Bobby.

"Can't we do anything?"

Joe looked around before sliding his hand into his inside pocket.

"Oh, shit!"

"What's wrong?" asked Bobby.

"I can't turn it on without looking at it. I don't know the buttons without looking."

"It's no big deal," said Bobby, "just take it out."

The pit manager, Charlie had just made eye-contact with Joe and smiled whilst looking down, as though inviting him to take up a free seat at the card table. Joe's hand dropped from his pocket instinctively and he smiled back. Charlie, like all good pit-men had a trained eye for spotting people who looked as though they had a little extra and Joe looked like one of them.

"Good evening, sir," he oozed, "I hope everything is to your satisfaction?"

"Actually, we just arrived," Joe revealed.

"Perhaps a friendly game of Blackjack to get you started, sir?"

"Well, er..." Bobby poked Joe in the back and he took a seat at the end of the table. Charlie slipped by the dealer and offered his hand to Joe. "Charlie, Charlie Rios."

"Joe, Joe LeRi...ski," stammered Joe, angry at himself for not having thought about that before.

Bobby almost burst into laughter at the ridiculous sounding name that Joe had just improvised. Then she thought about it. It didn't sound too bad after all, it was just the way Joe had said it.

Joe delved into his forever-shrinking wallet and took out a one hundred dollar bill. He waved it at the dealer who told him to put it down as he was unable to accept cash from the hand.

"One hundred cash change, green," declared the dealer whose golden name-badge introduced him as Dave, from Virginia. Charlie acknowledged Dave's words and watched his dealer ram the note into a slot on the table before giving Joe four green chips.

"Only four?" exclaimed Joe, feeling a little hard done by. Dave tapped a little plaque on the corner of the table that indicated that twenty-five dollars was the minimum bet.

"Do you know what you're doing, Joe?" asked Bobby, a little

concerned.

"I hope so," said Joe, "you've got to get twenty-one without going too high. Watch, you'll pick it up."

Joe knew that he had neglected his purpose but he felt that he had acted in the least suspicious way. He took a single chip and slid it onto the vacant betting-box in front of him. As his fingers brushed through the red baize surface, the tops of his fingers turned slightly grey as they picked up some of the deep-seated cigarette ash. Joe looked at his fingers and sniffed the musty waste before realizing what it was.

Suddenly, he felt nervous. Why? He thought. Why should he be feeling nervous? Was it because the tape wasn't on, or that Charlie was standing close in a menacing statement of body language? Joe frantically searched for the truth. It seemed to elude him. His first card was dealt and his pulse beat yet faster. Jack of Spades, worth ten! The fragments of truth were beginning to gel.

Dave dealt himself a six before giving Joe a Queen of Clubs. Twenty! Joe turned to Bobby excitedly and explained that his twenty was a strong hand. She looked a little confused at Joe's sudden enthusiasm. Dave pulled a nine followed by an eight. It was too much and Joe had won. Dave placed a single green chip in front of Joe's original stake.

It not only represented twenty-five dollars, but it revealed the truth that Joe had been searching for as he almost snatched it and renewed his starting pile, leaving one on the table. It dawned on him that he was actually enjoying it. His built in defense mechanisms of self-righteousness were now failing him. Gambling was like riding a bicycle. You never forget how to do it.

Charlie smiled at the winners as though they had been the

beneficiaries of the casino's endless generosity. Bobby tugged at Joe, before whispering in his ear, "Joe, don't forget why we're here."

This seemed to shake the stars from Joe's eyes and he put all of his chips on the box, displaying either a willingness to lose everything and quit the game or a bold move to double his pile. It was the biggest bet on the table and Charlie's eyes lit up.

"One twenty-five, green plays," reminded Dave.

Joe had already stood up as if to walk away. His first card was an ace. Unbelievable! The strongest starting card. He sat back down. Whether he would count it as one or eleven depended on his second card. An arrogant King of Spades worth ten announced 21, a *Blackjack!*

Joe brought his fist down on the table. He apologized immediately looking side to side at the other punters as if to gloat. After his winning hand had been paid at three to two, Joe's box was worth three-hundred and twelve dollars, fifty cents.

Joe's heart was thumping. He remembered the feeling of euphoria that used to come with a winning bet, but nothing in past could compare with now. He was actually here in Vegas, the Mecca of all gamblers' pilgrimages and this fact intensified the intoxication.

"I'm leaving, Joe," said Bobby.

"Hold on a minute," pleaded Joe.

"Can't you see what's happening?" she complained.

"I'm just killing a little time." Joe lied.

"Useless time. It's not even switched on, is it, Joe?" Bobby's veiled reference to the tape-recorder confused the listening Charlie whose straining ears were alert as ever. He ran a few possibilities through his cautious mind. He concluded that Joe was a seasoned gambler with a device to help him count cards all the way down the shoe. After all, he had watched for a little while before joining the game and on the second hand, he had pressed his stake, right on a Blackjack. It was too good to be luck. His act of pretending to walk away hadn't fooled anybody either.

He went over to the other side of the pit and picked up the house-phone. He dialed the usual digit and Luca Telesino picked up immediately. "Yes, Charlie?"

"I think we've got a device on the floor."

"What kind?" Telesino asked, curious.

"Counter. He pressed up for a 'jack," Charlie explained.

"I wasn't watching," confessed Telesino, "How much?"

"He's over two up, in two games."

"Two thousand?" blurted Telesino.

"No, Boss. Two hundred."

"It's hardly serious money, is it Charlie?" said Telesino, almost laughing at the paltry amount. Counters usually play big and a real counter would have pressed up further if he sensed a Blackjack was on the cards. Still, caution was always advised.

"There's something about him, I think you should watch him, Boss. He's that guy on Blackjack Two. Grey suit. Sounds like a Limey, but I'm not sure."

"Is he alone?" asked Telesino, searching for Joe's form on one of his many screens.

"No, he's got a young chick with him. She looks under-age."

"Leave her alone, I'll be watching them. Give them some comps. Good work Charlie."

"Yeah, thanks Boss," said Charlie, already scribbling out a complimentary ticket giving dinner for two. He walked back and handed the ticket to Joe, saying, "We've just opened a brand new restaurant, perhaps you would like to be our guests for dinner?"

Joe, who had increased his pile of chips to five hundred dollars in Charlie's brief absence, took the ticket and thanked him graciously.

"I'm starving, Joe," urged Bobby, "can we eat now, please?"

Joe finally gave way and he asked Charlie for directions to the restaurant. They left in the direction of Charlie's pointed finger, back past the machines and over to the small elevator which seemed to serve the restaurant.

"I've won enough to pay for your clothes, courtesy of *Eastern Promise*," laughed Joe, as the lift hauled them to the third floor.

"I'm pretty pissed off at you, Joe," declared Bobby. The lift stopped and the door opened to reveal a natural-themed restaurant that looked as though it contained the Garden of Eden. They stared in wonder for a second.

"What for?" asked Joe, resuming the original conversation, "Why are you pissed off with me?"

"You'll soon find out," said Bobby, sternly.

The maitre d' escorted them to a central table but gave way to Joe's request for one by the wall. Joe ordered a beer and Bobby followed suit. When they were on their own again, Bobby frowned at Joe. "You know what you remind me of?"

"What?" echoed Joe.

"You remind me of an alcoholic who goes around telling everybody not to drink, but when nobody's watching, you're off catching a slug or two of your own."

"What's that supposed to mean?" retorted Joe.

"You get on some kind of soap-box to preach and you do exactly the same thing that you're speakin' out against. If gambling's so bad, why are you enjoying it so much?"

Joe knew that she was calling him a hypocrite and he tried to convince himself that she was wrong. Bobby went on, "You can't fool me. You were enjoying yourself down there and don't deny it."

Joe could not face her as she spoke. However blunt, she was telling the truth.

"There was nothing stopping you from walking away to set your tape," she pointed out firmly, "You could have played on the one dollar table. It was only two tables down. It was like I didn't know you."

"I felt the feeling come back to me," admitted Joe. "I played a little in England while I was at university. A friend dragged me out." Simon's face formed before Joe's eyes.

"Now that's a friend," said Bobby. "Think, Joe. Why are we here?"

"To get the tape," he answered.

"Right, and if I didn't know any better, I'd say you were getting eaten by those sub... whatever you call them."

"Subliminals," clarified Joe. "You could be right, but how come it didn't bother you?"

"I know I ain't got a chance to win in these places, but you, you're only fooling yourself that you ain't got a chance. You actually think you can win. You don't believe what you say and that's sad. You've even got proof. Look at those chips in your pocket. I'd say it was a good job there's no gambling in your islands or else you'd be in trouble."

"Alright," Joe surrendered, "After we eat, I'll set the tape and we'll play on the one-dollar table."

"Wrong," corrected Bobby, "I'll play on the one-dollar table. You're watching."

Joe laughed it off and agreed to Bobby's terms. But she had been right and that bothered Joe as he felt embarrassed and ashamed for appearing so shallow. They fell silent, invisible thoughts real and imagined bouncing back and forth between them, interspersed by the odd eye contact which only magnified his shame.

About twenty minutes later, the two friends were half-way through their Italian dishes when a tall, heavy set man dressed importantly in a black tuxedo came over to their table.

"Good evening, I trust everything is to your satisfaction?" he reeled off smoothly, bowing slightly.

"Fine thanks," replied Joe.

"Luca Telesino, General Manager," said the man offering his hand.

"Joe Leriski, and this is my niece, Bobby Verrill," said Joe, shaking the offered hand.

Telesino leered at the youthful, pretty Bobby, assuming that she was fair game.

"Mr. Rios tells me that you're having a good run at Blackjack?"

"Just lucky," said Bobby, before Joe could speak.

"How long do you plan to be in town?" Telesino inquired.

"A few days, a few weeks, whenever our money runs out," said Joe.

"Well if you're staying and you can guarantee us your action, we can find a room for you. Complimentary, of course."

"Thanks, we'll think about it," answered Joe, now on his guard.

Telesino gave him an impressive-looking business card with his name embossed in gold on a pure white background.

"If you need anything whilst you're here, feel free to call me. I'll be glad to help in any way I can."

'I bet you will', thought Joe, as Telesino turned to walk away.

"Slimy shit," said Bobby, confident that the man was out of earshot. "He reminds me of a club owner I used to know in 'Louis. A shiny apple, rotten to the core."

Joe said nothing, knowing better than to question Bobby's proven judgment.

They finished dinner and Joe gave the maitre d' the complimentary slip and a service tip. He was feeling better for his talk with Bobby. He hoped that he could resist his weakness. If it hadn't been for his pushy little friend, his nightmare could have been real. He hated his apparent lack of purpose, forgotten amid the glitzy glamour of the gaming-floor.

In the elevator, Joe looked up at the ceiling and something that looked like a glass bubble caught his eye. Was it? It couldn't be? He refrained from taking out his tape-recorder and eyed Bobby fiercely. When they came out, Joe spoke in low tones, "Did you see the camera in there?"

"No, why?"

"I thought I saw one in the elevator, that's why I didn't set the tape," said Joe.

"Shit, look all around on the ceiling, there are cameras everywhere," exclaimed Bobby.

"I've heard of security, but this is ridiculous," declared Joe. "Come on, let's go outside and come back."

They left the building and turned left. Joe pressed the 'Play' and the 'Record' buttons and halted the machine using the 'Pause' switch. He regretted the fact that he hadn't thought of this earlier.

He accustomed himself to releasing the 'Pause' with the machine in his pocket. Then he stuffed some cash alongside the player to give himself a valid excuse for going into the pocket and they went back inside. Joe still had the chips with him and he doubted the wisdom of leaving the place with them as he remembered that casinos did not like their chips to leave the building.

He went straight to the casino bank and cashed his chips in. Bobby found a seat at the one-dollar table and turned to face Joe as if to ask for some money. Joe fumbled around his pocket, switched the machine on, and brought out some cash for the young gambler. It was finally going to plan, he thought as he watched Bobby trying to come to grips with the game. It wasn't long before she could hold her own and after an hour was up, Bobby was twenty dollars down and the machine clicked off quietly in Joe's jacket. No one noticed except Joe and Bobby, who right on cue, said that she had played enough and wanted to go home.

After they had left, a pensive Telesino paced up and down in his control room. He called Charlie and told him to come upstairs. Five minutes later, Charlie was sitting in Telesino's office.

"What makes you think he was a counter, Charlie?"

"I'm not sure. The skinny babe said something about 'it not being switched on' or something like that. What with the way he picked out that 'jack, I guess I had to come to that conclusion."

"They seemed to act pretty weird. After they came back from dinner, they played on the singles table and the guy just stood around."

"Perhaps they were testing something out?" speculated the Boss.

"Can't say for sure," said Charlie. "They didn't win."

"I can be sure of one thing, though."

"What's that, Boss?"

"If they come in again, we'll be watching them like hawks."

Charlie did not doubt his boss's resolve. The man hated losing, whatever the amount.

Telesino hoped that his secret tape had cast its spell.

It was nearly one a.m. in Vegas. Back at the motel, Joe took the tape out and was preparing to listen to it. He turned the volume up and strained to hear, but the orchestral, background music just played louder, interspersed by shouts and groans of the players. His heart sank. There was nothing. He sat in a chair and stared at the wall, thinking deeply.

"We haven't got the equipment," he said, shaking his head, "If there's something on the tape, we're going to have to separate the sounds."

"How are we going to do that?" asked Bobby.

"We need to use a mixing deck, like they use in recording studios," explained Joe.

"You sure?" asked Bobby, doubting any conviction in Joe's tone. Joe ignored her skepticism. He knew it could be done, but all the relevant technical principles had been forgotten a long time ago.

An idea flashed across his mind. No, it wasn't an idea; it was a face, Simon's face. Not only was Simon supposed to be visiting Joe in Grand Cayman in three weeks time, he was also brilliant with electronics. Perhaps Simon would know how to filter out the subliminals? Joe wondered. He was also worried that Simon's visit would have to be postponed unless he could finish in Vegas soon.

"I've got a friend back in England," said Joe, "He may be able to help."

"I guess anything's worth a shot," replied Bobby, unhappy at seeing Joe at such a loss.

"I think I'll call him and ask him if I can send him the tape. He's got an electronics repair shop. Maybe he'll know what to do?" Joe roughly calculated that the time in England would be mid-morning. Somewhat nervously, he picked up the receiver, dialed the operator, and requested information, United Kingdom.

It was nostalgically refreshing to hear the distinctive double ring of an English telephone, he thought.

A lady operator, whose voice was the epitome of the forgotten, English rose, blossomed onto the line.

"Information, can I help you?"

"Computer Cabin, Humberside," Joe requested.

Bobby listened intently as she tried to imagine England from the little she had seen on TV.

"Which town, please?"

"Grimsby," replied Joe.

She obliged and Joe wrote the number on the back of the Yellow Pages. He dialed the number direct and as the phone rang, his heart began to thump.

Although he and Simon had exchanged letters, they had not spoken in years.

"Computer Cabin. Simon speaking."

"Simon, it's Joe, Joe LeRice." The line crackled, the huge distance undermining its integrity.

"Joe, is it really you? I can't believe it, mate. I've got the ticket, thanks. I can't wait till next month. Everything's ok, I hope?"

Simon's enthusiastic voice had taken on a certain maturity, but the sentiment applied the other way as well.

"Yeah, everything's fine," Joe lied.

"You sound like a Yank, Joe."

Joe laughed, "That's me, adaptable as ever. Simon, I was wondering if you could give me some advice?"

"Fire away, dude," mocked Simon in his best American accent. He was taking the piss.

That sounded more like the Simon of old, thought Joe as he remembered his friend's merciless sense of humor usually delivered with a perfectly straight face.

Joe turned to the task in hand. "I've got a tape-recording and I think there is a subliminal message on it. Can you help me prove it?"

"Probably. Why? What's it for?" asked Simon, intrigued, yet taken aback by the directness of his friend.

"It's a long story. I need to know, yes or no?" Joe's urgency was getting the better of him.

"Yes, I'd probably digitize the tape and analyze the frequencies, or try and filter out the main theme," explained Simon. "There is probably more than one approach, but that's where I would begin."

"How soon?" pressed Joe, the technicalities not even registering.

"My, my, a real 007 job? Is it that urgent?" said Simon lightly, yet knowing that if it was important to Joe, it was important to him. They shared a deep bond forged over four years of seeing each other almost every day, living in grotty digs, studying for exams and drinking ale whilst listening to up and coming rock bands.

"Unfortunately, yes, it's that important," echoed Joe, knowing that if he could count on anyone, it would be Simon Ward.

"How soon can you get the tape to me?" Simon sensed the urgency in his friend's earnest voice and did not need to ask any more questions.

"I'll express the package first thing in the morning," promised Joe. "It'll take one, maybe two days. It's one of those small tapes."

"A micro?"

"I think so," said Joe.

"Send me the player as well, mate. It'll save time."

"Do me a favor, Simon, will you?"

"What's that?"

"Call me as soon as you find something. Anytime."

"No probs. If anything's there, I'll dig it out... Man, you should see my new deck. We're making our first album soon."

"That's great news, how about a demo tape?" asked Joe.

"I'll bring one with me to Grand Cayman."

"By the way, I'm in Vegas," said Joe.

"Las Vegas?"

"The same,"

"Oh shit, man," gasped Simon concerned. "I thought you'd grown out of all that crap, Joe,"

"It's not like you think, I'm not here for fun," retorted Joe, a little stronger than he intended, anxious that his friend would not arrive at the wrong conclusion.

"You'd better give me your number, so I can call you," said Simon, dropping the subject.

"I'll put a note in the package; it'll have all the details on it."

"Alright mate."

"Cheers, Simon."

Immediately after hanging up, Joe was annoyed with himself because it was the first time in years that he had spoken to his friend and he felt as though he had come across as cold and selfish. He resisted the urge to call back and apologize, knowing that he would have to enter into a lengthy explanation of recent events.

They called it a night. Joe lay restless, knowing that it would be a few days before he would hear anything from Simon; Bobby lay awake wishing that she was in Joe's bed.

Exhaustion crept up on them and their thoughts came to life. Early the next morning, Joe was left feeling grateful that his hopeless dream was just that, a dream, whereas Bobby was disappointed because her realistic fantasy had ended, leaving her alone with a damp emptiness. Half-asleep, she probed her bed for areas of lingering human warmth. She found none and was brought to her full senses by the sound of Joe talking on the phone to a company who did express mailing.

"Wake up, sleepy head," said Joe, after he had hung up.

"Why?" mumbled Bobby, "what are we doing today?"

"Good question. The couriers are coming for the tape in an hour, but after that, I haven't thought," admitted Joe.

"I've been reading some of that stuff they put in the room. Why don't we go to Lake Mead, or better still, the Grand Canyon," suggested Bobby. "I can't remember the last time I did anything like that."

Joe resisted the urge to remind Bobby that he wasn't on holiday, but a break sounded like a bloody good idea, he thought. Besides, nothing would be happening for a day or two and downtown Vegas and the motel room were beginning to wear thin.

"Grand Canyon sounds good. What does it say?" asked Joe.

Bobby thumbed to the relevant page and began to repeat snippets as she read them, "Grand Canyon...spectacular colors...Colorado River...crowded in summer...advance reservations...three hundred miles from Vegas."

"Forget it," declared Joe, "it'll have to wait."

"I guess," accepted Bobby, "but what about Lake Mead? It says here that it's only twenty miles away. It's also got the Hoover Dam. There's water-skiing, fishing and all kinds of shit. There's even a guided tour for all you oldies."

"I didn't know you water-skied?" said Joe.

"I don't, I'm a great watcher, though. If you ever need advice, I'm always available. "

"So I've noticed," laughed Joe.

"Joe, you bitch!" She jumped out of bed and clothed only in a pair of skimpy, light-blue cotton panties and a short t-shirt, she rushed over to Joe, playfully bowling him over onto his own bed.

The sight of him lying there, smiling at her, overcame any of her remaining excuses. She fell onto him and buried her head in his.

"Make love to me, Joe," she panted.

Joe was dumbstruck, his world dissolved into an ocean of confusion and yet, instinctively he embraced her. She moaned. A shard of sanity flickered before Joe's eyes and he struggled free and stood up.

"Bobby. This can't happen. It mustn't."

"I love you, Joe." She came close to him.

"No, Bobby. Please don't. Don't spoil it."

Bobby burst into tears and Joe held her, comforting her.

"I'm sorry, Joe. I just couldn't stop myself," she moaned.

"It's alright. I understand," said Joe, fighting for composure.

"I feel so... so stupid," stammered Bobby, "I should have guessed."

"It's not your fault, we were getting pretty close. I should have seen," confessed Joe.

Silence fell upon their small, embarrassing world. Joe went to the bathroom, not being able to offer any words that would console a sniffling Bobby.

Through the sound of the rushing water, Joe was sure that he heard the room door slam shut. His assumption that Bobby had gone out for a cigarette was revised when he saw the remains of what looked like a hasty exit.

He pulled on the closest pair of trousers and rushed out, sensing that he was too late. He was right; there was no sign of his little friend. He hung his head in his hands and almost wept. He wished that he could have told her that he loved her, with the love that true friends share, and now she had gone.

Back inside, he discovered that apart from a few dollars change that she might have been hanging on to, Bobby hadn't taken any other cash. He grabbed a shirt, slipped his bare feet into his shoes and headed down Fremont Street. He kept on walking, sometimes blindly crossing roads, until he came to Las Vegas Boulevard. He turned left and began to recognize some of the casinos that he had driven past over the last few days. He scanned everywhere in desperation, even peering into passing cars, trying to catch a glimpse of Bobby.

Three hours later, his feet blistered and his search fruitless, Joe called a cab back to the motel. He had left his money in the room and the driver waited impatiently for him to fetch the fare.

For Joe it was over, and an unconditional friendship, based on trust, had gone. Bobby had not been to blame, unless honesty was a crime. Joe was angry at not being able to spot an earlier solution to the awkward situation. Had he been so naive that he had unwittingly led her on? He tried to force himself to renew the purpose behind his presence in this god-forsaken place.

He was transported instantly back to his unhappy, lonely past and he sensed that a tried and true solution was near. He snatched some money from the dresser and walked over to the liquor store at the mall. He bought six cold beers, a bottle of vodka and a bottle of orange juice before destroying ten years of abstention with a packet of strong, menthol cigarettes.

The short walk back dragged sorely with his cracked feet. Once inside, he pulled up two chairs in front of the television. He flicked his shoes off, sat down in one chair, and cocked his legs up in the other. Making sure the drink was within reach, he lazily pressed the television power switch with a puffy toe, deciding to leave the channel selection just as it was, showing all-day news and sports reports.

With a cigarette burning, he opened his first beer and stubbornly headed towards oblivion. After the beers had created a seductively fuzzy feeling that slightly intensified with each one, the warm cocktail of vodka and orange juice made his empty eyes water. He winced and pulled hard on a cigarette, wondering how he had given up anything that tasted so good.

The television began to play tricks on his shrinking mind with the stories appearing to repeat themselves over and over again. His world began to rotate and he fought desperately to escape the decaying orbit. The only way out seemed to be down, yet he struggled to stand up, eyed his bed, and stumbled blindly towards it before he could forget where it was. The rattling noise of the empty cans and bottles that he tripped over was blanked before he hit the ground in an unceremonious heap. His limp body lay completely flat except for shallow breathing that disguised itself amidst ugly snores. His usually-taut face had turned to rubber and wobbled as he exhaled.

Four hours later, he awoke in a pool of what could only have been his own urine. His brain was trapped in a pounding shell that seemed hell-bent on revenge for the evil trick that he had just played on it, promising euphoria and delivering nausea.

The soured taste of beer in his sticky mouth was made more repulsive by the pockets of tobacco-flavored jelly that had formed during his alcoholic stupor.

He stood up, keeping his head as low as possible, and collapsed on his bed. He peeled off his foul-smelling trousers and threw them into the corner of the room. He squinted at his watch and gave up trying to work out the time in the Cayman Islands. It was close enough to calling time, but the uncooperative digits on the phone refused to come into focus and the receiver slipped from his hand to the floor.

He staggered to the shower and lay in the bath while the cold water bombarded him with icy reminders that he needed to call home. With the shower unable to flush the sickly feelings from inside him, he settled for a clean exterior. A real Pharisee, he thought, trying to inject humor into his dire situation.

He tried to call again; disgusted that he actually had to think to remember his own number.

"Rachael, it's Joe," he croaked.

"What's wrong, you sound awful," she remarked straight away, "Are you ok, honey?"

"Headache, terrible headache," mumbled Joe.

"What's that? What did you say?"

"I said, headache," repeated Joe.

"You haven't been drinking, have you?" She sounded concerned.

Joe's guilty laugh was strangled in his throat as if commanded by his furious brain. He knew there was no fooling Rachael. He felt as though he had gone back in time, to the early days.

"I had a couple, nothing serious." Joe hoped that his feelings would be mirrored by his lie.

"Joe, I know you're trying, but if it's getting to be too much for you, please come home. Please honey."

"It's alright," stressed Joe, "I've made some real progress, but I won't know for sure until the next day or two."

"I sent you that newspaper that you asked for. There are four of them; three men and a woman. "

"Great, thanks a lot." Joe tried to sound appreciative but the attempt didn't wash.

"What progress have you made, Joe?" searched Rachael, anxious to hear a valid reason that would keep him away from his home and hoping that he had not gotten into trouble.

"I can't explain now, but it could be something important." The line fell into silence amid Rachael's helplessness and Joe's apparent lack of effort. "I'd better be going, then," muttered Joe, breaking the silence.

A strained goodbye left Joe feeling as though every support in his life was strained to its limit and the fact that he was the one doing all the bending didn't help.

What he was going to do tomorrow, he had no idea, but whatever it was, it would have to be without this hideous head, he thought. He sunk to his bed and tried to block out the dull drone of the ever-present television, refusing to get up and turn it off.

His repentant brain requested a truce with his angry body and the latter agreed that he had been punished enough and released him for a while.

Chapter Sixteen

"Computer Cabin?"

"That's right," said Simon Ward, answering his telephone.

"Kwick Pak, international couriers, we've got a package for you."

"What, from Las Vegas?"

"That's the one," confirmed the voice.

"Can you deliver it right away?" asked Simon, amazed at the speedy service, as it had only taken one and a half days to come from the other side of the globe.

"Will do. I was just making sure that someone was there to sign for it. I'll send someone over in about half-an-hour."

"Cheers mate. I'll be here," Simon confirmed.

Simon also had no choice but to be there. His small, one man operation could hardly pay the rent, let alone afford any other staff. Things were quiet on the business front, most consumers seemed to want to replace their tired, broken machines with the latest technology, rather than have them repaired.

Simon was of the opinion that the major electronics companies acted like bakers, loathe to put their fresh bread out until the old had been sold. He was convinced that the computer companies had prepared their 'new generation' of products well in advance, and they were just waiting for their relentless sales drive to falter before stepping in with the next batch. Consequently, unclaimed, repaired goods would lie abandoned in the back of Simon's shop. He had resorted to selling them to recoup the cash that he had lost in fixing them.

It was now four-thirty p.m. and he hardly ever went home before seven. He pulled his long, straggly, black hair from his peaked face and held the resulting pony-tail with one hand behind his head, while he reached for his elastic band. Much practiced, he opened it with his thumb and forefinger and pulled his hair through the loop a couple of times. He hated doing it, but it was the only way to stop his locks from falling all over the circuit boards of the broken equipment that he was examining.

He had tried without it, but the acrid smell of burning hair that always accompanied his soldering jobs had made him accept this solution.

He attached two test probes to the circuit board of the cash register he was examining and looked at the resulting waveforms on his oscilloscope.

"Alright, you beast, where are you?" he whispered, as he hunted for the offending component. Methodically, he worked his way around the integrated circuits, testing every output for each input. Simon was smart. He knew exactly what a component was supposed to do from its cryptic model number.

"Got you, you bastard!" he declared five minutes later, as he found an input that had gone short circuit to ground and sucked power relentlessly from the supply. He had just finished releasing the component from its socket and was replacing it with a new one, when a uniformed delivery-man came through the door with his parcel. Simon scribbled his signature on a wad of triplicate and was given his copy along with the package. The man left and Simon, always glad of a new challenge, turned his full attention towards it.

Inside, was a new box that contained exactly what was depicted on it, a micro cassette player. He read the note from Joe. It didn't say much, but Simon concluded that it was so important, that Joe had assumed a divine right to ask him for a favor, without so much as a reason why. He always had been a forceful so-and-so. Simon thought back to their days together. Although domineering and somewhat opinionated, Joe had always been generous, treating his friends to movies, meals and interesting, if somewhat intense, company and conversation. Simon had also learned that if anything certain applied to Joe LeRice, it was to expect the unexpected.

Here was the only electronics student who had graduated and still not been able to program a computer. So how had he achieved an overall pass grade for his computer assignments? Simple, the crafty bugger would sit next to studious terminal users and watch as they accessed their files. He would sneak glances as they typed in their passwords on the Cyber Mainframe.

After they had finished, he would access the same file and transfer the program to his own directory. Then he would cosmetically modify the work to make it appear original. That was as far as his computing inclination had taken him, just doing enough. He was a resourceful son of a bitch, never cut out for a place in the system.

Simon smiled affectionately as he remembered his friend. If anybody was going to make it in life, it would be Joe LeRice, but he was safe in the knowledge that Joe had not harmed a soul on the way to his success. Simon wondered what Joe had got himself into this time, especially now that he was in Las Vegas, of all places. The poor bloke had been in danger of losing a lot of his inheritance money as a student by getting involved with a casino. Simon recalled almost threatening Joe to get him to pack it in. Besides, if Joe had run out of money, there would be no more late-night meals, evenings at the cinema or lunchtime pints of beer at the university bar.

Simon switched the cassette player on and heard what sounded like a medley of easy listening tunes along with drones of background talk with the odd shriek thrown in. Bloody hell, he thought, it *is* a casino.

The first task was to analyze the noise, to see if there was anything obvious that would indicate a hidden soundtrack. He unscrewed the back of the recorder and attached the two 'scope probes to the two contacts of the loudspeaker.

He turned the tape back on and watched the waveform created by the sounds. Since music was a combination of high and low frequency sounds, he decided to filter out the higher pitched sounds and see if anything lower was hiding beneath them. He lashed up a simple electronic filter on a prototyping breadboard using some basic components. His experience told him to use adjustable components so that he could examine a range of signals. He had his filter, now he had to connect it in. It made sense to connect it before the loudspeaker, so any change would be audible.

The resulting signal showed that there were indeed some low frequencies, but audibly the result was an indecipherable drone.

He amplified the drone and it became a loud drone, still guarding its secret. He adjusted his filter, rewound the tape, and watched and listened. Again, he had no joy, but the fact that something was there still remained. Perhaps it was the background noise from the casino floor where the awful recording was obviously made? If that was the case, then he was barking up the wrong tree. Two hours and many permutations and combinations later, he felt as though he were running out of options.

He needed to think, to forget his failures and start over again. He threw his tools down, picked up his faithful leather jacket and walked out of his shop. It was getting cold at nights now, he mused, as his warm breath formed a cloud of condensation. It mixed with the chill, evening air, hazing his view of the orange street lights. He went to the Shearbridge pub across the road and picked up a couple of cans of beer and a cheese and pickle sandwich which he took back to his workshop.

Inside again, he sat in his second-hand swivel-chair and looked out into the road, watching the blurs of passing cars as they sped by. One of the cars sounded as though it was slowing down. The familiar, tired engine ground to a halt in the nearby darkness. April, Simon's petite girlfriend appeared in the doorway and smiled at her pensive lover.

"No hellos for me?" she joked.

"Not tonight," he replied sullenly, throwing an empty can into the overflowing wastepaper-basket. "I've got a real tough one on right now."

"Aren't you rehearsing tonight with the guys?" asked April.

"I doubt it; it's getting late. They'll cope without me. They've got all my solos on tape. I would have liked a little more time on this job."

April knew better than to ask about Simon's work. Technical electronic theory was a subject that was best avoided.

"Don't worry love; you'll soon be soaking up all those rays in the Cayman Islands with that Joe chap. I wish I was coming with you."

"So do I. If we could afford it, you would be."

"It's alright, Simon. You need a break. I'll just keep our bed warm." They kissed. Simon realized that he was indeed a lucky man.

"I'll just record this tape onto a standard cassette and then we'll head home."

Simon had the band's mixing deck at home and he had decided to try a different angle by coding the tape digitally so it might be easier to examine and at least it was a different approach.

He connected the micro-cassette player to a normal-sized machine and played it. He wasn't going to record the whole thing, that would have meant another hour or so in this freezing hole. The first song began to play and April began to laugh. Simon looked at her disparagingly.

"What's wrong? What have I done now?" he complained.

"Since when have you been into James Last and his orchestra?" she grinned. "That's a terrible recording. You could have asked my Mum, she's got all his records."

"How did you know what it was?" asked her bemused boyfriend.

"We grew up on it. That sounds like 'La Vie En Rose'; at least I think it does."

"April. You're brilliant!" whooped Simon triumphantly.

"What are you talking about?" She looked totally confused.

"I reckon you've just solved my problem. Tell me, what's one minus one?"

"Nothing, at least it was the last time I checked," answered April, baffled.

"Then I'm in business," Simon declared. "Quick, we mustn't waste any time. Let's go to your Mum's house."

"Hold your horses. What's going on?"

"The long and the short of it is that I've got a music tape with a hidden message on it, like rock bands sometimes do, except this one has been done cleverly."

"What's that got to do with James Last?" April was lost.

"If I have a recording with no message on it, like your Mum will have, and play it in direct opposition to the one with the message, then the music will cancel out; like combining a signal with its anti-signal. One minus one. Zero." He paused for the final re-calculation, "Make that one and a little bit minus one, is a little bit. It's that little bit that I want."

"Whatever you say, sweetheart," said April knowing that any other response would be futile.

Simon, far too excited to notice April's lack of enthusiasm, went on, "So when the music cancels out, I can see whatever's left. It's just like tearing the suit of armor from your enemy."

Simon passed the telephone to April and told her to ask her mother if they could come over. She did so, and a few minutes later, they were driving the ten miles to her parents' house.

When they arrived, Simon played the tunes for April's mother. She recognized them all within seconds of hearing them and told him on which album in her vast collection he could find the recordings.

She was a little reluctant when Simon asked her for all the relevant records, but his promise of an immediate return helped to allay her fears; she consented, knowing that she would not have to be without her idols for too long.

They drove back to the shop. Simon had managed to convince April that he wouldn't be too long, although he hadn't convinced himself. She resigned herself to take-away fish-and-chips and yet another evening in the cold workshop.

Speaking only to his equipment, Simon became one with his job. His first task was to see if the two recordings of each song were of the same tempo. He decided to start with 'La Vie En Rose', and soon, it became quite obvious that although the artists were different, the tracks were pretty faithful to each other. If not, this would have posed a problem although not insurmountable as he could have forced the tracks to match perfectly although it would have been extremely time consuming.

He played the clean melody on a record player and recorded it onto tape. He then synchronized the two recordings to play simultaneously, Joe's one normally, and the other through an inverter to create the anti-signal. The two resulting signals were then combined onto a single track.

With bated breath, Simon watched as a tiny waveform flickered onto the screen of his oscilloscope. When 'La Vie En Rose' had finished, he rewound the mixed tape and played it. The background noise was now clear; most of the music had vanished except for the odd note and out-of-time drum beat. He could hear gamblers asking for cards and talking amongst each other. Straining his ears he could hear what sounded like a low whispering.

"That's it!" he roared, "I've got you now, you bubonic chancre." Vivid descriptions had always been his forte. "Come here, April, listen to this."

He turned the volume up to maximum, adjusted the treble response for a crisper sound, and they listened, trying to ignore the chattering of the gamblers. The mysterious whisperings became audible. "You are a winner. *Eastern Promise* is your home. You can be rich. Yes, rich. Bet now to win. Go on, do it. *Eastern Promise,* it's your home. .."

The alluring theme continued for the duration of the recording. Simon was absolutely dumbfounded. "The filthy, rotten bastards," he muttered, shaking his head.

"What is it, Simon?" asked April.

"It's a subliminal manipulation technique."

"I hate it when you talk dirty, she said, reminding him that his 'high tech' jargon had just flown right over her head.

"Brainwashing, if you like," he explained. "This one coaxes people to gamble, making them think that it's the best thing since sliced bread. These sods are particularly clever. They're drilling the name of the place into your brain, so whenever you think about gambling, the name of their place always springs to mind first."

"Can we go home now?" She had no other questions.

"Yep, after one phone call."

Simon picked up Joe's note, looked up the procedure for dialing direct to the United States and punched in the resulting string of numbers. He reached the motel reception and asked for Joe's room. Joe's phone had not even finished its first ring when it was picked up which was quite surprising, given the early hour of the morning in Vegas.

"Hello," said Joe cautiously.

"Joe, it's Simon. I've got something."

"Really? Oh that's fantastic! What is it?" Joe was ripe for some good news. He had spent a couple of depressing days alone, wrestling unsuccessfully with his ebbing conviction.

"It's definitely subliminal control. I've managed to isolate the messages crudely. Basically, it's enticing people to gamble encouraging them to bet and that *Eastern Promise* is their home. I assume that's the name of the place?"

"That's right," confirmed Joe. "Here's the bad news. *Eastern Promise* is planning to operate in the Caymans." He paused, "I'm trying to stop them."

"The utter bastards!" Simon cried, "How can you stop them?"

"Well, your news is a start. It shows that they're pretty unscrupulous."

"Yeah, but is it illegal? It might be morally off-base, but what about legally?" questioned Simon.

"I hadn't really thought about it, I just assumed," admitted Joe, regretting his blatant lack of research. "I'm not too bothered about Vegas laws; it's the Cayman laws that concern me. Perhaps we could legislate against this type of thing."

"What do you want me to do with the tape? Send it on to you, or what?"

"Listen, mate," said Joe, attempting to revert to his best English accent, "How would you feel about delivering the tape in person? Think of it as an early start to your holiday."

"Bombshell," said Simon, flatly.

"I thought you might say that," countered Joe. "What do I have to do to make it worth your while?"

"My God, you are serious?" stated Simon, caught off guard by the intensity of his friend. He had almost forgotten how persuasive Joe could be.

"I need your expertise on the tape," lied Joe. The honest truth was that he was faltering and that any genuine support was welcome, even if it would cost extra money. Just having his trusted friend would be a welcome asset.

"I've got a business to run, Joe. I'll be losing time in the Caymans as it is."

"How's business?" Joe tried another angle.

"Not brilliant, but it's paying the bills." Simon delivered a lie of his own.

"Alright then, you've got a ticket from me already, I'll even subsidize your business for all your lost work," persisted Joe.

Simon was beginning to feel embarrassed by the concessions that Joe was making. He didn't want to humiliate his friend any more. One glance over at April tapping her fingers convinced him that in his hand he held his last chance to see any of the world as a single man. Recently, April had been suggesting that eight years of courtship would have to result in something more concrete. Simon had been clinging to his mandatory, single, rock-star status for dear life and his continual failure to hit the 'big time' was causing him to run out of excuses.

"Ok Joe, you win," conceded Simon, successfully concealing his excitement.

"You don't know how happy that makes me," enthused Joe. The lines were too far apart for Joe to hear Simon's muttered agreement.

"What do I do next?" asked Simon, sensing that April would soon cotton on to the direction of the conversation, if she hadn't done so already.

"Here's the deal," conspired Joe. "Your ticket is valid for Miami, anyway. Get to Miami, clear Immigration and Customs and go to the main Eastern Airlines Information Desk. There'll be a ticket waiting for you to get you to Vegas. If you've got time, call me from Miami, if not call me from the airport in Vegas."

"So I get to Miami and go to Eastern Information Desk?" repeated Simon, eyeing April's obvious concern. She didn't like this Joe fellow any more.

"That'll do," confirmed Joe. "Get the first flight out. If you can't get on one airline, try another. They usually honor each others' tickets."

"I'm on my way, mate, tape and all."

Simon hung up and turned to April who had a face like thunder; it was time to hatch the ultimate excuse.

Chapter Seventeen

Knowing that Simon would be bringing the tape in person, Joe reckoned that Brogan would like to hear the good news. Before contacting him, Joe had a few chores that had to be taken care of. The first was to ask Rachael to make a cash payment on his credit cards, before his purchasing power faded completely, the second was to make sure that Simon had a ticket waiting for him at Miami. After these jobs were completed, he called Brogan.

"Brogan, it's Joe. It looks like we've got something. The subliminals showed up, I can prove it."

"That's good news, Joe. Can you come over? I'd like to hear them."

"I won't have the tape until tomorrow," Joe admitted. "I'll bring it over then. It's coming from England. Perhaps we can discuss a plan of attack. I could use your advice."

Brogan was beginning to admire Joe's tenacity and found himself more willing to help, although he still held little hope that his brother's killers would be brought to justice.

"Listen, Joe. I'm having a barbecue tonight. There'll be steaks, beers and company; all the good things in life. How about joining us? What do you say?

"Sounds great, Brogan. I could use some company," confessed Joe.

"You can bring your friend too, er."

"Bobby," Joe reminded him.

"Yes, Bobby. Bring her as well."

"I would, if I knew where she was," sighed Joe.

"Why, what's happened?"

"Don't laugh, but things got a bit messy between us. I think I gave her the wrong message and she wanted to sleep with me. She vanished in a hurry," explained Joe, ignoring any personal embarrassment.

"You know what they say about a woman scorned," reminded Brogan.

"True," said Joe, "I'll get over it, but I don't think it was like that. I think she was crushed. I feel so bad."

"We can talk about it this evening. Meet me at the shop at about four-thirty. I'll give you a ride over to my place after I close. You're in for a treat, Joe. I'll show you my party tricks."

"Alright. I'll see you then," agreed Joe.

They hung up. It was almost mid-day in Vegas. Since his binge, Joe had spent the next day recovering and cleaning up. He had taken his dirty clothes to the motel owner who had offered to clean them. Hoping that they were ready, he went to the reception desk to collect them. The middle-aged receptionist disappeared into the back and re-emerged clutching Joe's clothes. They were neatly piled and Joe took them from her and pressed them to his nose. They smelled pleasingly fresh.

He was about to walk back to his room, when she called him back,

"Mr. LeRice, these came for your room. I assume they're yours." She waved a couple of envelopes at him. Joe turned back to face her and said, "Probably. Just stick them on top of the clothes; I'll hold them down with my chin."

She obliged and held the door open for him as he left.

Having managed to get into his room, Joe set his bundle down and looked at the envelopes. The large one was from Rachael containing the newspapers that he had asked her to send. The smaller one was posted locally. It was addressed to Bobby. Knowing that he would probably never see her again, he decided to open it. It was from the doctor's office that she had been to. Joe read and as he did so, his jaw dropped with horror.

"...I am sorry to inform you that the results of your recent blood tests give conclusive evidence that you are HIV positive which has developed into the AIDS virus..."

The letter went on to say that Bobby was advised to contact a support group whose literature was enclosed within the letter.

Joe sat down; his shaking legs no longer able to support him.

Thoughts of Bobby dying of AIDS raced through his mind, hurting him more as they spawned vivid images.

Rough justice, indeed, he thought. No it was not justice, it was just rough, he concluded. Even if she had managed to change her ways, there was no reprieve. Sentence had been served. She was on 'Death Row' and her right to appeal had been permanently withdrawn. Perhaps it was better that she didn't know? Joe surmised, but what about all those people that she had slept with? What about all those she was going to sleep with? Joe's own escape replayed itself and he inhaled deeply and sighed with relief. Then he felt dirty for thinking such a thing at his friend's expense.

He put the letter and the pamphlet back in the envelope before opening the larger one. There was a note from Rachael urging him to be careful. His resolve firmed as he read her reminder that no matter how tough things were, she would always love him. He closed his eyes and imagined her coming towards him, her eyes piercing his soul with love that came from her clean heart. He shook the image from his vision; it was the sort of truth that hurt.

On the second page of the newspaper was a photograph of the *Eastern Promise* delegation. Joe recognized Luca Telesino immediately, but the other three faces were foreign to him.

Joe killed a few hours by doing some sentimental shopping at the mall. He even plucked up enough courage to buy some lingerie for his wife. With schoolboy embarrassment and fear of ridicule conquered briefly, Joe felt strangely brave, wanting to tell the world what he had just achieved.

After a freshen-up and a change, he took a taxi to *The Store*. Whilst he waited for Brogan to finish the daily sales report, he let Chris show him some of the jewelry that was on offer. He bought Rachael a pair of gold, leaf-shaped earrings. Two tiny pave diamonds shimmered in their eighteen carat gold settings, while a couple of baby pearls simulated the fruit that they bore. It was the overall beauty of the pieces, combined with their small, unassuming size that appealed to Joe, not to mention the attractive price that Chris gave him.

In the thick traffic, Brogan's house was about an hour's drive from
his shop. Joe watched the dense city spread out as they headed towards Boulder City. He saw signposts to Lake Mead and wondered if Bobby would ever get to see the water-skiing.

"Boulder City," said Brogan, as they approached, "The only city in the whole state of Nevada where gambling is outlawed."

"Is it catching?" asked Joe.

"I doubt it," said Brogan drily, "It's got a great golf course, though."

Brogan began to slow down and pulled into a long, winding

driveway that hinted a pretty special house would be found at the end of this path. On purpose, Brogan drove slowly up to his house as he milked the compliments from Joe on his immaculate garden.

Brogan accompanied Joe towards sounds of frivolity that came from the back of the house and introduced him to his wife who was grilling chunks of marbled meat on a cast-iron barbecue. A swimming-pool was occupied by a few golden leaves that had accumulated during the day and the men opened a couple of beers and hung around the inviting aroma of the grill, making small talk until their food was ready.

After eating, they went inside the house and Brogan took Joe to his study. On an oak table in the far right corner was a full-sized roulette wheel complete with betting baize.

"I didn't know you were a gambler?" said Joe, surprised at this sight.

"I'm not," stated Brogan flatly, "The wheel was left behind as part of the furnishings. The previous owners seemed in a hurry to get away and left everything included in the asking price."

"Why would they do that?" asked Joe.

"Any number of reasons," started Brogan, "My pet theory is that they used to have illegal gambling parties. Don't forget, this is Boulder City. Perhaps they got in trouble and needed a speedy exit."

"Do you use it?" asked Joe.

"Not really. When my brother started to get involved, I read some books about gambling. I used to imagine that I had a whole load of cash riding on one spin...basically fucking around. Every gambler dreams of breaking the bank..."

"That's true," interrupted Joe nodding in agreement.

"Well, it happened once," Brogan continued. "Some English guy named Wells did it at Monte Carlo, at the turn of the century. In fact he did it six times in three days."

"How did he manage that?" pressed Joe, rapt by the impossibility of the tale.

"A lot of explanations have been offered, psychic force, a special system or just plain luck."

"Which one do you reckon?" Joe probed deeper.

"I read that he used a method called the Martingale system. Every time you lose a bet, you double your stake. I got pretty interested and I tried it, playing here by myself."

"Did it work?"

"Hardly, I lost eventually," admitted Brogan, "But I noticed something strange. Occasionally, I would hit the same number twice. One after the other. So there had to be some common factors, agree?"

"Sounds logical enough," replied Joe.

"So, I decided to try and standardize everything. Where I stood to spin, the speed I put the ball in with, the force with which I spun the wheel and most importantly, it seemed, which number was passing me as I let the ball go."

"What happened?" Joe was captivated.

"I hit sometimes but if I didn't get it exactly, it would only be a few slots off. Practice makes perfect and I practiced releasing the ball as the green zero passed me. At the speed I do it, the ball usually lands between five slots either side of sixteen, red."

"I get it," realized Joe, "If you've got a bent croupier, then you can take a signal knowing where to bet."

"That's my guess, or else you bet and the croupier tries to hit," said Brogan, nodding. "That Wells guy turned four hundred into forty grand. He was a convicted crook back in England, and it's my guess that he played the same croupier or croupiers and they knew all about it."

"What about these days?" Joe asked.

"Croupiers try and beat the gamblers for the most part. The better they do, the higher their wage. Even if a gambler thinks he's got the measure of one of them, management changes croupier. You can't win."

"I had no idea it was *that* complex," sighed Joe. "I thought it was a game of luck with the odds slightly against you."

"It is *that* complex, but only for the more seasoned pros. Most people play small and the odds take care of them anyway. The casinos have about three percent more chance in their favor than the gambler. It's enough to keep them in business. When you factor in the experience of the atmosphere, the décor, the drinks, heck even subliminal messages now, well I'd say they can't lose."

"Show me how to hit, then," said Joe, anxious to see the proof of the pudding.

Brogan picked the white ball from out of the wheel. Deliberately, he put his hand on the green zero and pulled it, putting the numbers in motion. His hand went back, setting himself up to put the ball in. As the green zero passed him for the third time, he spun the ball along the wooden rim. After several circuits, the ball lost speed, slipped through some diamond-shaped notches and bounced several times before settling into the five red slot.

"It's not sixteen," remarked Joe.

"No, but it's only two slots away. If you'd bet eleven chips, one on sixteen and one on each of the five numbers either side, you'd have lost ten and won thirty-five back. I'll hit eight out of ten. That's a damned good return. I've worked it out; if you bet a dollar a chip, over ten games, you'll be one hundred and eighty-six dollars up."

"Ever thought about being a croupier," laughed Joe before realizing what a stupid statement he had just made, knowing Brogan's aversion to gambling.

"It's a load of unproductive, false bullshit," sneered Brogan predictably. "Ask my brother. He'll tell you."

"I'm sorry," murmured Joe, "I didn't mean to joke about it."

"No offence taken, but I'd like to see those bastards at *Eastern Promise* put out of business. It's one thing glamorizing bullshit; it's another to take your choice away."

"You'll be able to listen to their tape pretty soon. I sent it to a friend in England. He's analyzed it and he's bringing it over himself."

"Impressive," Brogan nodded pensively. "When do you expect him?"

"Possibly late tomorrow night," replied Joe.

"I'll look forward to it," said Brogan. "In the meantime, let me show you my favorite gadget." He brought out an ungainly machine that looked like a ticketing device. It hung by a black, leather shoulder-strap and had a cable coming out from it.

"What on earth is that," grinned Joe.

"It's a card-counter," explained Brogan, "otherwise known as a 'device' or a 'beast'. It counts the cards that have gone by and tells you the probable next card."

"No shit," exclaimed Joe. "Are you familiar with Blackjack, Joe?"

"Yeah, I suppose I am," came the coy but honest reply.

"Say I've got a bag containing three balls, a red, a white and a black."

"Alright," agreed Joe, imagining the scenario.

"If I take a ball out and it's red, what's left?"

"Simple, a white and a black."

"You'd bet on that?"

"Everything I've got," stated Joe.

"And you'd win," Brogan affirmed. "Card counting uses the same principle. It allows you to predict what's coming from what's gone."

"It's got to be more difficult than with the balls, hasn't it?"

"Right," confirmed Brogan, "but the basics are the same. To start with, it's totally unrealistic for a card counter to look at some digits and expect to see in a split second that three queens have gone, two jacks, one king etc, etc. All the high cards are worth the same, ten, so we divide the deck of cards into categories of similar cards. That cuts out a load of dicking around."

"Fair enough," agreed Joe. "So what are the categories?"

"There are four categories of cards, kings down to tens are called *Highs*, nines down to sixes are called *Mediums* and fives down to twos are called *Lows*."

"So the fourth category is aces?" added Joe.

"Correct." Brogan slung the device over his shoulder, it hung by his left thigh. "A sports jacket can hide it pretty well. Users would try and avoid suspicion by playing it cool."

"There's only three buttons on it," observed Joe. "You said there were four categories?"

"That's right, aces are the fourth, but because they can count as only one instead of eleven, they can be ignored. That makes things nice and easy."

"How's that?"

"It means that there are equal numbers of cards in each category," explained Brogan.

"You mean king, queen, jack, ten for highs, nine, eight, seven, six for mediums and five, four, three, two for lows. Four cards for each group."

"Exactly," Brogan confirmed. "So if you've been counting what's already been dealt, say twelve highs, six mediums and eleven lows.."

"The next card will probably be a medium," interrupted Joe, eagerly, "Because there are more of them left in the deck. Right?"

"Bingo. Simple isn't it. So if you need a medium, you ask for a card."

"Does it work? I mean, is it possible to make a killing using it?" asked Joe enthusiastically.

"It used to be. It's illegal now. This type of machine was discovered and outlawed in the 'fifties. The trick was to play small until the cards fell heavy to one category. Then you would bet big, knowing that the deck would have to even itself out."

"What happened if they caught someone using the device?" asked Joe.

"One of two things. If a casino wanted to bother with the legal side, you would end up with a ten grand fine."

"And if they didn't," prompted Joe.

"Then you would get a free fitting for a concrete overcoat," explained Brogan drily.

"Show me how the machine works," requested Joe.

Brogan slipped the cable up through his sleeve and asked Joe to deal out half a deck of cards. Brogan registered their category as quickly as Joe dealt them. At the end of the cable was a tiny revolving display which Brogan concealed in his hand. The machine made no noise at all.

"Right, stop there, and deal me two cards. The count now is eight, seven, four," said Brogan.

"So eight highs have gone, seven mediums and four lows," calculated Joe, giving two more cards to Brogan. They were a king and a six.

"I've got sixteen. That's another high and a medium," said Brogan as he pressed two buttons in a twinkling of an eye and stated, "The card count goes to nine, eight, and four. So I'm expecting a low. Not only that, I need a low to improve my score. Anything else won't do."

"Except an ace," added Joe.

"Yeah, but I'll still need a low." Joe dealt the next card. It was a four, a low.

"Twenty," announced Brogan. "That's the low one I was expecting. The laws of chance leaned on it."

Joe was impressed, but still curious. "Isn't the machine a bit awkward?"

"Yeah, it is. That's why one person played and a spectator operated the machine. He would pass instructions to the player, nods, winks, pulling on cigarettes, that kind of thing."

"Insane!" exclaimed Joe.

"It was, until you got caught," Brogan reminded him.

"Did you tell your brother about all this?" inquired Joe.

"I never got a chance, when I became really interested, it was too late for him. It was his way or the highway. We drifted apart; He became a mess. His hands kept shaking; he couldn't keep still, couldn't look me in the eye so I knew he wouldn't listen to me. He kept coming to borrow money from me and then he couldn't pay it back. Eventually I turned him down and he became too ashamed to face me. End of story."

"Thanks for showing me all this," said Joe, changing the subject.

"My pleasure, just don't get any ideas. The bastards are far too smart these days."

"No fear of that," smiled Joe. "I'd have to settle for good, old Lady Luck."

"You can leave that whore out of it," muttered Brogan. "In fact you can keep the whole sordid business. For every millionaire they make, you don't get a mention of all the poor suckers they've broken."

"You couldn't tell anyone that. They'd be determined to prove you wrong, thinking that they were one of the chosen few," stated Joe drawing on his own experience.

"I suppose you're right, Joe," concurred Brogan, turning to leave the room. Joe followed and accepted Brogan's offer of a ride home.

Chapter Eighteen

Thinking that he had convinced April of the possibility of returning with an engagement ring, Simon had managed to talk her into driving all night to Gatwick airport. It had taken five hours, but she drove with a selfless determination that she hoped would be a reflection of Simon's conviction to return. Simon dozed most of the way, avoiding any deepening of the theme of marriage.

They arrived at the airport at five a.m. Once inside the terminal, Simon scanned the departure information board and spotted a TWA flight leaving in three and a half hours time. Staunchly, he waited by the ticketing desk until two freshly made-up women appeared, looking as though they were opening for business.

Simon, clad in his leather jacket, pounced up to the desk and explained his need for a hasty departure. One of the agents looked his ticket over and confidently tapped at a computer keyboard.

"Yes," she said, "we can accept this ticket. Just sign this transfer slip and I'll get you a boarding-pass."

Simon scribbled on the document and passed it back, beaming. This would be the furthest he had ever travelled, his previous cheap trips to the Costa Brava paling into insignificance alongside this transatlantic crossing.

"Do you have any luggage that you would like me to check through for you, sir?"

He handed over a battered sports bag and smirked as the agent prodded what looked like a pair of protruding underpants out of sight, before putting it on the conveyor belt.

A few more taps at the keyboard were followed by a gracious

smile and the handing over of his ticket. "You'll be in first-class, sir. That will be towards the front of the aircraft."

"First-class?" echoed Simon. Of course, it came as a surprise to Simon because he hadn't even bothered to try and decipher the strange cryptic codes on the document.

"Your original ticket was first-class, sir."

"Fair enough," conceded Simon. 'Joe LeRice, you are one, cool dude', he thought, nodding in acknowledgement of his friend's gesture.

Assured of his new elevated status in the world, he took April by the arm and jaunted off to find a restaurant. After a hurried breakfast, Simon made his way to the departure lounge. Carrying only a white, plastic bag, his dark figure faded from April's sight as he was whisked down a long corridor on a motorized walk-way.

Now sitting down in the departure lounge, Simon found himself thinking about April already. How could that be? he thought. He was so used to her being around, and now she wasn't. It was an unusual feeling that went against the grain of his free-spiritedness. The implications of this were cast aside as he rose from his seat to answer the boarding call.

During the eight-hour flight, he fought to stay awake in case he missed any of the pampering that was being lavished around the first-class cabin. Consequently, when he arrived at Miami, he felt as though his body was held together with weak glue that would dissolve the moment he closed his eyes. This feeling of exhaustion diluted his ecstasy of being in the exciting, United States of America.

As an aura of foreign energy filled his senses, he wondered how long it would take for him to adapt.

Eastern Airlines had his ticket, as Joe had promised, but this time it was economy class.

Back to reality, he thought, as he signed for it. He found an impressive-looking circle of telephones. Spoiled for choice, he walked around them, marveling at their superior design to the ones that he was familiar with back home. He decided that now was the time to change the little money that he had. Finding a *Bureau de Change* was certainly not a problem; they were everywhere. There was one just a few yards from where he was standing. He was beginning to like this place already.

As his pounds were being exchanged for dollars, he checked his watch. It showed four-thirty, p.m. U.K. time. He mentally knocked off eight hours and calculated the time in Las Vegas. Eight-thirty in the morning, time for Joe's friendly wake-up call, he thought, getting to grips with the absurdity of it all.

He fed his chosen telephone with a combination of American coins, looking at each one before inserting it. He dialed, reached the motel, and asked for Joe's room. After five rings, Simon grinned mischievously as he imagined Joe struggling to wake up.

"Hello."

"British Telecom here. Wake-up you lazy chunk of shit."

"Simon, is that you, you old..." Joe searched for a suitable, friendly insult.

"Spare me the compliments, Joe. First-class to Miami, eh?"

"I thought you might appreciate it," said Joe.

"For a minute, I thought I had my own harem, the way they took care of me."

"So you're in Miami?" Joe cut in.

"Yep, there's a flight to Vegas in an hour."

"I'll meet you at Vegas Airport, then," confirmed Joe.

"Sounds good to me."

Five hours later, Joe's emotions swelled as the familiar black leather jacket that protected his perennially-thin friend came into view. The two old friends were re-united at the arrival gate of McCarran International Airport.

"Joe, you old bugger. It's good to see you."

Their handshake melted into a warm embrace.

"You haven't changed a bit, Simon."

"You have, Joe," observed Simon, still as blunt as ever.

"I'll bet you're tired," said Joe, "But before we go to the motel, I must warn you that's it's not exactly the Ritz. I'll book your room when we arrive."

"I bet it's no worse than that shit hole we used to share on St. Margaret's Street," laughed Simon remembering one of the hovels that they roomed in during their college days.

"In that case, you're in for a treat. It's got running water and wait for it; TV as well."

"You still sound like a Yank, Joe."

"Give yourself a couple of weeks and you will too. The Americans will think you're English and the English will think you're American. You can't win."

"Two weeks?"

"Well, if we finish here before then, I'd like you to see the Cayman Islands as well," said Joe.

"Oh man, you're blowing me away with all this generosity." Simon was shaking his head.

"Forget it. Money can't but friends, at least not my friends," said Joe.

"Yeah, but don't try too hard," joked Simon, "I come cheap." The taxi ride to the motel avoided *The Strip,* and Simon got his first real look at American suburbia as they drove up the eastern side of the city.

"These Yanks really know how to lay out a city," he remarked.

"Yeah," agreed Joe, "They had plenty of our mistakes to learn from."

At the motel, Simon dumped his bag on the spare bed and asked if anybody would be sleeping there.

"No, it's free," said Joe, "all the rooms have two beds."

"Then why don't you save yourself the expense of two rooms and let me have it. I'm about as fussy as a pig in shit."

"Then you'll feel at home," laughed Joe. "But no singing during the night," he added, a wicked grin turning the corners of his closed mouth. They laughed raucously at this comical reminiscence.

"Where's the tape?" asked Joe.

Simon fished it out from his hold-all and gave it to Joe.

"Excellent, Simon. Thanks a lot."

"It was a little tricky, but I cracked it with a little divine inspiration or should I say inspiration from the missus. After I separated the sounds, I re-recorded back onto to your micro-tape."

Joe played the tape. Simon motioned him to turn the volume up. He did so, and listened intently.

"What a bunch of fuckers, eh Joe?" said Simon, reminding Joe that his command of descriptive English was as good as ever.

"I'm forced to agree with you," replied Joe, unable to find a more appropriate phrase that would convey his sentiments as accurately.

Joe turned it off and suggested that they should get something to eat. He hoped that Simon would be able to accompany him to Brogan's later on in the evening.

Joe took Simon to the same Chinese restaurant that he had been to with Bobby. Simon was beginning to look visibly worn out. The soporific effect of a glass of beer made his eyeballs loll about as he strained to stay awake.

"It's either finish this food and kip on the floor, or back to the room for some shut-eye," declared Simon.

Within ten minutes, he was a snoring heap of leather and denim on the spare bed. Joe watched some news on television, figuring that any other noise to concentrate on would be a god-send.

An hour later, Simon woke up and Joe called Brogan who suggested a meeting at his house late that evening.

Joe had one more call to make. He dialed his home and Rachael's mother answered. She sounded pretty lively, considering her circumstances, thought Joe hoping that he would be able to talk with her without putting his foot in it.

"Elene, how are you?"

"Oh, I'm making it, Joe," she replied with her lilting Caymanian brogue. "Which is more than I can say for your wife? How long do you expect me to look after her while you're away?"

"Is Rachael..."

"You get yourself home, Joe," interrupted Elene, "you've got a wife that needs you. She's missing you something terrible."

Still reeling from the matronly barrage fired by Elene, Joe heard the phone change hands at the other end. Rachael took over the receiver and was still laughing as she greeted Joe.

"There's nothing wrong with *her,*" he exclaimed.

"Pay her no mind," said Rachael affectionately towards her mother.

"Any news, sweetheart?" Joe asked.

"Lots, I'll tell you in a minute," enthused Rachael.

"Is your Mom still there?" asked Joe.

"She's just gone into the kitchen; I'll tell you the news."

"I'm all ears," said Joe.

"I read in the paper that *Eastern Promise* has bought a big piece of land on Seven Mile Beach, so I checked the Land Registry. It cost them nearly ten million dollars."

"So it's public knowledge?"

"For the most part," explained Rachael, "But here's the real news, they don't own it outright. There's a lien on the property. They loaned money from a local bank to do it. Not only that, apparently they've got financing from the same bank to build the hotel and casino."

"I'm not surprised; all their cash must have gone when they bought the gambling rights. I bet the banks lined up to lend them the money," deduced Joe, "They probably loaned the money under condition that *Eastern Promise* keep all their business accounts there, once they start operating."

"I never thought of that," admitted Rachael.

"Do you know which real estate company sold the land?"

"No, but I can find out," responded Rachael. "The company should be mentioned on the contract. Government should have a copy of the contract filed away. If they do, I can find it."

"When you do, check also who are registered as the directors of the company," Joe requested.

"That's a completely confidential area. I'll probably end up with a lawyer's name for the registered office. They've got a stranglehold on the system, but I'll try. I know some of the girls in the Registrar of Companies' office. Fancy, foreign lawyers can't change the fact that we grew up together."

"That's fighting talk, honey," Joe gushed, proud at his wife's strong stance.

"You're damned right it is, Joe. Every day I see what's been happening to the place since all this started. Business people are climbing like rats over each other to get involved. You should hear some of the rumors going back and forth. It's unbelievable. People are fighting over who should get retail space in the hotel, who gets to supply the building materials, who buys the adjoining property, it's crazy. Convention has gone out of the window."

"Just be careful and keep low," advised Joe. "I've got some news of my own. I've got proof that *Eastern Promise* try and brainwash their customers by using hidden messages on tapes."

"And that's what they plan to do here, I suppose?" concluded Rachael.

"Unless we stop them first. Can you find out if they've applied for any work permits yet? If so, then they've had to submit affidavits or police clearances, right?"

"That's true, it *is* standard procedure," confirmed Rachael. "I'll check that too. I'll try and get the information before you call tomorrow. Mummy's alright now. I can go back to work full-time."

"I've said it before, and I'll say it again," urged Joe. "Be careful, darling. You never know who you can trust."

"This is my country, Joe. I'll do my part."

"Yeah, I know. But still be careful. I'll call you tomorrow then."

They re-affirmed their love and after Joe had hung up, Simon spoke, "Sounds as though it's getting pretty heavy?"

"True, but things may just fall in our favor. Come on, let's go and see a friend."

As Simon showered, Joe lay on his bed trying to piece together the blurred fragments of this complex jig-saw puzzle. If he spoke out, would he be the lone voice in the wilderness of sanity? Perhaps he was in a minority and the Caymanian people were ready to embrace this addition to their culture. As soon as Joe doubted himself, he wondered why *Eastern Promise* had resorted to such underhanded tactics and his conviction returned with a vengeance.

At ten o'clock that evening, Simon and Joe arrived at Brogan's house. Joe introduced Simon to Brogan. The two of them hit it off immediately, Simon's natural calm leaping over Brogan's defensive walls and into the corridors of his acceptance.

They wasted no time and went into the study. Joe gave the tape-recorder to Brogan.

"Turn the volume right up and try to ignore the foreground racket," Joe told him.

Brogan's face tightened with concentration as he picked out the urgings that had deceived his brother. From deep hate sprung bitter tears and Brogan was now closer to being on the team.

Joe pulled the machine back and waited until Brogan had regained his composure. He explained what Rachael was doing back in the Cayman Islands to help their cause. Joe and Brogan spoke with such fervor, that Simon wanted a reason to be part of the crusade against *Eastern Promise*. Not able to find one that affected him directly, he decided to hate them anyway.

Brogan's wife, Janie, brought them some drinks before leaving them within their male bastion. Joe decided to lighten the theme and asked Brogan to show him some of his gambling trivia. Brogan brought out the card counter and showed Simon how it operated. "When was this made?" laughed Simon, "during the Stone-Age?"

"Close," smiled Brogan, "Late 'forties, early 'fifties."

"What did people who used it say? Pardon me while I wheel in my abacus? It's bloody massive."

Brogan showed Simon how it was possible to conceal it. "Yeah, but there's no excuse for anything that big," ridiculed Simon, "At least not today, not in the age of silicon chips."

"It's only a toy, Simon," interrupted Joe. "An antique, if you like."

"I bet the bastard who wore it didn't think it was a toy," retorted Simon.

"Or the bastard who caught him wearing it," laughed Brogan, continuing Simon's description.

"Wait a minute!" Joe stopped the conversation dead. "Simon, could you make something like this, only smaller?"

"I could make it bloody invisible compared to that."

"Joe, I hope you're not gonna say what I think you are?" said Brogan.

"I probably am." Joe's eyes went wild as possibilities glinted from inside them. "It's perfect. Listen to me."

The room fell silent. Joe grabbed his chance, "*Eastern Promise* have just shelled out a hundred million dollars or so in cash, for exclusive gaming rights in Cayman. So that's where they're weak, they are weak on cash. In fact they are probably gambling that nothing too expensive happens right now, agree?"

The two other men nodded in acceptance of Joe's argument. He went on, "So we hit them where it hurts...in the pocket. You make me a counter, Simon and I'll do it. I'll nail them to the wall. It would be my pleasure. I've always liked a good game of Blackjack."

"You've overlooked one thing, Joe," said Brogan. "If you want to win big, you've got to bet big."

"If that's what it takes, that's what I'll do. I've got a trust fund with about nine-hundred thousand Caymanian dollars in it." Joe revealed.

"How much is that in American dollars?" asked Brogan.

"Over a million," clarified Joe. Simon's jaw dropped. His friend really had made it. Joe went on, "Cayman dollars are stronger than U.S. It was supposed to be for an early retirement, but I'll chance it."

"What about your wife, Joe?" asked Simon. "What's she going to say when you empty the family purse?"

"It might not be necessary for her to find out. My signature alone is good enough. I can have the money wired up here to a bank."

"You crazy mother, Joe." Brogan shook his head.

"It can work, Brogan," said Simon, coming to the defense of his friend.

"Another insane Limey. This is too much."

"In or out, Brogan?" Joe pressed him. Brogan didn't like it one bit. The *no* that formed in his mind was overwhelmed by the *yes* from his heart.

"Oh hell, I think you're mad," he said, shaking his head slowly, "Count me in for two hundred grand and damn me for listening. Shit! Outnumbered by a couple of loony Limeys in my own home."

"Count me in," said Simon, putting his last hundred dollars on the table.

"So it's settled them," announced Joe. "While I get the money, Simon makes the device."

"Whose gonna play?" asked Brogan.

"I guess that's my department," elected Joe.

"So whose gonna work the device?" explored Brogan further.

"That job's got to go to Simon," stated Joe. "It'll be his toy."

"Simon, do you know how to play Blackjack?" Brogan was

serious. "I mean, even if you know the count, how are you going to decide whether Joe pulls a card or not?"

"I know the basics," professed Simon, "But if you can teach me the intricacies, I'll only need to be told once. I do know that twenty one is the score to aim for."

"Then we're going to spend a lot of time together, mate," stated Brogan, affectionately patting Simon on the back. "You'll be doubling down and splitting aces before you know it."

"Can Simon stay here for a couple of days?" hustled Joe. "While I'm getting the money, he can build the device and you can teach him the game?"

"No reason why not," agreed Brogan. "I can take a few days off. Chris is more than capable of handling *The Store* by himself." Whilst Brogan called a taxi, Joe gave Simon some cash to buy the equipment that he would need. Ten minutes later, the cab appeared and Joe arranged to return the next evening. As Joe's taxi pulled up in front of the motel, he noticed a figure huddled in the dim light outside his door. He paid the driver and rushed over. It looked like Bobby. She was sitting, her arms wrapped around her legs and her head between her knees rocking gently.

He went over and raised her slowly to her feet. She looked terrible, her face was bruised and she couldn't speak. Overcome by pity for his dying friend, Joe held her gently and guided her into his room where she sat on the spare bed. He was tortured about informing her about the blood tests.

"I'm sorry, but you're going to die," was what it amounted to. Perhaps he should just give her the letter and she could read for herself. On the other hand, he could say nothing and let her waste away, one short stop in a hospital before getting a look at the Big

Black Book. She didn't look in much condition for anything at the moment.

"Come on, Bobby. Let me put you in bed," begged Joe.

She nodded, feeling safe in his company. Joe sat on the end of the bed and unstrapped the shoes from her limp feet. He managed to ease the blankets from under her featherweight, frame before covering her with them. She lay on her side and nuzzled up to the pillow as though it were her mother's breast.

"Can I get you anything? A drink? Something to eat, maybe?"

"Vodka," she croaked from a half-smiling face, the other half hidden by the pillow. Joe took her words at face value, knowing that it was a bit late for her to refrain from under-age drinking. She would soon be running out of any pleasures in life.

"Vodka it is, then," he announced. "Just give me ten minutes each way."

As Joe jogged down to the liquor store, he recalled his first meeting with Bobby. *Bloody Mary, on the rocks.* She'd like that, he thought. He picked up some snacks along with some of Bobby's favorite cigarettes as well.

Back inside his room, he set his goods down before fetching a quarter's worth of ice from the machine outside. Now he had the rocks, it was the last ingredient.

He mixed up a strong drink and took it over to her. She struggled to sit up. It was obvious that she had been savagely beaten. The dim bedside-lamp brought out the shades of yellow that surrounded her swollen eyes. Her lips were dry and cracked and she winced as the burning alcohol flowed into the tiny crevices. She tried desperately hard not to smile, it would have only brought more pain, but there was no denying the soothing glow that began to caress her from the inside out.

"What happened, Bobby? You look like hell."

The smile that she had been holding back erupted onto her face and the centre line of her lower lip glistened red with blood as it split. She took the lit cigarette which Joe held out to her.

"*Eastern Promise*...I don't know why," she mumbled, her smile having quickly vanished as she recalled the ordeal.

"You went to the *Eastern Promise*?" echoed Joe.

"Thought I might find you in there..."

"I was here all the time, you know that," groaned Joe.

"Not that easy... it would be too obvious."

"Too obvious for what?"

"Didn't want you to think...I was crawlin' back." She looked lost in the absurdity of the truth.

"You foolish girl," said Joe warmly, "I wasn't angry with you. You were just being honest."

"I thought you'd be mad at me?"

"No way, Bobby," reassured Joe, "You just get some rest, you hear?"

"He raped me...that man," continued Bobby.

"What! Who, who raped you?"

"That man...The fucking manager."

Joe grabbed his Caymanian newspaper and showed Bobby the photograph of the *Eastern Promise* people. Bobby looked the faces over before pointing emphatically to Luca Telesino.

"The bastard!" Joe snarled, secretly drawing morbid pleasure from the fact that he was now probably a dying bastard.

"He asked me about you. I said we had an argument and that I was going home to St. Louis. He took me to a room and locked me in." Bobby flinched with sore recollection. "I tried to call you but the phone didn't work. He punched me and raped me, again and again."

She tried to cry, but couldn't, years of cold street living icing up her tear ducts.

"It's alright, Bobby. You're safe now," lied Joe, in his most compassionate tone.

"I didn't tell them anything. Honest."

Joe realized that he only had Bobby's word for that, but his gut told him to believe her. Right now, he would leave her to rest, but in the morning, she would have to answer some questions.

He watched her as she faded away into sleep. Beyond her mask of anguish and pain, Joe sensed an unusual serenity about her that seemed to surround her like a halo and in a strange way, he was envious.

Chapter Nineteen

Luca Telesino sat in the control room that adjoined his office. He was taking immense pleasure in watching the demise of a wealthy Japanese businessman who, having entered the fray as a big-betting 'whale', now held the status of 'minnow'.

The man's million dollars worth of chips now stood for ten per cent of their original worth. For Telesino, this was the ideal reply to the pressure that he had been put under by Durant and Medini. Although they had secured their gambling contract in those godforsaken islands, it had cost them nearly every penny of their own, not to mention the cash from those rough-bastard Colombians. The resulting nervousness had been relayed down the company's chain of command and Telesino had found himself to be the buck where everything stopped. He loved it, the intensity of it all turned him on and if it was not necessary for a human being to sleep, Telesino would have been content to stay awake permanently.

As he watched his prey squirm and sweat, Telesino thought back to the excitement that he had experienced with that little bitch, Bobby, or whatever her name was. He didn't expect to see her again, or that trumped-up, half-breed Limey who said he was her uncle. He hoped that he had smashed her into recognizing his power.

The fear in her eyes as he struck her, again and again; he loved it, every brutal second. His most enjoyable part had been when he dragged her cowering, beaten body out from the corner and thrown her over a chair where he had forced her. He had to admit that he didn't have to force very hard, but he enjoyed it, nevertheless.

These thoughts brought him to a state of arousal so he went into his bathroom and stroked himself to a climax. It didn't take long, he was good at it, but the only problem was that he had decreased his sexual stamina to about ten thrusts, sometimes less. Anyway, the way he saw it, it was his wife's problem not his and he always got what he wanted.

He heard his private phone ring. Telesino wiped his hand affectionately; it was Charlie.

"Mr. Osaki's up for a marker."

"Good," said Telesino, sensing that now was the time to turn the screw. "Write him up for a hundred grand."

"How much?" gasped Charlie.

"You heard me, Charlie. A hundred grand. Now, you fool."

"Yes sir, right away." Charlie didn't need telling a third time, although it was the most credit his boss had extended to a first time customer.

For Telesino, it was more than a calculated gamble. He knew that if the man could blow one million, he could blow another, but it would be on management's terms. Giving him only a hundred thousand at a time would take away the gambler's option for a one-hand sting, where he could recoup his losses at the drop of a hat.

No, things were never that easy and it was Luca Telesino's job to make sure that was exactly the way they stayed. He laughed loudly as he watched Mr. Osaki humbly accept his marker with a little bow that conveyed respect for the service that had just been extended to him. Those bastards didn't cut any ice with Luca Telesino, underneath all that oriental mystique and politeness; they were just nervous men, unable to control their pathetic weakness.

Suddenly the door burst open, Durant and Medini appeared and quickly scanned for any reason to belittle their manager. They found none.

"How's business tonight?" asked Medini.

"Excellent," replied Telesino. "I'm in the process of milking that 'whale' from Japan. He's on markers now."

"I'm glad to hear it, Luca," interjected Durant, "Very glad, because there's no room to fuck up now during these trying times."

"I understand, sir. Perfectly."

Durant and Medini went over to their private safe. They had chosen to locate it in Telesino's office as they were rarely there, but their faithful hound had a true sense of loyalty and was sworn to guard it with his life. The safe had two separate combinations to it, one for each of them. One could not open it without the presence of the other. From time to time, Telesino had seen his bosses come in and either take out, or put in piles of cash that certainly did not come from the casino floor. Recently, he noticed that there was a lot more removing than replacing, but he kept his eyes open and his mouth shut.

Telesino retreated into the viewing-room to carry out a few of his midnight chores. The first was making sure that the eight people who worked in front of his security screens did not slack at their stations. Once again, he insisted that it was coffee time. His reputation for mixing the bitterest coffee that any of them had ever tasted was secretly accepted as not being one of the perks of the job. Although some of them suspected, none of them dared question what ingredient it was that could foul such a simple pleasure. Whatever it was, it sent them home with glazed, wide-open eyes.

After covertly adding the neat, powdered caffeine to the urn, Telesino filled up his workers' cups and paced around with a threatening posture until the drinks were finished. The scanners knew it was pointless to protest, so they drank in unison, creating a fresco of contorted faces.

Now that his workers were wide-awake, it was time to extend the same favor to his customers. Not only were they at liberty to enjoy free, doctored coffees, they were about to experience the wonderful effects of oxygen-enriched air. This simple necessity of life worked wonders for alertness in the early hours of the morning, sustaining the players who would then be entitled to boast about their staying power.

Telesino punched a few buttons on a command console and the gas began to infiltrate the gaming-floor in a concentration that was just significant enough to give the desired effect. In very high ratios, this gas was potentially explosive, but as it was, cigarettes burned a little faster and lighter flames leapt a little higher. With more important things to worry about, the odd singed fringe was laughed off as a humorous error of judgment. Satisfied, Telesino took the opportunity of retiring to his penthouse suite on the top floor. He felt safe there as he locked himself in with the memories of his sexual encounters, many of which he had recorded on video tape to fill his quieter moments. If his wife was lucky, he would turn up at their home on the west side of town to give her the pleasure of his company, but so far tonight, that seemed unlikely, his job came first.

Chapter Twenty

Joe had changed and sat patiently, waiting for Bobby to wake. With her puffed eyes, her cheeks seemed more sunken than ever. She laid perfectly still, any commands to toss or turn, being refused by her debilitated body. Eventually, at nine o'clock that morning, she groaned as she awoke, her pain now real.

"Good morning, Bobby," lied Joe.

"Hi, Joe," she moaned, sounding slightly improved on the night before, "It's good to be back."

"Listen Bobby, I know it might be painful, but you've got to tell me what you said about me to that man, Telesino."

Bobby nodded, hinting that she was equal to the task, "Not much, I mean I didn't say what you were doing, if that's what you mean. I told him that we had an argument, but also that you would meet me there."

"At the *Eastern Promise*?"

"That's right. I waited and waited, hoping that you would show. After a few hours, he came back and we got talking. I mentioned that I could use a job and he asked me to go upstairs with him."

"And you did?"

"I didn't really have much choice, Joe," Bobby pointed out.

"I suppose so; he is a pretty forceful character," conceded Joe.

"He took me to a room and we had a drink. He asked about you, and I said I hated you for throwing me out and not coming for me. Then he dropped the subject and made me watch a video. That's when it all started."

"When what started?" demanded Joe.

"He started coming at me. I was afraid. I would have let him, but he didn't want it like that. He was a big, strong bastard. He enjoyed hurting me. Fucker didn't even pay me."

"The bastard!" was all Joe could say. He could not comfort her physically, a rooted fear prevented him.

"Joe, I'm not going to make it, am I?"

"What do you mean?"

"I'm not going to make it. I can feel it. I've been bad for a while now. Everything's getting harder. I think I'm awful sick."

Joe didn't know what to say. He shook his head, "I'm sorry, baby."

"So help me, if you cry on me, Joe," she rasped, "It don't look good."

"What am I supposed to do?" Joe looked torn. "Bobby. It's AIDS. You're dying." He passed her the letter.

"Thank God for that," she muttered, dropping it to the floor without even looking at it. Joe stopped and stared at her. She was serious, she meant it.

"Don't worry, Joe," she continued, "I haven't gone crazy. I've had enough, that's all. I've had enough of this bullshit world."

"You can't give up, baby," begged Joe, unable to understand her wish to forfeit.

"Why not? People say they care. That's all it is. It's only words and I don't mean you, Joe. You're the only person who's ever made me smile just lately. You were fun. I didn't deserve you."

"I should have done more..." started Joe.

"Hold on," Bobby broke in, "Let me finish. When you hit rock bottom, you're just a hassle, but when you've gone, people make a big fuss over you. I'm only gonna be a hassle a little longer. It'll be fun, watching them come to my grave, giving me flowers. Do you know Joe; I never got any flowers while I was alive?"

Joe uprooted his fear and hugged her. "I love you, Bobby," he whispered.

"I know, Joe. I love you, too. I understand now. At least, I think I do, you know...what love really is?" She smiled and lay back in bed.

"I think I'd better get you somewhere where they can take care of you," Joe suggested, completely unprepared for this moment.

"No, no doctors now. I need a favor from you, Joe."

"Tell me, what can I do?"

"Get me a ticket to St. Louis. Today," demanded Bobby firmly.

"It's already done, Bobby."

Joe called the airport and reserved her seat for late that afternoon. He told her that after he had taken care of some business at the bank, he would return to take her to the airport. He left the room and walked quickly, trying to stay ahead of his thoughts.

Joe knew that he would have to go through a lot of red tape at the bank, so he equipped himself with enough identification to get the job done.

Joe used the same bank where he had made the cash withdrawal on his credit card. He asked to speak to the manager, who on finding out what service Joe required, eagerly escorted him to his office, whilst mentally totaling the charges that he could tack on to this gambler's obvious misfortune.

After identification was formalized, the two participating banks agreed on a transfer procedure and Joe left, feeling that he had paid a high price for the service, but he accepted his lack of options. Although he would have to return for his cashier's cheque tomorrow, he stopped to withdraw some money for Bobby.

When he arrived back at the motel, Bobby had already showered and changed and was lying on the bed gazing aimlessly at the ceiling. The true seeds of her predicament had sprouted and brought forth their dark fruits, but her upper lip remained stiff and she was ready.

"Let's go, Joe."

"You sure you'll be ok? Who's going to look after you?"

"I'll have to go home, Joe. I think it's right. My kid sister will keep me company. "

"What about your parents?"

"It'll be their last chance to accept me. It might do them some good," she smiled weakly.

At the airport, Bobby began to feel wobbly. Joe held her and looked around for some help. Faces flashed by, passing glances denied by their owners. Joe managed to get Bobby to the security check. She stumbled through the doorway and had to steady herself on the machine that X-rayed hand-luggage. Joe surged through a couple of officials to get help for her. They wheeled around to stop him. He glared back at them saying, "Can't you see? She needs help."

"I'm sorry, sir. You can't go beyond this point without a boarding-pass," one of them explained.

"Then get her some help. Don't just stand there."

The two men looked lost. At that moment, a stewardess arrived on the scene. "Can I help?" she asked, in a friendly tone.

"It's my friend," said Joe, "She's feeling sick."

"Shall I call the doctor?"

"No," said Bobby firmly, "No doctors. Just get me to the plane."

"What flight is she on?"

"St. Louis, half an hour," explained Joe.

"That's my flight. Just wait here," said the stewardess, "I'll be right back."

She left, returning two minutes later pushing a wheel-chair. Joe eased Bobby into the seat and bent down to hold her hands.

"This is it, Joe. Take care of yourself. Kick some butt in that casino for me, you hear?"

He passed her an envelope. "There's a few dollars here for your parents to use to look after you. Don't let them abuse it. There might be some left over for a Bloody Mary." They laughed, weakly.

"Joe?" whispered Bobby earnestly, "Would you have tried this hard to keep me?"

"Shit..." Leveled by the question, he choked on guilt.

"Sorry, bad call. But like I said, Joe, I won't be a hassle much longer."

Bobby had made her point, perfectly.

Joe whispered a request in the stewardess' ear before she wheeled Bobby away. She nodded before turning to push the sick girl towards the departure gate.

A few minutes later, Bobby was safely in her seat and preparing for take-off. When the craft was airborne, the stewardess brought her a small bouquet of flowers. Smiling weakly, Bobby opened the note. There was only one word. It said, 'Joe.' Knowing exactly what it meant, she tucked it in with the two thousand dollars that he had given her.

Travelling to Brogan's house, Joe was getting to grips with two emotions, relief and the guilt of it. When he arrived, he was grateful that he had something to turn his attention to. He found solace in the destructive intent of his plan to take on *Eastern Promise*. His rage had to be channeled or he would be in danger of an emotional eruption.

He envisaged Telesino's motionless body lying on the floor and he was still pummeling it, his own tears mixing with the bastard's blood.

"What's up, mate?" asked Simon, "You look a bit off."

"A shit day."

"How about a beer?'

"Yes."

In Brogan's study, the desk was littered with bits of wire, the guts of a cheap, digital watch, electronic components and pieces of paper that had calculations scribbled on them.

"How's it looking," asked Joe.

"Not bad, not bad at all," replied Simon, showing Joe the digital watch that he had obviously modified.

"There are basically three components to these things," he explained, "The display, the chip and the battery. I got rid of the battery and the chip, but the display proved perfect for my needs."

"How's that," asked Joe, intrigued by his friend's ingenuity.

"I can use the hour display for *high* cards, the minutes for *mediums* and the seconds for *lows.* Here's the good part. It's got a date display. I'm using that for aces. That way, we can count every card that goes by."

"So the display goes on your wrist?" checked Joe. "How are you going to register the cards?"

"Simple. As it stands, the watch is just a display. It will only show what I want it to show. It needs input." He showed Joe a wafer-thin card with six pocket-calculator type buttons protruding. A small battery was attached to the back of the card and a five foot-wire hung from it.

"I chopped up a cheap calculator for the buttons. They're soft and make no noise when you press them."

"What are the two extra buttons for?" asked Joe.

"One resets the display to zero," replied Simon.

"Very handy after a shuffle," interjected Brogan.

"And the other allows me to signal you," continued Simon.

Simon put the buttons in his right trouser-pocket and passed the wire through his shirt and down his left sleeve. Then he connected the wire into the belly of the watch and pulled the excess out of sight. The watch sat at the junction of his cuff, with no sign of any wire.

"Look at the display, Joe," said Simon.

Joe saw that the previously blank display now showed six large digits and two smaller ones, all reading zero.

"How many cards in a single deck, Joe?" asked Brogan.

"Fifty-two."

"Right, sixteen highs, sixteen mediums, sixteen lows and four aces," elaborated Brogan.

"Now deal out some cards, say thirty," instructed Simon.

"How fast?" asked Joe.

"You've seen it done," said Simon, "As fast as that."

Joe began to deal cards, mentally counting how many had gone. Simon stood watching them intently, his right hand in its pocket pressing the appropriate button for each card that Joe dealt.

"Right, that's thirty, "confirmed Joe.

"The count says 5-12-11 and 2 aces gone," stated Simon. "It's a total of thirty cards."

He showed the two other men the display and they both agreed.

"Now deal me a couple of cards." ordered Brogan. Joe dealt him a two and a ten. Simon adjusted his count.

"I can see Brogan's cards," said Simon. "He's got a ten which changes the high count from five to six and a two which pushes the lows from eleven to twelve. The count changes to 6-12-12 and 2 aces. Brogan can hold the game up long enough for me to change the count."

"So, I've got twelve," affirmed Brogan. "Judging by the fact that only six highs have gone by, I'd say we were due some more."
"So what would you do?" Joe asked, "Take a card or not?"

"No. Because the cards have to even out," replied Brogan, "We're due some high ones. If I pull a high on twelve, I hit twenty-two; I'm bust and I've lost my stake. No I'll stay at twelve."

"So I have to play now, as the dealer?" asked Joe.

"That's right," said Brogan, "Give yourself a couple of cards."

Joe did so, turning them face up. A jack and a six. Sixteen.

"Stop," ordered Brogan. "We're still expecting highs. Now, deal. You're on sixteen. The rules say you have to take a card."

Slowly, but deliberately, Joe turned over the top card from the remainder of the deck. He looked at it, shielding it from the others. They stared at him.

"Bingo!" He threw it down. It was the king of clubs, a high! The dealer had bust: the players had won!

"Deal the rest of the cards, Joe," said Brogan, "But keep the last one back."

Simon adjusted his count for the king before tracking the other cards. Now holding only one card, Joe stepped back."

"16-16-16 and three aces," said Simon to Brogan.

"Without looking at that card, Joe," declared Brogan confidently, "It's an ace."

"Of spades," added Joe as he cast it down. "It looks like we're ready, gentlemen."

"Not quite," said Brogan, "In the little game that we played, it was hardly true to life. You've got to receive instructions from Simon without anybody suspecting."

"Shit. You're right. In the excitement, I forgot," admitted Joe.

"There are a couple of options," declared Brogan. "Simon can stand at the corner of your vision and you can watch for a visible signal..."

"You did say *visible* signal, didn't you?" Joe interrupted.

"That's right," confirmed Brogan.

"So if it's visible to me, it'll be visible to everyone else, right?" he concluded.

"True, if they know what to look for," replied Brogan.

"If they play video recordings of all the hands that I take a card on," stressed Joe, "And Simon draws on a cigarette every time, or does the same movement, they'll put two and two together, surely?"

"Which brings me to the second option," declared Simon confidently.

Brogan fell silent and glanced at Simon who stood up and casually ran his hand through his hair.

"The *invisible* signal," grinned Simon, taking centre stage. He lifted some papers from the desk to reveal some more minute gadgetry.

"Take your watch off, Joe," he ordered. After Joe had complied, Simon made sure that Joe's watch had a metal casing, before carefully re-positioning it on top of a tiny metal box that he placed on the moist part of Joe's wrist.

"Is it uncomfortable?" Simon asked.

"Not unduly, but I'd have to get used to it. Anyway, what is it?"

"It's a cheap and nasty receiver," laughed Simon. "If I send it a signal, it'll vibrate and give you a tingle. Your watch is acting as the antenna."

"Bloody amazing," declared Joe

"It's bullshit really. Anybody could make one. I've hardly spent a hundred and fifty qui...I mean dollars. Forty of that was for the soldering-iron."

"Alright Simon, tingle me," taunted Joe.

Simon pressed a button on the transmitter and Joe laughed.

"Yep, I felt that alright," he confirmed.

"Before we start," said Brogan, "You two need to work out a code, say one tingle for a card and two to stay as you are. That way, if you don't get a signal, you know something's wrong."

"Don't forget doubling down and splitting," reminded Simon, anxious to share his newly-learned jargon with his friends.

"When do we start?" Joe asked, feeling like a child with a new toy.

"When we polish up our act," declared Brogan, bringing him back to reality. "This ain't going to be a walk in the park. If you give them any reasons to suspect you, they'll fuck you."

"So we practice." Joe responded to Brogan's caution.

"Correct," said Brogan. "I'll play manager. And If I so much as catch a whiff of emotion or suspected communication, I'll come down on you so heavy, I swear."

They spent several hours playing the game, with Brogan

dealing and Simon casually watching, but communicating with Joe who sat at the desk, playing the super-cool, high-roller.

As night traversed into early morning, confidence soared and they adjourned for cold beers.

Joe asked Brogan if he could call Rachael.

"Hi, Sweetheart," said Joe, "Got any news?"

"A little. It's not too good, though."

"How come?"

"So far, *Eastern Promise* has applied for three senior management work permits, their names are, Alex Durant, Giovanni Medini and Gianluca Telesino. All three have Las Vegas police clearances that have been verified by Caymanian Police. So until they commit a crime in the islands, we can't stop them, or unless you can prove that the certificates are false, which means that you're calling their police liars?"

Joe remembered Brogan's advice about the near impossibility of penetrating the bureaucratic beast, but with his new approach coming to fruition, the news didn't hurt too much. Right now, they were going to fight fire with fire.

"What about the real estate company that sold the land?"

"The company is *Exclusive Caribbean Properties;* some American guy is registered as the principal, but that was as far as I got. Public knowledge of ownership ended at a lawyer's office and I hit a brick wall at Registrar of Companies. The girls swore that they couldn't find any files."

"Shit. I hope nobody's onto you. I think you might've gone a little too far. Just back off for a while, something big is happening here. I won't need any more information right now."

After the call, Joe shared the new information with his friends.

Simon felt it was time to clarify something that was bothering him.

"Joe, how much did you say that *Eastern Promise* paid the Cayman government?"

"A lot. More than one hundred and thirty million dollars, I think."

"Do you realize how many tourists would have come through the doors to lose that kind of money?"

"It is lucrative, isn't it?"

"No, there's more to it than that. This has really been bugging me since you said it. They must have really needed that place, real bad."

"What for?" asked Joe.

"From the little I know about the Cayman Islands," explained Simon, "Finance seems to be pretty big."

"It's the biggest," said Joe.

"If you had dirty money, say several million or more in drugs proceeds, and you wanted to deposit it, could you go to a bank in the Caymans and make a cash deposit?"

"No way," stressed Joe. "The law would come down heavy on a bank that did that."

"So what if the money was processed through a legitimate operation, before deposit? Say, lost on purpose through a casino? Then it would be laundered, right?"

"As clean as a whistle. Good God! I think that's it, Simon," exclaimed Joe, as the seriousness of the situation dawned. "The bastards will be so powerful; they'll have government in their pocket, especially if government is on a cut of the takings."

"Then we'd better hope that *Eastern Promise* is a little short on cash and high on commitments," said Brogan before offering to drive him back to the Golden Palace Motel.

Joe promised to show up at Brogan's the next day, after he had collected his cheque.

Chapter Twenty One

Stricken by fear of the unknown, Joe LeRice had spent a restless night playing out the possible outcomes ranging from total triumph to complete disaster. Success seemed to hinge on a knife-edge and it was getting sharper all the time.

Late that morning, he paid a visit to the bank; they had his cashier's cheque ready, minus their 'insignificant' deduction for services rendered. Armed with his supply of ammunition, Joe headed for his rendezvous in Boulder City.

At Brogan's house the atmosphere was electric as the three men acted out their roles over several decks of cards. Brogan's job would be to stand slightly to the right of Simon to obscure any obvious movements in his pocket. Brogan had already advised them that playing high stakes would bring spectators. Extra bodies would certainly be a beneficial distraction, but the possibility of them blocking Simon's view would have to be countered.

They planned to make a late entry to the *Eastern Promise.* That way, they hoped that they might be fortunate to catch some late-shift staff who would rather be in their beds than dealing cards.

Joe removed Luca Telesino's business card from his wallet and dialed the number. The switchboard put him through.

"Luca Telesino."

"Mr. Telesino, it's Joe Leriski. We met several days ago at your casino."

"I meet lots of people Mr. Leriski; you'll have to be more specific."

"I was with my niece, Bobby Verrill; you met us in your

restaurant."

Telesino almost choked, he remembered, completely. What could this insignificant little fuck be getting at, he thought, as he said, "Ah yes, I recall now. How's your vacation going?"

"Pretty good actually, thanks."

"I'm glad to hear it," Telesino lied. "Now what can I do for you?"

"You may not remember," Joe started, "But you said that you could arrange a room for me there if I guaranteed you my action."

"That's possible, I may have said that."

"Well, I'd like to take you up on your offer."

"That depends on the action. How much can you put up?" Telesino asked, suddenly interested, but surprised that Joe had not said more about Bobby.

"Three quarters of a million, cash," said Joe flatly, hoping that his flippancy would be regarded as a weakness.

"That will more than suffice. I suppose you'll be wanting a room each, you and your niece?" Confusion gripped Telesino. He wondered what the hell was going on.

"Oh no, just one room," said Joe, matter-of-factly, seizing the opportunity to allay Telesino's suspicions. "My niece just left. Apparently, a taxi that she was in crashed and she was a little bruised up. Nothing serious, though. She's back in St. Louis with her mother."

"Vegas traffic is pretty intense. I'm pleased she's alright," Telesino lied again, his heart reverting to normal time.

"Yeah, it was a shame, but I'm having the time of my life and I'm not done yet," Joe sensed that he had successfully defused the situation to his favor.

"Mr. Leriski, it will give me great pleasure to reserve you one of our luxury suites. Do you want me to send a limousine to pick you up?"

"No thanks. That won't be necessary. Expect me tonight at about nine o'clock." Joe hung up.

The remainder of the afternoon was spent fixing Simon up with some suitable clothes. A smart, baggy suit was democratically agreed to be the most practical attire.

Joe turned up at *Eastern Promise* ten minutes after nine. Telesino met him personally and escorted him to a suite on the thirty-second floor. He showed Joe around the lavish quarters ending with a breathtaking view of Vegas at night from the balcony. At that height, chill gusts of dry desert air quickly drove them back inside.

After Telesino had left, Joe decided to unpack, surreptitiously looking for hidden cameras or bugs as he did so. Not really knowing what bugs looked like, he realized that he would simply have to behave as normally as was possible in the given circumstances.

Just before midnight, adrenalin output in Joe's body reached peak levels. He breathed deeply, shaking his arms and legs to release the tension. This was it. He had to strike; it would have to be swift and brutal. There would be no compassion, he thought. These snakes did not deserve it.

Through one of his cameras, Telesino watched Joe descend to the gaming floor. He was a little disappointed to see Joe leave the building, but his hopes and suspicions were raised when the man walked back in a few minutes later.

Joe, with the receiver now under his watch, made his way to the casino bank. Special arrangements had been made for him to have his own chips that were worth ten thousand dollars each. He collected fifty of them, belittled by the fact that years of his hard work could be transformed into a pocketful of fancy discs. A security guard accompanied him to a vacant Blackjack table. He set his chips down and waited for something to happen.

Five minutes later, convinced that his intended victim had stewed enough, Telesino showed up with a pretty, female dealer. Joe acknowledged her beauty with a wry grin before reminding himself of why he was here.

She was carrying a tray of chips that were identical to Joe's. The word spread like wildfire. There was a high-roller about to play! Minimum stakes were ten grand! The immediate area behind Joe was cordoned off in a semi-circle as a small crowd began to form. Joe looked around.

Thank God! His friends were standing to the left of him. No recognition registered between them. Quickly, he looked back. He felt two tingles on his wrist and the feeling of relief was indescribable. He scratched his head. That was the signal that the test had been a success.

Michelle, the dealer, looked nervous. Twice, she had lost count of her chips as Luca Telesino stood menacingly behind her. Junior pit bosses surrounded by their small-time gamblers stole glances hoping that one day, they would get their chance to land a 'whale'.

Four brand-new packs of cards, still sealed in cellophane, were placed in front of Joe. He nodded and they were opened. Deftly, Michelle spread them out before Joe, achieving four colorful arcs. Joe scanned each deck, making sure that there were no anomalies. Satisfied, he sat back and watched as they were all combined and shuffled.

Michelle passed Joe the black, plastic marker-card, which he used to cut the deck and she separated the cards where the cut was made and finally put the cards in the shoe. It was time to play.

Joe became aware of the eerie silence that had fallen on his world. He took a single chip and placed it on his stake-box. He knew that he would have to play 'small' until he got the signal to bet big. It could take as many as ten hands. Card-counting relied on *probability* not *certainty*, so Lady Luck would have to play her part as well.

In the twinkling of an eye, four cards were dealt. Joe had two queens or two highs, worth twenty. He did not need Simon to tell him that he should stay on that total. Nevertheless, feeling the signal reassured him that he was not alone. He pushed his cards under his stake, indicating that he was happy.

The dealer, showing an eight, turned over her other card. It was a nine. Seventeen. Incredible, he had just taken them for ten thousand dollars in about thirty seconds. The rules said that the dealer could not take any more cards at seventeen and above, so Michelle pushed a chip over to Joe. His pile had been restored to its former glory and it was the casino's money that he was now playing with.

Simon's watch said 2-2-0 and 0 aces. The next ten hands were traded evenly. The count had been dutifully followed and stood at 15-21-23 and 4 aces. Simon felt it was time to increase the stakes knowing that some high cards were due. He signaled Joe to press his stake up. Tentatively, Joe pushed fifty thousand dollars onto his box. His gut twisted with fear. Adrenaline began to flow freely and his heart was almost unable to cope with the ferocity of the onslaught and a pain seared through his chest. A thumping beat pulsated between his temples clouding his vision. Michelle dealt. Droplets of sweat rolled off his fingers and disappeared into the thick carpet.

His fingers shook visibly as he picked his chips up. A six and a five. 'Help me, Simon,' he prayed. He felt three buzzes. What the hell! It couldn't be a double-down, surely? Not on fifty thousand?

He scratched his head, asking for verification. It came again, three buzzes.

"Double-down, please," croaked Joe, hoarsely. His score of eleven entitled him to double his stake in exchange for only one card.

"Double-down, fifty thousand. One card only," declared Michelle, sounding very important while trying to conceal her excitement. Telesino nodded, his face like granite.

Joe counted out another five chips and put them on his box, making two neat piles and totaling one hundred thousand dollars. Michelle dealt. Ten of hearts. Twenty-one!

A roar was heard from the gallery. Admiration for this hard pro' was rife. Joe allowed himself a sideways glance as if to acknowledge the plaudits from his audience.

The game wasn't over, but Joe's twenty-one proved too strong for the eighteen that Michelle achieved. Secretly, she was happy for this man, but having witnessed the downfall of so many like him, she kept any emotion well in check. She was just doing her job, after all.

Joe felt as though a huge burden had been lifted. He smiled and requested a beer. Telesino clapped his hands loudly and demanded cocktails. A pretty girl scurried over to take the order.

Another ten hands later, betting one chip only, Joe was another thirty thousand dollars up. It was a start, but he would have to maintain his steely nerve if he was to cause any real damage. He would need to win at least three million or so to make an impact he had estimated.

Two important-looking men brushed through the pit and walked up to Telesino. Joe recognized them from his newspaper photo as Giovanni Medini and Alex Durant, the owners. This was beyond his wildest dreams, the owners in person, ready to witness their own demise.

Telesino scowled at the sight of them. It was poor practice for owners to be seen 'sweating the action'.

During the next hand, the black marker card that had been sitting three-quarters the way down the deck showed as the next card. It signified a re-shuffle and a reset of the count to zero after which Joe lost the hand, and a chip, but one look at the size of his own pile softened the blow.

Telesino had managed to convince his bosses that their presence would only be detrimental to the atmosphere and reluctantly they left, their final expressions displaying a brooding foreboding.

Telesino was in his element. He had seen this all before. This man was obviously a 'natural', with the ability to count through the shoe or he had some kind of help. He glanced across the onlookers and drew a blank. It was now time for him to play a card of his own.

He whispered in Michelle's ear. Her face dropped, visibly disappointed. She too had seen all this before.

After Joe had cut the newly-shuffled cards, Michelle took the black marker and placed it only one third down the deck. The audience buzzed. Simon's heart sank. The bastard! he thought. By doing that, the casino had just about removed any hope of them making the sting that they had intended. As soon as the cards would show a pattern, the marker would re-emerge and it would be time to shuffle, all over again heralding a disastrous turn of events for the gambler.

As Joe lost the next three hands, he realized that the impetus had shifted and that they were now playing on Telesino's terms. As soon as he felt ready for a large bet, it was time to shuffle. Unable to commit himself, Joe felt his pile dwindle in dribs and drabs. That suited Telesino, who didn't mind winning, at whatever pace.

Soon, Joe was back to where he started. Anxious to recover, he pushed ten chips out. Hushed groans transformed the idle chatter that had broken out. It was Simon's turn to go into near heart-failure. What was Joe doing? There had been no signal for a press, nor had there been for a long time. This was a maverick decision, but he still had a job to do. He checked his count. It read 13-14-13 and 1 ace. It was too bloody close to predict anything; the three main categories were nearly all even; anything could happen. Sitting on twelve, Joe threw caution to the wind and pulled a king. Twenty-two, bust! The bottom fell out of his rattled world.

Now he was down. He imagined Telesino laughing in his face. From his position of disadvantage, Joe glanced up at the manager. The sneering glare that he received bristled down his neck. Moving a stack of about twenty chips for his stake, Joe glared back. Telesino smiled. Joe had just played into his hands. It was just like the old boxing adage, 'mad is bad', and Joe was mad. Simon nearly fainted. Joe was just another gambler. Nothing had changed since those days at university. Joe was not the captain of his own ship.

Joe braced himself. He closed his eyes as his cards came. Tentatively, he opened them, immediately wishing he hadn't. Fourteen, a useless hand. It was one of those moments when he wished he could go back in time. He waited for Simon's signal before scratching his head, reminding his friend that he needed help. No signal came. He looked at the dealer. She had ten. Still no signal came. He was on his own.

"Card, please," he mumbled, stroking his original two on the table as if to infuse them with luck.

The eight of clubs dropped in front of him. Twenty two. Bust! He buried his head in his hands and wept. He turned around to look for Simon and Brogan. They had vanished. He was over three hundred thousand dollars down and he motioned that he would not be playing any more for the time being. Michelle looked at him compassionately, but her concern did not register in his vacant brain.

Visions of him explaining to Rachael what he had done caused a plug of vomit to leap up to the back of his throat. He swallowed and winced as he imagined the foul lump retreating back inside himself.

The bank of observers behind Joe began to disperse, their need for excitement fulfilled and happy that someone else was worse off than themselves. It had been good entertainment.

Whatever Brogan and Simon had done, Joe knew that the blame lay with him. He had played their game and lost. At least he had the guts to face up to his mistake, but that did not make it easier to swallow.

He decided to go to his suite and drown his sorrows in a bottle of something or other. The elevator trip lasted forever. Joe wanted to shake his fist at the camera that watched him, but he knew it was hopeless. He had chosen to forsake the normal channels of action and play away from home; so consequently, he would have to accept the home-team rules.

Joe paused outside his door to find his key. He put it in the lock and turned it, deciding that if he was going to be miserable, it might as well be in luxury. As he pushed the door in, he noticed a piece of paper lying on the floor. It had obviously been pushed under his door.

He picked it up and read. "Sorry for leaving, Joe, but Brogan and I had to stop you before you lost all your money. You fucked up big time and you know it. Stay exactly where you are. In a day or so, we will be back in touch. Relax, and take it easy. Trust us."

It was signed by Simon. Joe tore up the note and flushed it down the toilet. The need to trust remained in his mind giving him hope. He tried to nurture the sentiment, for it was all he had. Shelving his plans to get drunk, he climbed into his bed where he lay uneasily, perplexed by the fact that he had not called Rachael. After all, exactly how he was going to explain what he had done, he could not begin to contemplate at that moment.

He considered leaving and accepting his losses, but having erased the fruits of several years of his life in such a short time, gave him the inclination to hold on and see what Brogan and Simon had in store. Joe drifted in and out of sleep hoping that the nightmare of his reality would evaporate when he awoke.

Chapter Twenty Two

Anxiously, Joe prepared to kill some time hoping to hear from his friends sooner rather than later. He was getting ready to go to the restaurant for breakfast when he became aware of a throbbing in his wrist. Removing his watch, he saw that his tiny receiver was still there, which proved that the nightmare that he just had woken from was a reality. He peeled the device from his skin, revealing a red, raw patch of skin that stung as he replaced his watch.

He took the elevator down to the gaming-floor and headed towards the twenty-four hour restaurant. As he walked past the tables he felt eyes mocking him, he tried to avert his gaze, but the sight of a familiar person made him look twice.

The man was sitting at a Blackjack table and appeared tense, wrapped up in his immediate surroundings. Joe stopped, squinting for confirmation.

Mike Ackroyd, one of the most senior politicians in the Cayman Islands! What the hell was *he* doing here? Joe did an about turn and hurried away from the scene. As the elevator opened to accommodate him, Joe glanced back to see if the mirage had vanished. It hadn't, but Joe was confident that Ackroyd had not seen him, since Ackroyd's head was still buried in his cards.

Possible explanations pounded at Joe's logic. This was too bizarre, even for the strangest of coincidences. The politician *had* to be involved somewhere and the cogs of Joe's rationale turned as they sought a solution. Perhaps Ackroyd was on a 'fam trip' getting familiar with the operation that would soon be in his islands.

Bullshit! Joe thought, concluding that was about as likely as a daytrip to Chernobyl. Besides, Ackroyd wasn't using *Monopoly* money on that table. Suddenly, Bobby's words came back to him. *A set-up!* That's was it was. A fucking, monumental set-up! The pieces were beginning to fit.

Mike Ackroyd had been the inside link, the reason for *Eastern Promise's* amazingly swift progress in the Cayman Islands. So the bastard was probably in cahoots, and had set up his whole, bloody country.

Then Joe remembered that Mike Ackroyd had studied in Los Angeles, which wasn't too far away. He had probably begun to gamble then, eventually getting into debt with *Eastern Promise*. So Ackroyd had targeted Arthur, leaving *Eastern Promise* to do the rest.

Joe wondered how many of Ackroyd's so-called, international public relations visits included detours to this place.

Joe wanted to go back to the gaming-floor and beat him to a pulp, for Arthur, for Bobby, for the unwitting country that had been duped by him, and finally, for himself.

In a sudden burst of clarity and compassion, Joe realized that Ackroyd might not have had a choice, but had become a victim and been forced into this situation, but a line had to drawn somewhere, surely?

Unable to draw that line, Joe retreated to the safety of his suite. An ugly possibility struck Joe. If Ackroyd knew that Rachael had been digging into *Eastern Promise* files, then she might be in danger.

He decided to warn her that it would be best if she left the islands for a few days. Somewhat concerned, Joe found an alternative way out of the building, initially taking the lift down to the first floor and then using a stairway that brought him out near the reception. On the street, he found a public telephone and called collect. Rachael answered, sounding tired. It was nine a.m. in Grand Cayman.

"Rachael, darling. You've got to listen to me."

"What's wrong? Why didn't you call last night? I was so worried. I called the motel. They said you'd left."

"I don't have time to explain. You've got to leave the island."

"Why? Are you in trouble?"

"Not yet, but you might be," Joe explained hurriedly.

"What's happening, Joe? I'm getting frightened."

"It's Ackroyd, he's gambling at *Eastern Promise* here in Vegas. He's been in on the whole thing from the start. You've got to leave. He probably knows that you've been checking up on him."

"I found out last night, that he owns Exclusive Caribbean Properties," explained Rachael. "I couldn't tell you, because you never called."

"I'm not surprised," said Joe. "But he's giving all his commission right back where it came from. The man's a gambler." As soon as Joe judged Ackroyd, his own conscience judged him and threatened to pass sentence. Joe felt confused, his holier-than-thou façade totally exposed in the flaws of a man that he had so easily condemned.

"When do you want me to leave, Joe?" She sensed the urgency.

"Next flight. Don't waste any time. Please," he begged.

"What about Mummy?"

"Take her too," Joe insisted.

"Where shall we go?"

"Miami or Tampa, whichever flight leaves first. Get a hotel, anywhere. You can't call me, but you can call Brogan Higgins. Tell him where you are. Take this number down." Joe gave her Brogan's number.

"The noon flights will be checking in soon," said Rachael, "We'll get the first one up to the States"

"Hurry, but be careful."

Feeling a little more secure, Joe walked back inside the hotel.

Chapter Twenty Three

Luca Telesino was a very happy man. Not only had he let down a couple of inflated gamblers in as many days, but that pathetic fool of a politician from the Caymans was back again, and appeared to be losing the sales commission that he had creamed off from *Eastern Promise's* land acquisition in the islands. He had to hand it to Durant and Medini, sometimes those arrogant bastards deserved to be his bosses.

Apart from several scanners reporting glitches that caused their screens to lose integrity briefly, things were perfectly routine. The explanation provided by the maintenance manager that a power surge had infiltrated the system seemed plausible enough and was dutifully logged in Telesino's daily report. The system appeared to be functioning correctly now and that was all that mattered.

Meanwhile, Joe was pacing up and down in his suite, waiting for something to happen. It was like being in a war zone expecting the break-out of hostilities. Joe's situation was worsened by his lack of orders, having no idea who was going to fire the next salvo. He knew it would not be him, the fragile fabric of his psyche so easily torn last night, exposing him as just another weak man. Joe recoiled as he relived his shame.

By now, the amount of time that he had killed in front of the television had made him an expert on internal American affairs and sports. Deep down, he wanted out, this was no longer a game and he had suffered real losses to prove it. The rose-colored glasses through which he had become accustomed to viewing his idealistic world were now scratched, fissures of cynicism distorting every value that he thought he held dear.

Evening appeared to sublime from morning and a little after eight p.m., there was a knock at his door.

"Good evening, Joe LeRice." It was Mike Ackroyd. "What a surprise. Perhaps I should call you Mr. Leriski, the big time gambler." He laughed.

"What the fuck do you want?" Mike Ackroyd was the last person who should be knocking at his door.

"I've come to make sure that you know exactly where you stand."

"What's that supposed to mean?" Joe tried to look surprised.

"I don't know what you're doing here, but it's my guess that you're going to end up in serious problems if I inform the owners what you've been up to."

"What are you getting at?" Joe parried.

'It's come to my attention that your wife has been looking into my business connections and then I bump into you up here of all places. What exactly are you trying to accomplish?"

"I don't know what you mean."

"I think you do and if you reckon that you can jeopardize my legitimate rights, you'll be in some serious trouble," threatened Ackroyd.

"Don't give me that crap, Ackroyd," countered Joe. "You're in this up to your neck. Since when was it considered legitimate to fuck democracy and another man's life?"

'I don't know what you're talking about."

"Bullshit! You set up Arthur Downing. I hold you personally responsible for his death."

"That's a very serious allegation."

"And not without proof," Joe bluffed. "You know the snakes at

Eastern Promise are the lowest of the low and yet you selfishly decided to inflict them on your own people. You hid behind Arthur Downing and used him. You are not fit to hold your position. You are for you and God help the rest of us."

Ackroyd appeared visibly shaken as he realized that Joe was right. He thought back to the early days when he became involved in casino gambling. In spite of having brokered many legitimate and lucrative business deals, he remembered all the cash that he had frittered away over the years. He recalled the web of lies that he woven to mask his movements, the backhanders that he had to accept to feed his voracious habit, the excuses and worst of all, the torment that he had found himself living with. The only thing that held his family together was the extravagant generosity that bought their silence, but even those relationships were frayed. For the first time in years, Ackroyd stood speechless, his dark world utterly illuminated by the light of truth.

"Sir, you are a gambler," Joe continued, "And if anyone should know, it's me. Essentially, we are all the same. At first, I wanted to hate you, but in hating you, I would have to hate myself."

Joe's desperate words seemed to strike a chord in the politician, but Ackroyd's well-trained defense mechanisms intervened.

"Listen, Joe," Ackroyd's voice softened. "You can't stop them. They're too powerful now. Why not be reasonable? I can probably get you contracts to build for them. You'll be rich. I know you need the money, I watched you last night."

Joe feigned genuine interest.

"This is a big boat, Joe," Ackroyd continued, "Neither you nor I can rock it. Anyway, I've done nothing wrong and although it was unfortunate what happened to Arthur, there's nobody to blame."

Joe detected an element of fear in the politician's voice, fueling the argument that Ackroyd was more of a pawn than a player.

"I'll have to think about it," said Joe, hoping that he would not be put to the test immediately.

"I know you like Blackjack," stated Ackroyd, "I'll be playing later tonight. Why don't you join in? Maybe you'll get some better luck."

Ackroyd opened the door to leave and a bell-boy appeared with an envelope which he announced was for Mr. Leriski.

Embarrassed, Joe took it and slipped it into his pocket before tipping the young man. Ackroyd waited until they were alone again before saying,

"So I'll see you tonight? Perhaps we can talk some more?"

"I'll think about it," Joe said again.

With Ackroyd out of the picture for the time being, Joe turned his attention to the note. It was from Brogan.

"Rachael called my wife. She and Elene are safe. Come down to Room 101 at one o'clock tonight. Do not telephone."

Brogan had signed the letter and underneath his own name, he had written the name, Charles Wells. Who the hell was Charles Wells? The name certainly rang a bell, albeit a small one. Joe pushed it to the forefront of his mind, commanding his subconscious to locate any reference to it.

Joe called downstairs for room service and ordered a plate of salad sandwiches and a single bottle of beer. He had this light supper on the balcony, preferring the icy gusts outside to the heavy atmosphere of his room. He felt his head clear as frayed nerve endings meshed back together. He started thinking about Ackroyd and found himself incapable of judging him, having ridden the same tsunami that is the gambler's turbulent emotional world.

At five minutes to one, he walked out from the elevator onto the first floor. The corridor before him appeared dusty and neglected, in total contrast to the world from which he had just descended. The walls were in need of a coat of paint and cigarette butts lay strewn on the floor. A glance around revealed none of the sophisticated observation equipment that was prevalent throughout the more important areas of this place.

Room 101 was right at the end of the passageway and opposite the emergency staircase. Joe knocked lightly on the door. It opened immediately.

"Come in, Joe," said Brogan, smiling. "Welcome to the poor part of town." Joe walked in and Brogan closed the door.

Simon was sitting at a computer keyboard that was plugged into the room television. On the screen was a picture of a roulette wheel on which was superimposed some computer graphics.

"That's a closed-circuit TV picture, surely?" observed Joe.

"Correct, with additional graphics by Simon Ward."

"So you just went downstairs and asked politely if you could hook up a camera to the ceiling?" surmised Joe, intrigued by this sudden turn of events.

"Better than that, this is their camera that we're using; and we didn't ask permission," Simon grinned confidently. "We tapped off their signal." He stood up and beckoned Joe to look behind the dresser that the television set rested on. A panel had been partially removed revealing an array of coaxial cables, one of which passed through an electronic box of some sort. A lead from the same box plugged into the television set.

"How did you know which cable was which?" asked Joe.

"Good old-fashioned trial and error," said Simon. "The door hasn't been beaten down yet, so I assume they haven't noticed. On second thoughts, they probably noticed a brief loss of picture, but it wouldn't have been for more than a few seconds while I disconnected and reconnected the main signal"

"Won't they be suspicious? If you're tapping off the signal, then won't it be weaker in the observation room?" Joe suggested.

"I've thought of that," said Simon, "The box is just a signal booster from an electrical store; it doubles the signal, half for them and half for me."

"Weird, but how did you know that the cables came through this room?" Joe was certainly surprised at their preparations.

"Building blueprints are a lot easier to look at than criminal records," said Brogan.

"Yeah," chimed in Simon, "and although the building plans weren't too specific, this was one of only two ducts that the cables could be passed up. There are telephone lines in there somewhere, too."

"So you've checked records, tapped into the cameras and programmed a computer in less than forty-eight hours?" asked Joe.

"Not exactly," Simon pointed out. "I had the idea when Brogan showed me his 'man who broke the bank' trick. It was Brogan's idea about using their camera."

"Of course, Wells," realized Joe.

"That ain't true, Simon and you know it," retorted Brogan playfully, "I just mentioned that they sure had a lot of cameras and Einstein here gets a brainstorm."

"How does it work, Simon?" asked Joe, before adding, "Make it simple."

"Simple, eh?" said Simon, massaging his jaw. "Alright then. If you walk at four miles an hour, where will you be in one hour?"

"Four miles away, of course. I said simple, not kindergarten."

"Listen, will you?" Simon cut Joe short. "So if I know the starting speed of the roulette ball, I can calculate when it will fall to the edge of the numbers."

"How can you figure out the speed of the ball?" asked Joe.

"From the TV screen. I've done a little graphics program that tracks the ball based on its shape and the color of its pixels. As soon as the ball is put in, I can get a figure for its speed. Watch this."

The threesome watched the live action that was coming up from the gaming-floor. Soon they saw the croupier's hand release the ball into the rim of the wheel. A bright, white dot superimposed itself on the roulette ball and tracked it. Almost immediately, several figures appeared in the left-hand corner of the screen.

"That's the speed, then?" remarked Joe.

"Correct," answered Simon.

"But the inside wheel is also moving."

Simon tapped at the keyboard. A roulette wheel made from computer graphics materialized and sat on its real-life counterpart revolving in perfect unison with it. Another figure appeared in the right-hand corner of the screen.

"That's the figure for the wheel speed at the instant the ball was put in," explained Simon. "The numbers are irrelevant. The calculation takes care of everything behind the scenes. Let's go back to the example. Imagine there are two people, eight miles apart. If they both start walking towards each other at four miles an hour, where will they meet?"

"In the middle, after one hour," answered Joe.

"You are absolutely right. This is a fancy version of the same thing. Watch again."

They sat and waited for another spin of the wheel. As soon as the ball was injected, the two speed figures appeared simultaneously and changed rapidly; a few seconds later, the twelve, red segment began to flash.

"It's calculated where the ball should come to rest," said Simon.

"The scenario has already been processed in the computer, using the initial data, the dimensions of the wheel and the history of all the previous spins. The program has been learning all this time. Now keep watching and you will see real-life catch up with it."

Real-life did indeed catch up. The ball landed in the twelve slot.

"Incredible!" gasped Joe, bereft of words.

"Yeah, but it doesn't hit smack on every time," interjected Brogan

"To be safe, it's best to bet two numbers either side."

"How are you going to get the signal downstairs?" asked Joe.

"Pretty much the same way as before, but the transmitter's been beefed up. We're not really that far away. It's only one floor down."

"What signals are you using?" asked Joe.

"We're pulsing so Brogan can play without having to look at a watch every spin. That would be too suspicious. Three pulses followed by another three is thirty-three," explained Simon. "So you'd bet thirty-three and two numbers that are either side on the wheel."

"But that's tough," deduced Joe, "because the numbers are all mixed up on the wheel. How would you know which numbers to bet?"

"4, 16, 21 and 6," smiled Brogan confidently. "I know those damned numbers off by heart."

"Impressive, but what about twenty-nine?" asked Joe, "That's two pulses followed by nine. You'd run out of time."

"You're right, Joe. It would be a close call, but we've been practicing. Brogan's got it down pat."

Brogan's face denied the allegation.

"When do we start?" asked Joe, controlling his rush of enthusiasm.

"You won't be playing roulette, Joe," stated Brogan.

"Why not?" Joe groaned, as though his chance of redemption had been cruelly stolen.

"Because you'll be playing Blackjack, all by yourself. You're the decoy. "

"But what about all the money I've lost?"

"Perfect, wasn't it," grinned Brogan.

"What the fuck do you mean?" demanded Joe.

"I'm sorry, Joe, but let's be honest. You're just another gambler. You need the thrill of the chase and then you can't think straight. We're not going to gamble. We're going to win."

"You bastards," muttered Joe, shaking his head angrier at himself for realizing that other people too had seen his weakness. "And you've been planning this all the time while I was getting into the shit?"

"No mate," soothed Simon. "It wasn't like that," he explained. "We wanted you to win, just as much as you did, but you took the decisions. They were the decisions of a gambler and you lost."

Joe felt dizzy as the truth penetrated. As the sensation waned, he felt strangely free sensing that in spite of his mistakes, his friends were still that, his friends.

"Yeah, I guess you're right," he accepted, "But you didn't have to let me humiliate myself like that."

"Actually, it was your choice. Perhaps now you realize once and for all, what you're up against?" said Brogan.

"Yourself," declared Simon.

Joe nodded in agreement and accepted the criticism in the spirit that was intended.

"Your losses will be taken care of," said Brogan, "So don't worry about that. Any money that you have left in chips, I'd advise you to convert it to cash and put it in a safety-deposit box in the casino bank."

"Why?" inquired Joe.

"There's gonna be a lot of angry people when they find out they can't be paid," explained Brogan, "We'll be converting our winnings as we go along. Chris, my salesman, will be playing courier, getting to the bank as soon as we get paid for our wins."

"So what's my next move?" asked Joe.

"After you've changed your chips, take some cash to a Blackjack table and make out that you want to play high stakes. Put cash on the table. They'll have to count it there and then, it'll waste valuable time."

"When do I start?" asked Joe, happy with his new role.

"Only a few minutes from now." Brogan confirmed, taking a typed document from his briefcase. "Look at this. What do you think?" he asked, giving it to Joe, who glanced over it, before acknowledging its importance.

"I would have said impossible before, but I'd settle for ambitious now," said Joe. "What makes you think that *Eastern Promise* will sign it?"

"They might not have a choice," declared Brogan, "If they sign this document, then they relinquish their hold on the gaming rights to the Cayman Islands. After that, it's up to your government to set things right."

"What can I say...?" started Joe, fighting for words that could convey his gratitude.

"Nothing. Not yet anyway," said Brogan. "Just get down there and do your job and we'll take it from there. Just keep Telesino's attention at whatever cost."

Joe made his way downstairs and breezed onto the gaming-floor with a new found air of confidence. He did as he was told and spent the next twenty minutes converting his money to cash before storing it in two boxes.

He took five wads of five thousand dollars with him to the Blackjack table and sat down, a cocky grin on his face. This display of arrogance had the desired effect. Five minutes later, Telesino had crawled out of his woodwork and was pacing his pit. He dismissed Charlie's request to oversee the game and walked over to Joe. Telesino was blinded by hate for this pathetic creature who did not know his place in his kingdom and he was going to enjoy publicly dismantling him.

"I hope you have better luck, this time, Mr. Leriski," he sneered.

"Oh, I intend to," replied Joe nonchalantly. "In fact, I'm confident, that none of your little dealers' tricks will stop me from getting my money back."

"I may be mistaken, but do I detect just a drop of bad blood?" oozed Telesino.

"Come to think of it," said Joe, "I can smell a lot of bad blood around here."

The veiled reference to Telesino's impending ill-health flew over the manager's head as he commanded a male dealer to count the wad of money that Joe had just thrown down. Before the cash had been fully counted, an enthusiastic Charlie tapped Telesino on the shoulder. Excitement pervaded through his voice and he was unable to keep it down.

"There seems to be some action brewing on Roulette One. Possible whale, maybe more than one."

"Keep your voice down," Telesino rebuked him. "Consider this your big chance, Charlie. You supervise the roulette. Give them a lot of leeway if they want to bet big. Kiss their asses, smile and wait. Check with me before you do any markers."

"Will do, Boss." Eagerly, Charlie hurried back to his section of the pit; his god-given authority swelling his head as he looked menacingly at his croupier.

A glance in the direction of roulette table number one told Joe that Brogan was in position at one end of the table and if his eyes hadn't mistaken him, at least two of his employees from *The Store* were at the other.

"Better start small," said Joe, toying with Telesino by placing a stake of one thousand dollars on the table.

"Me too," came a voice from behind him.

Joe turned to see Mike Ackroyd take up a seat beside him.

Telesino was happy to see this second man for whom he had signed many markers over the years on the instructions of his bosses.

"Hello, Joe," said Ackroyd, "Glad to see you made it. Are you feeling lucky?"

"We'll soon find out." Joe began to feel unsettled, but the situation became clearer when they won the first hand by virtue of the dealer busting.

"Yes!" Ackroyd hissed triumphantly, as soon as he realized his hand was a winner. "Good start eh, Joe?"

"Yeah, not bad at all," agreed Joe. The fervor that Mike Ackroyd displayed was befitting a true gambler, thought Joe as he imagined the subliminal messages flooding the politician's brain and strangely, he had to make a concerted effort not to feel sorry for the man.

Suddenly, a loud roar was heard from Charlie's section. It certainly caught Telesino's attention and almost everyone else's in the room.

Charlie beckoned Telesino over. When Joe ruled Telesino to be out of earshot he turned to Ackroyd, careful to speak in low tones, "Mike, it looks like you enjoy winning?"

"Why else am I here?" Ackroyd laughed, sounding as though he had indulged in a few drinks.

"Tonight, you can win big. I know it."

"What are you talking about?"

"That's why you're playing, isn't it?" Joe stated.

"That's why we're all playing. You know that."

"If I said you could win a lot, what would you say, Mike?"

"I'd say, how?"

Joe seized his opportunity. Ackroyd's gambling instincts were ruling him, as they probably had done for years. "There's a guy over by that roulette table. He's been winning all night."

"Which guy?" asked Ackroyd, straining to see.

Joe, sensing that his trump card was turning into an ace, pointed Brogan out and said, "Follow his bets and bet big. He'll carry you through."

"What about you?" Ackroyd sounded suspicious. "Why aren't you there if you're so confident?"

"Why do you think I'm playing small? I thought it was obvious. The guy on the roulette is playing for me." Immediately, Joe wished that he hadn't been so explicit, but it did the trick. Ackroyd left the table and went over to the roulette wheel, and in doing so revealed that his true loyalty to the gambling cause outweighed the fear of his masters at *Eastern Promise*.

Telesino stalked back wearing a face like thunder. He had admonished Charlie for not changing his croupier quickly enough and consequently the casino was several hundred thousand in the hole. Suitably scolded, Charlie stood forlornly at his post as the new croupier checked in.

"Having problems?" said Joe, smirking at the manager.

"Are you playing or talking, sir?" Telesino snapped.

Joe pushed a stake onto his box. "Playing. To win," he replied, as he looked at his cards. "Hmm, to double down or not to double down, that is the question," he mused. Telesino looked irked by these brash ramblings. Joe threw down another pile of cash and asked that it be converted into chips.

Another roar was heard with extra decibels added by Mike Ackroyd. It was difficult to see what was happening now because quite a large crowd had gathered around the roulette table.

"Looks like you're at the wrong table," smirked Joe, collecting the winnings from his last hand. "I don't know though, if you stick around long enough, you might be in trouble here too."

Telesino seethed. He wanted to punch Joe's words back down his throat. Charlie came over again, looking distraught. "I did what you said, and now they're all winning. We need more chips."

"Get more chips, you idiot. When you do, take over at this table."

"No need," said Joe, not finding it difficult to overhear their anxious voices, "I know when to quit."

Joe rose from his seat and casually walked over towards the

crowd that was swelling around Roulette One. It was impossible to get a good vantage point. Frenzied gamblers, pumped up by the invisible orders to bet, jockeyed for positions, waiting for the signal from the oracle that sat at the end of the baize. Brogan, his face betraying no emotion, ignored the fuss and concentrated on the signals that were coming from Simon.

Telesino barged past the croupier who was counting out a new batch of chips. The original chips now lay in huge piles around the rim of the table waiting to be multiplied yet again. Joe strained for an update on the state of affairs. Brogan had amassed a vast pile of chips and was using the lull in activity to send Chris to the bank to fill up yet another deposit box.

Telesino reconnoitered the mass of armor that was arrayed against him. In fact some of the players had started playing with special, high value chips. Charlie had done his job well, giving them the leeway that he had been instructed to.

Brogan beckoned Telesino. The manager obeyed.

"All of it. One spin," announced Brogan.

Groans of disbelief were followed by a proverbial, pin-dropping silence. Telesino wilted under the wall of oppressive stares that waited for his verdict. "One spin?" his voice quivered, "All of it?"

Brogan nodded.

Telesino plucked the ball from its last resting place. The possibility of a pay-out had to be avoided at all costs. "One spin. My spin," he countered.

He pushed Charlie out of the way and braced himself for the moment. He pulled on the numbers wheel, setting it into motion.

"Place your bets, please."

No one moved to break the ominous silence. All eyes fell on

Brogan. Telesino steadied himself before introducing the ball. Brogan concentrated. Telesino released the ball.

Suddenly, Brogan felt it. One pulse, a pause, then more pulses. One, two, three, four. Come on, Simon! Five, six. Six! Sixteen. The ball began to slow. There wasn't any time to bet the numbers either side of it. Brogan shoved the marker chip representing his whole pile on to the table, shouting, "Sixteen, all of it!"

Hordes of chips followed shouts of, "Sixteen! Sixteen!"

"No more bets!" screamed Telesino. "No more bets!" He pushed shaky hands away as the ball descended towards its pre-calculated destiny. It fell into the numbers and hopped, once, twice. Sixteen was miles away. It seemed impossible. Then the ball seemed to hang on the inner rim and finally, its energy spent, dropped.

"Sixteen, Red!" Pandemonium followed. Telesino backed away, leaving Charlie and his croupiers to sort out the mountain of chips that would have to be paid, all at thirty-five to one. It was millions of dollars.

Joe felt a tugging at his jacket. It was Brogan, "Come on, Joe. We've got some unfinished business. Chris can sort out the cash."

"Too bloody right...Wait! Wait a second," shouted Joe as he dove into the crowd of exuberant gamblers and hauled Mike Ackroyd out. The politician was clutching handfuls of chips and his expression was one of a child whose new toy had been cruelly snatched away.

What's happening? What's going on, Joe?" he squealed.

"Your reprieve," exclaimed Joe, "No questions. Just come with us," he ordered and offering no further resistance, Ackroyd duly followed.

Five burly security guards converged on the gaming area while another few stood ready at the bank. Telesino was nearly at the staff elevator when Brogan caught up with him. Joe and Ackroyd were in hot pursuit.

"All aboard for going up," shouted Brogan, pinning Telesino in the corner of the lift.

"Get your fucking hands off me," he shrieked.

"Brogan, meet Mike Ackroyd," said Joe, "He's decided to help us."

"Pleased to meet you, I'm sure," replied Brogan coldly.

Ackroyd flinched under Brogan's stare.

"Top floor, please. Now!" commanded Brogan.

Telesino punched the necessary button and the confined space became a heaving tomb of hot breath. Ackroyd looked stunned, a couple of his chips falling on the floor as they slipped from his sweaty hands. He picked them up, ignoring the contempt that he had just incurred.

Once on the top floor, Brogan shoved Telesino out and the others followed.

"Where are your bosses?" he demanded gruffly.

"I don't know," lied Telesino.

"Where?" shouted Brogan.

"In the office," Telesino quickly surrendered.

"Open it. Now!"

Telesino turned his key and Brogan dragged him by the collar as he burst angrily into the room. Durant and Medini were crouched in front of the safe. They wheeled around shocked at this sudden turn of events.

"I think you'd better take that money downstairs to pay your gamblers," said Brogan, "It looks like they've broken the bank."

"Then we'll pay them," said Durant. "You have no right to be in here. I'm going to call security."

At that moment, the telephone rang. Durant answered it, his jaw dropping as he uttered, "How much?" He whispered the amount to Medini whose jaw joined Durant's on the floor. They glared at Telesino. He bolted. Joe caught him as he tried to escape, tripping him to the ground before placing a vicious kick in his belly. Telesino groaned in agony.

"No violence, Joe," demanded Brogan firmly.

Joe reached into his pocket and removed the letter to Bobby from the clinic. "Express mail, from Bobby Verrill. Read it and weep." he said icily, dropping it to the floor by Telesino's pained face.

Brogan took centre stage, "We've come to do a deal, gentlemen," he announced.

"What deal?" snapped Durant, angrily.

Brogan looked over to Joe as if to cue him.

"Mr. Ackroyd here has changed his mind about letting you people operate on his island," said Joe. "He wants you to sign a contract that refunds the money that you paid for the gambling rights to the Cayman Islands, don't you, Mike?"

Ackroyd looked down at the floor, unable to face his controllers, but deep resentment harbored over recent years came to bear and Ackroyd realized that he was tired of the slavery he had found himself in.

"Don't you, Mike?" repeated Joe.

"Yes," declared Ackroyd firmly, looking Medini in the eye.

"You must be crazy. Where are the guards? Guards!" screamed Medini.

"All your guards are probably trying to keep a bunch of crazed winners at bay," said Brogan, with a wry smile. "If you don't sign this paper, then we'll have to take you downstairs and introduce you to your customers as the people who have spent years taking their money and causing misery by preying on their weakness. And now that the boot is on the other foot, you won't pay up? I don't think so."

"Even if we sign, they'll still want paying?" Medini scowled.

"That's your problem," rasped Brogan feeling the anger rise up inside him as he realized he was face to face with his brother's murderers.

"We should call the police," said Durant weakly, knowing that if anyone was guilty it was them.

"Most of the winners are *my* people," declared Brogan. "About half of the money that you've lost belongs to me. It adds up to an awful lot. Shit, I lost count at a few million. Two of my men were draining your bank all the time."

Durant took Medini aside. A minute later they were nodding their heads. "What guarantee do we have that we get our money back from the Cayman Islands deal? Most of it's not ours anyway."

"You have my word," said Mike Ackroyd. "You will be refunded ninety percent as there is still some mess to clean up. You've done way too much damage. You turned me against my own country. Now you will help me make amends."

The document was changed to reflect this modification and Durant signed reluctantly before giving his pen to Medini to do the same. Joe picked up the contract and turned to Mike Ackroyd, "You'd better cash your chips in before you go home."

Ackroyd pulled the chips from his pocket and threw them on the floor in front of Durant and Medini. "I won't need this blood money," he declared, turning to Joe thanking him.

"Don't thank me, thank Brogan here," said Joe, "Anyway, you've got a plane to catch. I remember you saying something about calling a special sitting for the Legislative Assembly."

Mike Ackroyd did not need any more encouragement. As he was leaving the office, Simon walked in smiling broadly. "It's bedlam down there," he announced.

Joe patted him on the back, "Well done, mate."

"How did you do it?" begged Durant. "Tell me, I have to know."

"Well, if you really must know," started Joe, "Imagine two men, eight miles apart, walking at four miles an hour-"

"The same way we'll do it tomorrow and the day after, and the day after that," interrupted Brogan. "You're finished, all of you."

Epilogue

Joe LeRice soaked up the last few rays of the Caribbean evening sunshine. As he watched the sun dip down under the horizon, he cast a loving glance at his wife as she slept serenely on her recliner, her beautiful baby bump stretching her bikini bottom in a sexy, yet holy way.

Thanks to modern science, they knew in advance that their long awaited first-born would be a girl and that she was healthy and strong. They had already named her Josephine after her father and her frequent, vibrant kicks gave her parents ample warning of the independent life that she intended to lead once released from the safety of her mother's womb. Joe and Rachael would have had it no other way as they patiently waited for this new soul to shine her light in a darkened world.

Joe was so happy that his daughter would be born into a country where gambling was not permitted and he even mused that one day, she might become a lawyer and defend the constitution under which she was born.

Eastern Promise was duly paid off with Mike Ackroyd insisting that ten percent of the original fee be withheld for administrative purposes. Although he stood down at the next election, even today the Michael Ackroyd Technical College has a reputation of being one of the best in the region, its science and engineering graduates highly sought after.

Luca Telesino was forced to hand in his notice through ill-health and Medini and Durant sold their stake in *Eastern Promise Gaming Inc.* before going on a very long vacation to Colombia.

Kate Clementier initially found peace as a lesbian activist, joining the civil service and championing the rights of the vociferous minority, before she met and married a kind gentleman who had previously been a Catholic priest.

Elene rehabilitated fully, helped mainly by the tenacity of her plucky daughter and she eventually remarried, finding happiness with an American developer from Arkansas. Together they opened a large supermarket with a reputation for the freshest fruits and produce in the islands encouraging local growers and farmers to fill their shelves.

Brogan Higgins went back to running his shop in the heart of Vegas and became famous for introducing Caribbean black coral as an art form and jewelry medium to the elite. Even today, his one-of-a-kind pieces are highly sought after by famous actors, politicians and wealthy socialites.

Simon Ward never married April since his heavy metal band took off and he met a rock-chick on their first tour. He did however, remain friends with her mother.

Bobby Verrill passed away peacefully in St. Louis but not before she had personally opened the Bobby Verrill Centre for Homeless Women funded initially by Joe LeRice and Brogan Higgins. Her parents became sober with her father becoming a pastor.

Joe LeRice finally became a naturalized Caymanian and cast his first ever vote, voting for himself at the next elections where he stood on an independent platform of transparent government, but that is another story.

Dedication

This work is dedicated to the Caymanian people and all those residents, expat or otherwise, who are proud to call the Cayman Islands their home.

Having been first associated with the islands in 1973, I can honestly say that one would have to go a very long way to find a warmer, kinder people.

I would urge their elected leaders to fight fiercely, selflessly and honestly to protect the identity, heritage and values of the Caymanian people so that in the years to come, this little piece of paradise is preserved as an example to the world.

"He hath founded it upon the seas." Psalms 24:2

Made in the USA
Charleston, SC
06 August 2011